WILD EARL CHASE

Earls are Wild
Book Two

Anna Markland

ARE YOU SIGNED UP FOR DRAGONBLADE'S BLOG?

You'll get the latest news and information on exclusive giveaways, exclusive excerpts, coming releases, sales, free books, cover reveals and more.

Check out our complete list of authors, too!

No spam, no junk. That's a promise!

Sign Up Here

www.dragonbladepublishing.com

Dearest Reader;

Thank you for your support of a small press. At Dragonblade Publishing, we strive to bring you the highest quality Historical Romance from the some of the best authors in the business. Without your support, there is no 'us', so we sincerely hope you adore these stories and find some new favorite authors along the way.

Happy Reading!

CEO, Dragonblade Publishing

Dedicated to aficionados of thoroughbred horse racing.

"If you rile a tiger, he's going to show his claws."
~ Rob James-Collier

More Anna Markland

Anna has authored more than sixty bestselling, award-winning and much-loved Medieval, Viking and Highlander historical romance novels and novellas. Most recently, she has ventured into the world of the Regency.

No matter the historical or geographic setting, most of her series recount the adventures of successive generations of one family, with emphasis on the importance of ancestry and honor. A detailed list with links can be found at annamarkland.com.

GRIFF

Tattersalls, London, England, 1817

"I'D PREFER TO stay in the carriage," Edwina whined, a perfumed kerchief pressed to her pink nose. "Horses are so pungent."

Griffith Halliwell, third Earl of Pendlebury, patted his mistress' cold hand. "Of course, my dear," he replied, beating a hasty retreat out of the door held open by his footman. "Take Mrs. Waxenby home," he shouted to his driver.

"Sir," Bateson replied.

"Oh, but Griffith, my darling," Edwina sighed at the window. "I'm willing to wait until you come out of that dreadful place."

Griff forced a smile. "I'll be hours. It's best you return home."

"When will I see you next?"

Never.

"I'll call on you in a day or two," he lied. "Off with you, Bateson. I'll find my own way back to the townhouse."

The shiny, black coach and four bearing the Halliwell crest pulled away. Heads turned to admire the lacquered vehicle and the magnificent beasts in the traces. It was the usual reaction of passersby, but Griff's pride swelled and he never tired of it. He felt no obligation to acknowledge the lacy kerchief fluttering out the window. Cologne water wasn't unpleasant but did Edwina have to drench every article of her clothing in it?

How had he ever become involved with a woman who couldn't stand the smell of horses? Too blinded by the copious globes. Thank goodness he'd only bedded her the once, or maybe it was twice. No great loss. London was full of willing widows, though he'd be wise to exercise more care in his choice of a future mistress. Horses were his passion, so a paramour would have to love them, as well as possess a glorious pair of breasts—and hips a man could get a good grip on while she rode him.

He chuckled as he entered the subscription room of Tatter-salls. Perhaps he'd stumbled upon the reason his Welsh-born mother had wanted him to bear a name that meant *strong grip*.

Continuing his musings as he savored the heady smells of leather and manure, horseflesh and money, he decided to add *lusty* to his list of criteria. And, of course, a beautiful face. Blonde hair, naturally, and lots of it. And absolutely no bluestockings. A woman's place was in his bed, not a library.

"Griff, old man."

Recognizing the voice, he turned and immediately extended a hand to the friend who'd hailed him. "Richard, how goes today's bidding?"

Tattersall accepted the gesture with his usual firm grip. "The fillies are fetching a good price, but you're not interested in those."

"Indeed. Any news on the Arabian? You're certain he's a descendant of the original Godolphin?"

"Yes, he's clearly listed in the General Stud Book as a grandson of the great Eclipse, but the seller is still making arrangements for transport. I want to make sure you understand this horse's racing days are over."

"Yes, yes, a problem with the coffin bones. I know. I want him for stud."

"No worries, then. Once he arrives, he's yours."

"If I meet your price," Griff said.

Grinning, Richard slapped him on the back. "Of course. Business is business, after all."

Griff pumped his shrewd friend's hand again. "While I'm here, I'll take a walk around, perhaps pick out a mare or two."

"I'll be in touch," Richard assured him before striding off.

Griff held Richard Tattersall in high esteem. The jovial fellow had inherited a prosperous and renowned horse auction business built up by his father and grandfather. However, Richard had something his sires lacked—a certain ease with nobility and common man alike. This ability had enabled him to become the intimate of the best sporting men of the era. Griff counted himself fortunate to have Richard as a friend. The friendship had certainly helped build the reputation of Griff's Pendlebury Stables as a premier stud farm.

Scanning the excited throng of men clustered around the bidding arena, Griff fished in his frock coat pocket for his pewter hip flask and took a few swallows of French brandy. Thus fortified, he headed for a gap in the noisy crowd. He didn't need more mares, and should save the blunt for the Arabian. The stallion was going to cost a pretty penny but owners would pay handsomely for the chance to breed a winner with a thoroughbred stud. Pendlebury Stables might even attract the Prince Regent—horse racing fanatic that he was, as well as a close friend of Richard Tattersall.

After several more swigs of brandy, Griff placed a winning bid on a mediocre filly, ignoring the incredulous sneers of other patrons. If a man made the effort to come to Tattersalls, he had to bid on something. He could always consign the nag to a glue factory if she proved useless.

When he exited a short time later, it was a relief to find Bateson had, as usual, disobeyed his directive. A light drizzle had begun. Despite the crush of carriages, his own was parked within spitting distance of the auction house. Frederick had the step down and the door open. "It's amazing you always manage to find a spot close by," he shouted to Bateson, truly thankful for his driver's uncanny ability as he climbed aboard with some difficulty.

Three more sips of brandy did nothing to ward off a worsening headache. A brief visit to one of his clubs might help remedy a sudden melancholia. "Head for White's," he shouted to Bateson.

When he entered the club a short time later, he sensed excitement in the air, something that had been lacking since Brummell's flight to the Continent. "What's going on?" he asked Lord Sefton as the dandy hurried by.

"Alvanley's placed a bet on the raindrops."

When he'd first been accepted into White's, Griff had striven to become part of Brummell's clique. He'd since had reason to be glad they'd shunned him, probably because of his Lancashire roots. They drank to excess and gambled ridiculous amounts of money on trivial things. "How much?" he asked, feigning interest.

"Three thousand pounds on which of two raindrops will make it to the bottom of the pane first," Sefton replied with great glee. "You don't want to miss it."

Griff dutifully sat within sight of the bow window, ordered a brandy and watched entitled men make idiots of themselves. Alvanley loved being the center of attention, having taken over leadership of Prinny's Pals after Brummell's departure. Griff's only interest in the Regent was his love of horse racing. He'd sooner bet on a prized thoroughbred than on a raindrop.

The raucous atmosphere was doing nothing to soothe his headache, so he drained his brandy and left the club before the outcome of the "race" was decided. He had more important things to do, like deciding how to end things with Edwina without hurting her feelings. He recalled her opinion that horses were pungent. "The smell of money, my dear lady," he snorted, though the real reason he'd gone into horse breeding wasn't for the profits to be made. He simply loved the magnificent creatures—had since he was a child.

Potts already had the front door of his townhouse open before he stumbled from the carriage. Griff accepted Frederick's arm and the shelter of the footman's umbrella. Admittedly, he was mildly foxed—not an acceptable circumstance this early in the day—but he already resented the admonition he anticipated from the straitlaced butler who'd previously served his parents.

He groaned when the poker-faced Potts stuck his chin further in the air and announced, "Bad news from your northern estates, my lord. The Luddites are at it again."

CHARGES LAID

Dower House, Thicketford Manor, Preston, England

Lady Susan Crompton breezed into the morning room, not surprised to see Rebecca Waterman already seated and enjoying a steaming cup of black coffee.

"You seem chipper this morning," Rebecca noted.

"I slept well," Susan replied, helping herself to a boiled egg from the sideboard. "However, this room always makes me feel cheery. You certainly have a good eye for pleasing decor."

Rebecca blushed as she always did when anyone paid her a compliment. "I simply contributed a few ideas."

Susan sliced off the top of her egg, pleased to see the yolk was still runny. "That's an understatement. Restoring this house after the fire was a massive undertaking. Thank goodness you moved to Lancashire right around the time Gabriel instigated the repairs. Laborers could have done the work, but it was your eye for color and furnishings that turned a sow's ear into a silk purse."

"You can hardly call this house a sow's ear. True, the fire did a lot of damage, but I've benefitted too," Rebecca allowed, rising to help herself to buttered toast. "It worked out rather well. You needed a companion to share the dower house, and there I was."

"Yes. Neither of us dowager countesses but living here in the lap of luxury," Susan replied with a chuckle.

"This place is certainly far more opulent than my late husband's house," Rebecca said as she regained her seat.

Susan made no reply. Her friend had hinted at the abuse she'd suffered at the hands of her parsimonious drunkard of a husband; his fists had driven away his stepsons. It was a source of constant regret for Gabriel and his mother that his older brothers had been killed at Trafalgar after running away from home to join the navy.

"I consider myself fortunate to be living here so close to my one surviving son," Rebecca said. "I'm glad I made the move from Kent."

Susan nodded. "It's amazing the twists and turns life takes, isn't it? Your son unexpectedly inherits an earldom from my late brother, falls in love with and marries his widow, then agrees to allow you and me to move into the refurbished dower house."

"And you hadn't lived at Thicketford Manor for years."

"Not since my father drove me out because I refused to conform to his perception of how the daughter of an earl should comport herself."

"I'm sure he'd be proud of you now. You're one of the most accomplished and well-read women I know."

"I doubt it. Papa was too set in his ways and, as you're aware, he went mad at the end of his life, hence the fire that almost destroyed this house."

She refrained from reiterating her father had died in the fire he'd set. Let sleeping ghosts lie.

A discreet cough from the butler drew their attention. Jenkinson excused the interruption as he handed her a copy of *The Times*. "What's this?" she asked.

"A footman brought it over from the main house," he replied. "Lord Farnworth thought you'd want to read it now rather than waiting until you join Lady Farnworth for afternoon tea."

"Must be something important," Rebecca remarked. "My son usually likes to read the ink off the paper before anyone else sets eyes on it."

Susan perused the front page. "I don't see…"

"Page three," Jenkinson explained. "Luddites Charged."

Susan's hackles rose when she located the article. "They've arrested the leaders of the weavers' march," she exclaimed.

"On what charge?" her companion asked.

"Sedition, and one would think *The Times* would know better than to refer to them as Luddites. They never intended to destroy machinery."

Rebecca frowned. "I was under the impression they were starving weavers who planned to march to London to beg the Prince Regent for relief."

Susan stared at the brief article in disbelief, grateful Rebecca Waterman also lived at the dower house, and not just for her decorating abilities. The current earl's mother was intelligent and shared Susan's interest in Lancashire politics. It was gratifying not to be the only female voice of outrage when things like this latest miscarriage of justice occurred. To date they'd devoted much of their energy to campaigning against the slave trade, but Susan now saw a dire need closer to home.

She passed the newspaper to Rebecca. "And, of course, the leaders of the march are all from the Earl of Pendlebury's estate."

"I'm not familiar with Pendlebury," Rebecca admitted.

"South of here. Closer to Manchester. The earl himself lives in London and rarely comes north."

"I think Gabriel has spoken of him."

"Yes, your son and Pendlebury have met on the infrequent occasions the latter has taken his seat in the Lords. Apparently, he's a womanizer and a wastrel known for neglecting his responsibilities."

Rebecca handed the paper back to Jenkinson. "I seem to remember my son mentioning the earl owns a lot of horses."

Susan salted her boiled egg, disappointed to see the yolk had hardened. "I suppose that's what he spends his money on. The weavers who live on his estates are on the verge of starvation. They have no work since the factories have taken over. They hoped to appeal to the Prince Regent since the earl has failed to provide relief. Pendlebury probably doesn't even know of their plight."

Rebecca narrowed her eyes. "He must know now, if he reads *The Times*."

⊰⊱

GRIFF WAS EATING breakfast in the morning room of his London townhouse when Potts brought the post. "Anything important?" he asked, aware his butler thoroughly perused every envelope as soon as it was handed to him by the postman.

"A letter from your solicitors in Manchester, my lord."

Griff clenched his jaw. He'd expected to hear from old Rowbotham after reading the article in *The Times* two days prior about the arrest of his tenants. "I wonder what he wants?"

"Most likely something to do with the unrest, my lord," Potts replied as if speaking to a dimwitted child. He left without waiting to be dismissed.

Slicing open the missive, Griff pondered again the possibility of letting Potts go. The man was insufferably rude, but it was improbable the fellow would find work at his age. He was a damned fine butler, and, admittedly, the closest thing Griff had to a father, though neither would ever admit to it.

As he read the letter, his appetite fled. "Potts," he yelled, too angry to get up and pull the bell-rope.

The butler's speedy arrival confirmed Griff's suspicion he'd been lurking nearby. Potts had an uncanny knack of knowing when his presence was required. "Sir."

"I'm summoned to appear at a special sitting of the Manchester Sessions in a week for the trial of my tenants. What a bother! I suppose I'll have to stay at Clifton Heights."

The prospect of returning to his ancestral home filled him with dread. However, there seemed to be no alternative. "Make the arrangements."

"Already in hand," the irritating fellow replied. "I assume you'll be taking Frederick?"

Griff would have preferred to take Potts himself; the butler would quickly make sure everything at Clifton Heights was running smoothly. However, the prospect of enduring endless hours of travel with the supercilious blighter…

Frederick's size and surly demeanor might be just what was required in a situation that might turn out to be hostile. "Yes. Tell my footman he's to accompany me. And I'll give you letters to post to Rowbotham and my estate manager instructing them to do what they can to get the charges lowered."

SUSAN NORMALLY ENJOYED the daily afternoon walk from Thicketford Manor's dower house to the principal mansion where she'd grown up and where the present Earl and Countess of Farnworth now lived with their children; the mile-long trek gave her and Rebecca a chance to indulge in intelligent conversation and enjoy the fresh air.

Anxious to discuss the appalling miscarriage of justice with Emma's husband, she decided to ride instead of walking, not surprised when Rebecca declined to accompany her. Before moving to Lancashire, her friend had never ridden.

A light drizzle began as she dismounted with the aid of a groom outside Thicketford Manor's stables. She hurried to the front door, relieved to see Frame ready to welcome her, the door already open. "You must be the world's best butler," she told him for what was probably the hundredth time.

The man who'd served the Earls of Farnworth since before she was born cracked a hint of a smile. "The lack of a porte-cochère keeps me on my toes, Lady Susan. I wouldn't want you exposed to the elements any longer than necessary."

"Indeed," she replied as he took her cloak, hat and gloves.

"Lady Emma is in the drawing room," Frame informed her, handing the outerwear off to a maidservant.

Her friend greeted Susan warmly when she entered the drawing room. "Just in time for tea," she exclaimed with a smile.

It was a pleasant ritual they followed almost every day. Susan had always enjoyed a firm friendship with Emma, her late brother's widow. She considered it a blessing that her friend had fallen in love with and married the stalwart fellow who'd inherited her brother's earldom. Some might turn up their aristocratic noses at the unique arrangement that had allowed the current earl's mother to reside in the dower house with the late earl's sister, but it had worked out perfectly as far as Susan and Rebecca were concerned.

She was very glad she'd returned to the Farnworth estate after her brother's death. Her late father's ultimatum forced her to leave. While he was alive, he'd refused to sanction his daughter's interest in anything other than bearing children and organizing menus.

"Is Gabriel joining us?" she asked, accepting the cup of tea Emma passed. "I want to ask his opinion."

"I sense this has something to do with the marchers who were arrested."

"Yes. I plan to attend the trial."

"I had a feeling you might," Emma's husband said as he entered the room.

"Someone has to speak on their behalf."

Gabriel shook his head as he accepted his cup of tea. "I understand your outrage, but I doubt they'll allow a woman to speak."

She didn't censure him for his remark. Earl Gabriel Smith championed her right to become involved in social issues, but it was nonetheless infuriating that he was probably right. "Perhaps a letter from you..."

He rolled his eyes. "I really shouldn't interfere in another earl's affairs."

Susan snorted. "I doubt Pendlebury will even put in an appearance. Too busy with his damned horses."

TRIAL

LOATH AS HE was to travel by public transportation, Griff heeded the advice of his butler. As Potts rightly pointed out, there were several perfectly fine carriages stored at Clifton Heights, and it would be foolish to risk his own expensive horses on the trek north.

Potts arranged a seat on a Royal Mail coach. "More expensive than the private coaches, my lord, but a good deal faster and fewer passengers. Less likelihood of the conveyance overturning."

Upon boarding the black and maroon mail coach, Griff was pleasantly surprised by the cleanliness of the interior. Three well-dressed elderly gentlemen were to be his traveling companions. They were clearly unacquainted and the gruff greeting each gave seemed to indicate a desire not to engage in small talk. Since Griff intended to sleep for most of the sixteen-hour overnight journey, that suited him fine.

Frederick sat outside next to the driver, but Griff paid no attention to the two passengers climbing to sit on the bench behind them.

Armed with a blunderbuss and two pistols, the guard, impressive in his immaculate maroon and gold post office livery, sat at the rear, next to the mail box locked in the boot.

Griff settled into his seat, fully intending to stay there until they reached Manchester, unless nature called at one of the stops or the passengers had to alight when the coach encountered a steep hill. The weather promised to be fair so he didn't foresee a problem with the roads, which Potts assured him were improving by the day. Traveling at night also meant less traffic.

All in all, the roads weren't too rough, although Griff only managed to doze as they made their way north. Fresh horses were supplied every ten or fifteen miles; frequent stops to deliver and pick up mail interrupted his sleep, although, sometimes, the guard simply flung the mailbag from the coach and snatched another from the postmaster without the coach stopping at all.

His three companions snored loudly no matter what was going on outside. Despite the disturbances, Griff enjoyed the experience. He admired the efficiency of the whole operation and was pleased Potts had arranged this mode of transportation.

He was awake when light filtered into the coach. One of his fellow passengers scowled when Griff rolled up the leather window covering, but he paid no mind. Dawn was breaking over what he assumed were the hills and dales of the rugged Peak District. The sight moved him more than it should have. It was a sign they'd traveled far from the lush, rolling downs of the south, and he felt an odd sense of belonging.

Upon arriving at *The Punch Bowl* coaching inn in Manchester, he settled into a reasonably clean room and dispatched Frederick to his solicitor's office with a message letting him know he was at the inn.

He dozed off in the room's easy chair and napped for most of the afternoon. Rowbotham's reply arrived two hours later, expressing doubt Griff would be called to testify since it was the Crown bringing charges.

The evening meal of liver and onions was palatable, but his mattress turned out to be lumpy. Tossing and turning all night, he wished he'd gone on to Clifton Heights, but it was located further from the court.

Breakfast turned out to be the usual Lancashire mixed grill—bacon, fried kidneys, eggs and black pudding—served by a buxom lass who assured him with a wink it would put hair on his chest. Swatting her bottom, he countered that he'd be pleased to show her his chest, and other parts of his anatomy—if only he didn't have an appointment elsewhere.

During the ride to the court in the hired clarence, he toyed with the notion of avoiding Clifton Heights altogether, but supposed he'd better show up since he hadn't been back to his ancestral home for over two years.

Entering the crowded court proved to be as unpleasant as he'd expected. A hostile, scowling mob glared, every last man clad in unrelenting gray homespun, and scruffy women cocooned in ragged black shawls. The place reeked of unwashed bodies.

The only bright spot was an elegantly dressed woman seated on the bench reserved for the gentry. She might have taken his fancy had she been blonde, though he had to admit her raven locks were striking—at least they would be if they weren't bound up in a severe bun. He normally liked the *English rose* type of complexion, rosy cheeks and all that. This woman's olive coloring gave her the look of an exotic gypsy. Her tits were shapely; big enough to fit his hands; a lower décolletage would have shown them to better advantage. He smiled politely as he sat on the other end of the bench, but she kept her lips tightly pursed and ignored him. A prude, clearly. The high neckline should have been an indicator.

When the justices entered and the proceedings got underway, a group of shackled and bruised men were shoved into the dock. To his surprise, he didn't recognize any of them.

A barrister came to his feet and began to explain the charges. "On the tenth of March, 1817, five thousand marchers, mainly spinners and weavers, met in St. Peter's Field, near Manchester, along with a large crowd of onlookers, perhaps as many as twenty-five thousand people in total."

Griff was shocked so many had been involved.

The barrister droned on. "Naturally, in the face of this subversive gathering, the magistrates had no choice but to read the

Riot Act. The mob was broken up by the King's Dragoon Guards, and twenty-seven people were arrested."

The woman sharing Griff's bench was becoming increasingly agitated. He supposed the notion of dragoons attacking unarmed people might be upsetting for a lady.

"Many marchers then dropped out or were taken into custody by police and the yeomanry between Manchester and Stockport. The majority were turned back or arrested under vagrancy laws before they reached Derbyshire.

"I therefore ask that the justices see fit to find these men guilty of sedition and punished accordingly."

Given the barrister's succinct summary, Griff estimated the whole farce would be over in a half-hour at most. His hopes were dashed when he was called to the witness box.

He returned to his seat minutes later, relieved the Crown counsel had merely asked him to verify his name and title. Since there appeared to be no counsel acting for the defense, he assumed the matter was at an end. He was astonished when the lady was summoned to testify.

⋙✦⋘

"THESE MEN ARE not Luddites, my lords," Lady Susan Crompton insisted. "Nor are they seditionists. They are weavers who merely want to feed their families."

The chief justice adjusted his steel-rimmed spectacles and peered down at her from the bench. "They intended to march to London. We cannot have a repeat of the recent attack on the Prince Regent, Miss...er..."

Gripping the wooden railing, Susan struggled to hold on to her temper. Anger would further alienate the three elderly justices of the peace whose portly stature and fat jowls indicated they hadn't missed a meal in their entire privileged lives. She strove for a more even tone. "The marchers intended to appeal to the Prince Regent for relief before they and their children starve. Heaven knows Parliament has done nothing to mitigate their plight."

Stern scowls and mumbling greeted her criticism of the House of Commons. "With the growth of the cotton industry, I'm confident these men could have found work," one of the judges averred.

Susan fumed inwardly. The pompous fellow clearly knew nothing of the hundreds of weavers forced to leave their rural communities to seek low paying jobs in the cotton mills of the larger towns. "Many have done so, my lords. However, the fact remains, thousands of hard working weavers in villages the length and breadth of Lancashire—men who have produced quality goods for decades in their humble cottages—are now without work as factories spring up everywhere. The failed harvests caused by last year's abysmal summer have made things worse. They cannot afford to pay for what little food is available."

The three graybeards gaped. She had a sinking feeling they hadn't understood a word she'd said, but couldn't hold her tongue. "The Corn Laws of 1815 were intended to protect British agriculture from cheap foreign imports but their effect has been to increase grain prices and decrease supplies, causing hardship among the poor."

Anger reddened the men's wrinkled faces. "My dear lady, women have no business criticizing the decisions of Parliament," the chief justice blustered.

And there it was. The same prejudice Susan had faced all her adult life. She'd actually been shocked they'd accepted Gabriel's letter and allowed a woman to speak on behalf of the men unjustly accused of inciting sedition. Trembling with frustration, she narrowed her eyes. A terrible injustice was about to be visited upon innocent men. She could not stay silent. "The marchers carried no weapons, only a blanket to provide warmth on the journey and serve as a symbol of their industry. Many of them came from the estates of a local earl with a seat in the great

Parliament of this land—a man who cares so little for the welfare of his northern tenants he spends all his time in London."

A murmur rose from the crowded gallery of spectators as backsides shifted on benches and heads swiveled to the arrogant aristocrat of whom she spoke. The chief justice banged his gavel and called for order.

Susan's gaze finally came to rest on the man dressed in expensive raiment who sat in the private bench far removed from those he likely considered riffraff. A burly liveried footman stood behind him. She'd never met the earl before, but had known who he was as soon as he entered and ogled her breasts. She despised his cool arrogance, his sense of entitlement, his perfectly proportioned physique and broad shoulders. She swallowed hard, momentarily distracted by the unsettling memory of his perusal of her breasts before regaining her composure. "The Earl of Pendlebury has deigned to travel north to be here today, no doubt thirsting to see his starving tenants punished."

Pandemonium ensued. Men shook clenched fists, shouting angrily. Women snarled.

The chief justice banged his gavel repeatedly, calling in vain for order.

The earl showed no sign of emotion as he stared back at Susan. She refused to look away, though there was something unsettling about the hateful man's hooded gaze.

When order was finally restored, a verdict of guilty was hastily pronounced on the so-called Blanketeers. They were sentenced to transportation for life.

"You have just condemned their families to death," Susan shouted as her anger exploded and pandemonium broke out.

CONFRONTATION

ETERMINED NOT TO let the riffraff see he was perturbed, Griff nevertheless seethed inwardly.

The journey north had been a time-consuming inconvenience. However, since the men on trial lived on his lands, he'd been required to attend the proceedings. He certainly had not expected to be harangued by some bluestocking who was certainly more sexually appealing than she ought to be.

What?

The whole affair was ridiculous. As if a few weavers represented a threat to the Prince Regent. The pathetic buggers wouldn't have been allowed anywhere near him. "Tempest in a teacup," he muttered over his shoulder to the faithful Frederick.

He had to admit, though, the harridan in the witness box was right in one sense. The sentences were harsh and would result in starvation for families deprived of a breadwinner. He'd be blamed, if the rude scowls on the faces of men consoling weeping women were anything to go by. It wouldn't hurt to visit the cottages of the condemned men. The working class were always appreciative of a few coins tossed their way.

Exiting a courtroom full of angry men and women took a while. He was glad he'd brought Frederick along. The footman's broad shoulders and surly temperament soon cleared a path.

Reaching the outdoors, he inhaled the crisp April air, glad to be free of the upsetting place.

He was surprised to see a sleek coach waiting alongside his hackney, a somewhat familiar coat of arms emblazoned on the door. Two women stood beside the second conveyance, deep in conversation. A dark-haired woman had her back to him. The second was an attractive blonde with the face of an angel.

He hesitated when Frederick held open the door of his cab. He'd always been partial to blondes. Perhaps if…

He regretted the impulse to dally when the brunette turned and saw him.

Bollocks! The bluestocking!

His instinct was to bolt when she hurried toward him like an avenging angel, but he stood his ground. A Halliwell worth his salt didn't retreat in the face of a tongue-lashing from a female.

⟩⟩⟩⟨⟨⟨

"HALLIWELL," SUSAN DECLARED, somewhat surprised the tall rogue hadn't retreated when he espied her. She itched to wipe the smug superiority off his handsome features. She fisted her hands, disgusted she'd even noticed he was quite good looking. "Lady Susan Crompton," she informed him, determined not to dip the slightest curtsey or offer her hand.

"Ah," the cad replied with a similar lack of courtesy, "now I recognize the crest on your carriage. I admit I didn't pay attention to your name when you were called to testify."

Momentarily thrown off balance by a cavalier answer she ought to have expected, she fought to organize her thoughts. How to explain her former sister-in-law was now married to the current Earl of Farnworth? "I live in the dower house on the Farnworth estate," she said, flummoxed because this information was the last thing she should have divulged. "My late brother was the previous Earl of Farnworth."

"Matthew Crompton," Halliwell supplied. "He and I were at Eton together. My condolences. Perhaps you'll introduce me to your blonde companion."

Never at a loss for words, Susan hesitated. Polite conversation wasn't what she'd been aiming for. The lecherous glint in his eyes when he uttered the word *blonde* was disturbing in so many ways. What color were those intriguing eyes anyway?

Drat!

"Lady Emma Crompton Smith is Matthew's widow. She is the wife of the current earl."

She was appalled when Halliwell shrugged, disappointment etched on his chiseled features. His reputation as a rake seemed well-founded.

"The retired soldier, if I remember correctly," he said with a hint of disdain. "I've chatted with him when our paths have crossed in the Lords. Fine chap."

Here was her opening. "Then you are aware some peers are concerned for the welfare of the common man and woman."

Halliwell frowned. "Your point, I presume, is that I do not take care of my tenants."

Had he not been listening in court?

Susan had a reputation as a woman who spoke her mind, but she'd never actually confronted a powerful male face-to-face. She filled her lungs to bolster her courage. "Can you deny it?"

He barely glanced at the timepiece he took out of his waistcoat pocket with beautifully manicured, elegant fingers. "Much as I would love to stay and chat, I have a prior appointment. Good day to you, Lady Susan. Hopefully, our paths won't cross again."

Not only had he dismissed her out of hand, he then had the audacity to wink. "My regards to Lady Emma," he quipped as he boarded his hackney.

FEELING MORE AT ease once the hack had maneuvered through the angry crowd milling about outside the court, Griff stretched out his legs as far as the cramped cab would allow.

The day hadn't turned out as he'd expected. He'd sent instructions to his estate manager to do what he could to get the charges against his tenants dropped, or at least mitigated. He might have known William Fothersgill would prove ineffectual. The fellow spent too much time wenching and drinking. Not that there was anything wrong with a man enjoying himself, so long as he didn't neglect his duties.

He frowned when a twinge of guilt pricked his conscience. Perhaps if he had come earlier…

He closed his eyes, trying to conjure a memory of the attractive Countess Farnworth in an effort to think of more pleasant things. Her image proved to be elusive. All he could see in his mind's eye was the infernal bluestocking and the anger blazing in her gray eyes. "Mind you," he chuckled, "she was rather attractive, for a brunette. Tempting tits, too."

He vaguely remembered Matthew Crompton as a stickler for following rules. His sister had the same olive complexion but, clearly, she wasn't the sort who obeyed the rules of behavior that applied to ladies of good breeding.

He'd wager she'd be a firebrand in bed. He laughed out loud. She'd likely faint dead away if a man even suggested sexual congress.

⤜⟫⟪⤛

"DON'T LET HIM bother you," Emma advised as the Farnworth carriage began the journey back to Thicketford Manor.

Susan nodded her agreement. "At least I got a cheer from the crowd outside the court. Not that I managed to do anything to help those poor men."

Emma reached for her hand. "Perhaps if Gabriel has a word with the Earl of Pendlebury, you know, one earl to another."

Susan snorted. "Your husband is a reasonable and persuasive man but I don't have high hopes for Lord Pendlebury. He'll head back to London right away. He doesn't care."

"You may be right. Apparently, he operates a successful horse breeding stable near the city."

Susan rolled her eyes. "As if he couldn't breed horses here in Lancashire."

Emma shook her head. "Something to do with proximity to Tattersalls, I believe. Gabriel said Pendlebury's one topic of conversation is an Arabian horse he hopes to purchase. A thoroughbred, whatever that means."

"Thoroughbreds apparently make excellent racehorses," Susan explained. "Pendlebury will spend an incredible amount of money on an expensive horse, but nothing on improving his tenants' lives."

"I suppose horses that win races earn monetary prizes," Emma said.

Susan closed her eyes, too exhausted and sick at heart to even reply. Until a thought occurred. "I wonder how much it costs?"

"What?"

"To buy an Arabian."

CLIFTON HEIGHTS

W HEN GRIFF FINALLY arrived at Clifton Heights later in the afternoon, the musty odor that greeted him in the foyer aggravated his bad mood. "What is that smell?" he asked the butler.

The fellow eyed him as if he'd spoken Greek. "Smell, sir?"

Griff let out an exasperated sigh. Clearly, his butler, and probably the rest of the staff, had become used to the odor of damp and didn't notice it. "Where's Fothersgill?" he asked, handing his hat and gloves to the servant he didn't recall meeting before. It seemed no one stayed long in service at Clifton Heights.

"Andrews, my lord," the butler replied, evidently sensing Griff's confusion. "I believe he's gone to the village," he continued in a nasal monotone.

Griff suspected that meant his steward was at the local inn. "This whole place needs a good scrub," he lamented, knowing it was a waste of time to complain to this man—butlers weren't responsible for the upkeep of the house. "I hope my chamber smells sweeter."

"I'll speak to Mrs. Brass, sir," Andrews replied with a sigh, as if he were dealing with a whining child.

Since he couldn't remember hearing the name before, Griff supposed Mrs. Brass was the latest housekeeper. "See that you do."

Andrews bowed and left. Griff doubted the man would report

his wishes to the housekeeper and, if he did, the woman was likely as bold as her name suggested. Fothersgill seemed to have done a piss poor job of hiring and supervising staff.

He wandered into the drawing room. The hearth looked like it hadn't been cleaned in months. No hearty fire blazed in the sooty grate. No wonder a damp chill hung in the air. Griff hadn't laid eyes on a maid or footman since his arrival. It was as well he'd brought Frederick with him from London.

Clifton Heights had definitely seen better days, a reality that produced a twinge of guilt. His mother must be turning over in her grave. She'd taken immense pride in the ancestral home of the Earls of Pendlebury. Griff had neither the time nor the inclination to take care of it.

He'd hated the loneliness of the immense place after a tragic road accident had taken the lives of his parents three years before. The emptiness only served to intensify the enormity of his loss. A visit to an old family friend in London had opened up a whole new world—balls, musicales, loose women, coffee houses, gentlemen's clubs, gaming halls. He'd never come back to Clifton Heights, lodging funds with Rowbotham for its upkeep and management.

Admittedly, he'd acquired some bad habits in London, but nothing he couldn't control. He'd fallen in love with horse racing and invested the inheritance money from his parents wisely. The breeding stables were on the cusp of reaping huge rewards. A lot was riding on the Arabian.

The *double entendre* had him chuckling.

He'd made his home in London and had no intention of coming back to live in the north. The obvious solution was to dismiss Fothersgill and hire a more efficient steward to manage the crumbling pile. That could take time. He'd have to postpone his return to London.

With that possibility in mind, he went to his study and penned a letter to his man of business in London with instructions to secure the stallion if it came up for sale in Griff's absence.

He underlined the words *NO MATTER THE COST* before sealing the envelope.

He dashed off another letter to Richard Tattersall explaining the reason an agent would act on his behalf when the horse became available.

He rang for Andrews and gave him the letters. "These must go in the post forthwith."

The butler took the missives and left without even a hint of a bow.

As he climbed the stairs to his chamber, Griff wondered if, in the long run, the expense of keeping up Clifton Heights was worth it. The house was an enormous financial drain, although, looking around, he wasn't sure what Fothersgill was actually spending the money on. It might be best to close it up and hire a caretaker. The home farm and the rents from hundreds of tenants were the main sources of the earldom's income, and, hopefully, the farm would recover quickly from last year's disastrous harvests. Thank heaven for hardy moorland sheep and the soaring price of wool. The colder the weather, the more the woolly beasts seemed to thrive.

Thinking of his tenants reminded him of the unfortunate turn of events at the trial. Perhaps if he'd paid more attention to what was going on in the lives of the people who lived on his lands…

It irked that a bluestocking from the Farnworth estate seemed to know more about his tenants than he did. As a brand new member of the Lords, he'd backed the Corn Laws of which she was so critical, but hadn't been aware of any detrimental impact on common folks. And was there truth to what she'd said about weavers losing their livelihoods? Sometimes, the responsibility of being an earl was overwhelming. He'd never expected to inherit the title until he was older—and perhaps wiser.

He remembered a conversation he'd had not long ago with the Earl of Farnworth when they'd bumped into each other in the House of Lords. Griff had at least known he would one day become an earl and been groomed since boyhood for the eventuality. Gabriel Smith hadn't even been aware he was in line to inherit an earldom—yet the career soldier seemed to have fallen into the role of earl with ease. He'd even increased Farnworth's wealth and productivity despite taking over the reins during an economic post-war downturn.

Thicketford Manor was only a couple of hours away. It might be worth taking a carriage ride to chat with Lord Farnworth about hiring an efficient estate manager. Perhaps he could learn a thing or two about investing in profitable ventures like the Leeds to Liverpool Canal. The only drawback would be the chance of bumping into the opinionated Lady Susan. She'd mentioned she lived in the dower house, so perhaps he could avoid her.

RESEARCH

O N THE WAY home from the court, Susan leaned out of the carriage window and shouted to James Footman perched beside the driver. "Tell Conrad to turn around and head for the Chetham Library."

"Why on earth do you want to go there?" Emma asked when Susan regained her seat.

"We're so close. I want to do some research," she replied, suspecting Emma might think she'd lost her wits. Perhaps she had. It was suddenly vitally important she disrupt the Earl of Pendlebury's life.

"Into what?" Emma retorted. "We spent hours there researching arsenic last year when we thought someone was trying to poison Gabriel. In the end, the solution came from elsewhere, not from research."

"This will be different," Susan assured her, hoping she was correct. "One of the world's oldest libraries is bound to have a wealth of information on horses."

Emma narrowed her eyes. "What are you up to?"

"I want to know why Arabians are so important when it comes to breeding horses."

Emma let out an exasperated breath. "You mean to tell me you plan to ask a Chetham docent where to find information on breeding horses. Are you mad?"

"Why should women not learn about such things?"

"It's scandalous. They'll throw you out."

Susan had a feeling her friend might be right. "I won't mention the word *breeding*." A naughty voice in her head goaded her to add, "Nor the word *stud*."

Emma closed her eyes. "I'll wait for you in the carriage. You won't be in there long."

Susan had visited the Chetham Library on numerous occasions in the past, sometimes alone. She was usually the only woman among a host of men. The glares of the tutting academics who frequented the library always let her know she had invaded a privileged male bastion of knowledge. She ignored them.

However, she'd never before embarked on researching a practice men would definitely consider unsuitable for women to even know existed.

When the carriage halted outside the library, Susan hoped Emma might have changed her mind, but her friend folded her arms and closed her eyes.

Head held high, Susan entered the hallowed institution, ignoring the disdain contorting every male face. She recognized many of them from previous visits. "You'd think they'd know me by now," she muttered.

At least the ancient docent greeted her politely, though he didn't smile. "Lady Susan. What can I find for you today?"

"I'm interested in learning about Arabian horses," she whispered. It was a futile hope no one would overhear. Her words bounced off the thousands of leather-bound tomes piled high on towering shelves. Every head turned her way.

"The Earl of Farnworth is thinking of buying one," she lied, ashamed she hadn't held fast to her conviction that women were just as entitled to learn about the world as men.

"History of…characteristics…breeding?" the docent asked.

Audible gasps stole her remaining courage. "History," she murmured.

He led her through the maze of narrow aisles. On earlier visits, she'd often had trouble finding her way back to the entrance, but now felt more confident. She chuckled at the memory of a suggestion Emma had once made that they leave a trail of breadcrumbs.

She extracted several volumes from the shelf the docent indicated, hefted them to an empty table, extracted the slim notebook she always carried in her reticule and settled in to read.

⟫⟫⟩✖⟨⟪⟪

EMMA STARTLED AWAKE when Susan returned to the carriage. "I must have dozed off," she said with a yawn. "How long were you gone?"

"About an hour," Susan replied with a smile as Conrad set the horses in motion. "Sorry it took me so long."

"I assume they didn't eject you?"

"No. And I found a lot of good information."

Emma rolled her eyes. She wasn't remotely interested in horses, but Susan would regurgitate everything she had learned. It was as if her former sister-in-law soaked up knowledge like a sponge then couldn't keep it all in. Her suspicions would be confirmed if the conversation opened with *Did you know.*

Susan took out her notebook and flipped the pages. "Did you know that during the reigns of James I and Charles I, forty-three mares—the so-called Royal Mares—were imported into England from North Africa?"

Emma, of course, had no inkling of such things, but Susan carried on. "A record, called the General Stud Book, was begun."

"Why was it called that?" Emma asked, wishing she hadn't when Susan explained. "They call the male horse a stud. Anyway, the General Stud Book listed only those horses that could be traced back to the Royal Mares in direct line, or to one of three other horses imported to England: the Byerly Turk, imported in 1689, the Godolphin Barb, about 1730, and the Darley Arabian."

Emma stared blankly. "I don't..."

"The horse Pendlebury plans to buy must be a descendant of one of these."

Emma had long ago given up trying to plumb the depths of Susan's convoluted mind, so she sat back and resumed her nap.

⇶⇇

LATER, SUSAN AND Rebecca were chatting about the day's events while eating their evening meal. "On a whim," Susan said. "I stopped in at the main house when we dropped Emma off, just to see if Blair was about."

Rebecca salted her soup. "Good idea. An estate manager must know a lot about horses."

"You'd think so," Susan agreed. "Unfortunately, he has no knowledge of thoroughbreds."

"Still, it was a good idea to ask his opinion."

"Yes, although I eventually had to confide why I was interested in such a topic."

"I don't think anything you say or do can shock Mr. Blair," Rebecca suggested.

"You're probably right," Susan replied. "He's known me since I was a child. Papa was adamant I refrain from what he called *my bluestocking activities*. Blair was sympathetic when I had to leave home."

"That must have been hard."

"It was, but Papa wanted me to be someone I'm not. I had no choice."

"You were fortunate to find refuge in Somerset with Hannah More."

"Yes, I learned a lot from her and, fortunately, Papa didn't cut off my allowance. I was able to leave a bad situation, unlike you, stuck with a monster of a husband."

Rebecca dabbed her mouth with a napkin. "Marrying Mr. Waterman was the biggest mistake of my life. It cost me my children. If Raphael and Michael hadn't run off to join the navy in order to escape his fists, they might be alive today."

Susan patted her friend's hand. "Who can say? They might have given their lives for their country at Trafalgar in any event. Now that you're free of your late, unlamented husband, you get to live close to Gabriel."

Rebecca beamed a smile. "And see him happy with his lovely wife and children."

"Anyway, I digress," Susan said while they waited for the second course to be served. "Blair did mention there is a racecourse not far from here, in Chester. He also told me of a rumor that a certain landowner who frequents Chester is apparently up to his eyeballs in debt. He owns a thoroughbred he wants to sell."

Rebecca clapped her hands. "We could go for an outing."

"I hate to admit it, but we'll probably have to talk Gabriel into taking us."

EXCURSIONS

GRIFF SAT DOWN carefully on a rickety chair in the morning room at Clifton Heights and stared in disgust at the breakfast that awaited him. The fatty bacon, shriveled mushrooms, and watery fried eggs only aggravated his queasy stomach. There was no way of knowing how long the unappetizing mess had sat there, except that the chipped plate was ice cold.

Admittedly, it was his own fault. He'd risen late, a consequence of drinking far too much brandy before retiring last night—but it had been a hell of a day.

However, the abysmal breakfast confirmed his suspicion Clifton Heights didn't even boast a competent cook. He'd never cooked an egg himself, but how difficult could it be to do it properly?

He'd hoped the copious amounts of brandy would induce a deep sleep, but his fitful dozing had been disturbed by memories of a court full of angry people and a sharp-tongued, opinionated bluestocking.

He didn't care for brunettes and had nothing but disdain for women who meddled in the affairs of men. Yet, he'd spent the night peeling off Lady Susan Crompton's clothes, imagining her naked, writhing beneath him, begging…

Disgusted when his body responded predictably to the erotic vision, he shoved away the plate of congealing grease, realizing glumly an efficient footman was unlikely to appear to whisk the abomination away.

He stalked out of the morning room, surprised to almost bump into Andrews exiting the drawing room, a burlap sack in hand. He wondered briefly what the butler was doing in the drawing room, but had more pressing matters on his mind. "Did you speak to Mrs. Brass?" he asked.

Looking annoyed, Andrews peered down his long nose. "I've spoken with the housekeeper on numerous occasions, my lord."

Griff clenched his jaw, resolved to be rid of the insolent fellow once Fothersgill found a replacement. "I mean about the sheets on my bed. They smelled musty, though I instructed…"

"Mrs. Brass comes every other day," Andrews interrupted.

"So, she'll be here today and you can tell her to change the linens and air out my bedroom."

Andrews sighed. "No, my lord, she'll be here tomorrow."

Griff stared, desperately trying to think what reprimand Potts would offer this cheeky…

That brought him to his senses. Potts would discern immediately that the inefficient Fothersgill lay at the root of the problems at Clifton. Replace him and all would be well. "I don't suppose my estate manager is about?" he asked, suspecting he already knew the answer.

"No, my lord. I haven't seen him for a day or two. If you'll excuse me."

With that, he was gone before Griff had a chance to ask him what was in the sack and if his letters had been posted.

There was nothing for it but to seek advice and guidance from the Earl of Farnworth. He set off to find Frederick, intending to travel to Thicketford Manor. There must be an inn on the way where he could procure a decent breakfast.

IT HAD TAKEN some convincing, both during and after last

evening's meal, but Gabriel had finally agreed to escort his ladies to the races at Chester. Susan's idea to have Patsy add her voice to the cause proved to be the winning ploy. She'd counted on the earl's inability to deny his eight-year-old stepdaughter anything she wanted.

Emma complained her husband spoiled their daughter, but Susan judged her friend equally guilty on that front. Patsy had even convinced her doting parents to provide a "chum" for her poodle, insisting Wellington must be feeling left out since all of Patsy's attention was now on her baby Rafe. Thus, Wellington and Prinny (quickly rechristened Princess when it was discovered he was a bitch) were constantly underfoot, snapping at anyone who dared think of petting one of their five equally bad-tempered offspring.

Susan supposed she couldn't blame Gabriel and Emma for spoiling Patsy after the terrible kidnapping ordeal the child had undergone. Heaven only knew what might have happened if Gabriel and his valet hadn't rescued Patsy from the clutches of their vile neighbor, Arthur Coleman, and his accomplice, the witless maid, Tillie.

Arthur had completely disappeared after Patsy's rescue but Susan suspected Baron Whiteside had spirited his son off to the family's plantation in Jamaica. The things people did for their children! It was heartbreaking that a kindly man like the baron had risked prosecution and the confiscation of his estate to save his reprobate son from the gallows.

As for Tillie, the last anyone had seen of her was outside the church after Gabriel and Emma's wedding. No grand house would employ her after her dismissal from Thicketford Manor. She was probably an inmate of the Preston poorhouse by now.

Susan hoped Patsy wouldn't turn out to be a brat like Arthur when she grew up. It wasn't likely. Arthur had been an obnoxious twerp when he and the Cromptons played together as children. Despite sometimes showing evidence of being spoiled, Patsy was a sweet girl.

"I've invited Bradley and his wife to come with us," Gabriel informed them after breakfast as everyone gathered in Thicketford's opulent foyer, ready for the off.

Some might think an earl who invited his valet to participate in a family outing had lost his mind, but Bradley had served as Gabriel's batman in the army. They'd fought together at Waterloo, and, well, Bradley had shot one of Patsy's kidnappers and helped save the child's life.

As the earl's valet and the countess' abigail, Bradley and his wife occupied an unusual status somewhere between valued servants and respected friends.

"Lucy's declined to accompany us," Bradley informed them when he appeared. "She don't cotton to horses."

"Right," Gabriel said. "That makes things simpler. Bradley and I will ride to Chester, the ladies can squeeze into the carriage."

"Perhaps I should stay with the baby," Emma said, though Susan knew she was keen to go.

"Nonsense," Gabriel countered. "Rafe is perfectly fine with Amelia."

"He's right," Susan said, "and you don't want to miss the fun. Amelia is well qualified to take care of one infant."

She didn't voice her opinion Amelia Southwell had always struck her as rather overqualified to be a nanny, but it was gratifying to see a young woman keen on learning new things from every book she could get her hands on. She reminded Susan of herself in younger days.

"If you think so," Emma conceded.

"Let's go," Patsy urged.

THE ROODEE

GLAD TO DISEMBARK from his carriage in the yard of *The Pheasant* in Chorley, Griff handed Frederick a few pence and sent him off to the taproom. He entered the dining room, his agitation calming when tempting aromas wafted to his nostrils. He'd hoped to be at Thicketford Manor by now, but it had taken a half-hour for him, his footman and a stable lad roused from his bed in the hayloft at Clifton Heights to rid one of the carriages of several roosting hens and their revolting mess. Locating and harnessing a horse that didn't look like it was on its last legs had consumed another half-hour.

It was fortunate Fothersgill was nowhere to be found. Griff was in a mood to throttle the fellow by the time they set off for Preston with Frederick taking the reins.

Waiting to be served in the crowded dining room of *The Pheasant*, Griff hoped no one would pay much attention to the abysmal state of the carriage in the yard. He almost wished he hadn't made the stable boy scrub the grime off the Pendlebury coat of arms. The Earl of Farnworth wouldn't be impressed, and Griff had no one but himself to blame for the disgraceful state of his stables. Two or three of the once pristine carriages might be beyond repair.

"What's thy wish and pleasure, lovey?" a serving woman asked, interrupting his thoughts when she plonked a tray of empty tankards on his table.

"I'm ravenous," he replied, hoping she didn't mistake his meaning. A bountiful bosom directly under his nose was difficult to ignore, but she was old enough to be his mother—or perhaps his grandmother. "What do you recommend?"

"We've a nice pork pie. Comes with chips and gravy."

"And bread?"

"Penny extra. Tuppence if thee wants it buttered."

"Sounds good. And a tankard of ale."

After smiling a toothless grin, she hefted the tray onto her hip and tottered off. On her way into the kitchen, she came close to colliding with a surly young man on his way out. She cringed when he raised his fist.

Used to dining at one of his clubs in London where clean, liveried adolescents served meals, Griff experienced a peculiar pang of disquiet. The woman should be sitting in a comfortable armchair in a warm cottage, chuckling at the antics of her grandchildren for whom she was knitting…

"Get a grip," he growled under his breath.

It wasn't his concern that an elderly woman had to tote heavy trays and probably endure all kinds of abuse from patrons and employers alike.

His appetite had diminished somewhat by the time she returned with his food. However, the thick slab of crusty pork pie and the heaping mound of chips smothered in gravy revived his spirits. There was only a faint hint of butter on the bread, but he willingly paid the price of the meal, slipping a shilling into the pocket of the crone's pinny. "For you," he said softly. "Not the landlord."

After glancing in the direction of the scowling youth who'd accosted her earlier, she peeked into the pocket. "Thanks ever so much, yer lordship. It ain't often a toff like thyself is generous with 'is coin. God bless thee."

Tucking into his meal after she left, Griff pondered her words. A shilling to him was neither here nor there. It had cost him nothing, but the pittance obviously meant a lot to her. Perhaps

Lady Susan Crompton was right—cocooned in his opulent London townhouse for too long, he'd given little thought to the daily struggles of people who weren't "toffs" like him.

However, that was the way of the world, wasn't it? He couldn't be expected to solve all the problems of the working class. The "great unwashed" were usually the architects of their own misery, according to the prevailing opinion among the members of all his London clubs. As he swilled down the last of his meal with the ale remaining in his tankard, he thanked his lucky stars he'd been born into wealth.

Exiting the inn, he found Frederick perched on the driver's bench. "On to Thicketford Manor," Griff shouted, holding his nose as he entered the carriage. At least his destination was only a few miles away.

"Don't like the look of yon wheel, sir," Frederick said.

Exasperated, Griff leaned out of the window and followed his footman's nod. The wheel looked odd. "Let's hope it gets us to our destination," he hissed.

They stopped to ask directions twice. Eventually, a gatekeeper opened an ornate black and gold double gate and the carriage pulled into a winding avenue that led to Thicketford Manor. The majestic weeping willows lining both sides of the avenue put the barren approach to Clifton Heights to shame. His driveway used to have trees and he wondered how it was they had disappeared. When the impressive manor house came into view, it was plain to see it was in better repair than his own.

Frederick took down the step and held the carriage door open. Adjusting his cravat, Griff strode to the front door, lifted the brass lion's head and knocked.

It took only a minute for a butler to appear in response to the sonorous thud of the knocker. The fellow's demeanor and immaculate livery reminded Griff of Potts as he narrowed his eyes at the grimy carriage.

"Griffith Halliwell, Earl of Pendlebury," he announced in an effort to divert the butler's attention from the ramshackle vehicle.

"Here to call on the Earl of Farnworth."

"Frame at your service, your lordship," Potts' twin replied. "I'm afraid the whole family has gone on a day trip to the racecourse at Chester, returning tomorrow."

Rarely at a loss for words, Griff was gobsmacked. Were the Smiths racing aficionados like him? The *whole family*? Including the bluestocking? "They've gone to The Roodee?" he babbled.

"I beg your pardon, sir?" Frame asked, clearly puzzled.

"Er…nothing. That leaves me in a bit of a predicament. My carriage…"

"Clearly, neither it nor your steed are equipped for the four-hour journey to Chester."

Frame had obviously taken note of the suspect wheel and decrepit horse.

"Precisely. Perhaps there's an inn nearby you can recommend, and a wheelwright who can effect repairs."

"Certainly, my lord. *The Coach and Four* in Preston. They'll know of a wheelwright."

⇥⇤

AFTER A BRIEF stop to stretch their legs and water the horses, Susan and her companions arrived in Chester just after midday and took rooms at the *Pied Bull Inn*.

After initially insisting he had no space available—*it's race week, don't ye know*—the landlord changed his tune when Gabriel identified himself.

Surprisingly luxurious accommodations were soon found—Gabe and Emma in one spacious chamber, Susan, Rebecca and Patsy in another. Bradley was happy to bed down in the stables, as was Conrad, their driver.

"Mummy's glad we got rooms," Patsy confided. "She was afraid we might have to stay with Aunty Priscilla."

Susan had met Emma's sister at Matthew's wedding and

again at his funeral. From what she remembered of the woman who lived in Cheshire with several undisciplined children, massive dogs and a sullen husband, she was also relieved.

After a quick luncheon of pickled egg salad spread on toast rounds, they joined the substantial crowd walking the short distance to the racecourse.

Fortunately, the landlord of the *Pied Bull Inn* had wisely provided an escort. The diminutive Oscar was clearly well known to the officials and they were whisked to the front of the lengthy queue.

Once they entered the grounds, Susan gaped at the spectacle of hundreds of people crammed into a huge grandstand and an equal crush in the field below.

Bradley abruptly excused himself and disappeared into the crowd below the grandstand.

"Newly built this year," Oscar explained with an expansive gesture.

"You seem to know a lot about this place," Gabriel remarked.

"Used to be a jockey, my lord. Too old now, but I love coming here. Oldest racecourse in the country. The Roodee gets in yer blood."

Oscar led them up an exterior staircase to a private box, all the while explaining how the strange nickname had come into being. Susan looked down at a grassy area where several horses were being paraded around a ring—and suddenly knew exactly what the retired jockey meant.

She'd grown up around horses, though she couldn't say she particularly enjoyed riding. The sleek, long-legged beasts in the paddock below bore no resemblance to any horse she'd ever seen.

Oscar discretely informed Gabriel he would willingly act as a runner to place any bets his lordship wished to make on the outcome of the races.

Susan felt compelled to interrupt. "Can we get closer to those horses?"

Rebecca wrinkled her nose as she sat. "I prefer to stay up

here."

"Me too," Emma echoed.

Oscar, however, smiled knowingly. "If you'll come with me, your ladyship."

"Can I go, Daddy?" Patsy asked.

Gabriel hesitated, but then agreed. "Stay close to Oscar and Aunty Susan. A quid on whichever horse you think will win," he told Oscar, handing over money retrieved from his waistcoat pocket.

Susan had a lifelong love of learning; discovering new things excited her. The excitement pumping through her veins as she followed Oscar wasn't remotely cerebral. There was something primeval about the proud steeds; the toss of their noble heads made it clear they knew they weren't ordinary horses. The flared nostrils seemed to declare, "We're descended from a long line of purebreds, and don't you forget it."

Oscar's voice penetrated her trance. "The jockeys perched on their backs might ride them, but only because the nags allow it. They won't tolerate a jockey they don't like."

As they neared the railing, Susan inhaled the heady smells. Grass, leather, sweat, horse, even the steaming piles of manure— she loved it all.

An annoying thought impinged on her euphoria—a new appreciation for Pendlebury's apparent fascination with racehors- es.

However, she shoved aside the rakish earl's intrusion when Oscar winked and whispered, "Would you like to place a bet, my lady?"

Careful to hide what she was doing from Patsy—not difficult since the horses had absorbed all the child's attention—she fished in her reticule for a guinea. "Which one?"

As he took the coin, Oscar nodded to the horse he favored. "Galiano. Lots of heart. He likes this track."

Her own heart did a little flip. He'd indicated the chestnut she would have picked. "Very well."

When he'd gone, Susan and her niece stood by the railing watching the parade of stallions.

"They're lovely, aren't they?" Patsy said.

"Magnificent," Susan replied dreamily.

"What's that between their back legs?" her niece asked innocently, jolting Susan from her reverie.

"Er…well…you remember when Wellington and Princess…"

"Wait till you see them run," Oscar exclaimed, rescuing her from having to explain protruding male body parts as he rejoined them. "You'll get a better view from the grandstand."

Susan gladly followed his advice as the thoroughbreds were led out to the starting gate.

EQUIPMENT

B Y THE TIME Galiano had been declared the clear winner of the first race, Susan was exhausted. Unabashed by the puzzled stares of people in the crowd below and determined to ignore the undisguised amusement on the faces of her family members, she closed her eyes and relived the excitement.

She'd cheered for her favorite like a fishwife until she was hoarse, the pounding hoofbeats echoing in her ears. Jockeys clad in vibrant colored silks clung to their mounts like demons on a mission to wreak havoc atop the hounds of hell. Clods of muck flew through the air as hooves churned the earth.

But it was the sheer power of the horses that would stay in her memory forever. She imagined their forebears streaking across desert sands, handsome sun-bronzed sheiks stripped to the waist, riding bareback.

Overheated and shocked by her wanton thoughts, she blinked rapidly, further dismayed when an unwelcome vision compounded the embarrassment—Griffith Halliwell rode with those devilish sheiks. She retrieved the fan from her reticule. The image was enough to make a lady swoon.

"You enjoyed that," Gabriel remarked.

How did he know I'd imagined Pendlebury…oh!

The fan was proving useless.

She struggled to regain her composure. "Yes. I had no idea it would be so exciting. Especially since our…er…your horse won. I would love to own such an animal."

"To race?" Emma asked, her voice laden with doubt.

Thoughts of Griffith Halliwell intruded again. "Not necessarily. As we know, there's money to be made using a horse for…er…breeding other…er…baby horses."

Annoyed with herself for suddenly becoming a tongue-tied henwit, she took a deep breath and explained. "Stud fees, they call it."

"Indeed, Lady Susan," Oscar confirmed, coming to her rescue yet again. "And, if you are serious about buying a thoroughbred for breeding purposes, I can put you in touch with someone anxious to sell such a horse, a grandson of Eclipse."

"Eclipse?" Emma asked.

"Greatest thoroughbred that ever lived. Undefeated in eighteen races, including eleven King's Plates. Descendant of the original Godolphin Barb."

Susan was sure that must be an impressive achievement. "I doubt I could afford it," she admitted.

"Well, this gent's willing to negotiate," Oscar whispered, tapping the side of his nose. "His creditors have him in a bind. And I think he'd prefer to sell the stallion to someone in the north, otherwise he has to get him transported to Tattersalls in London."

"Can't they simply have someone ride it there?" Gabriel asked.

"There's the rub, my lord. The horse no longer races because the coffin bones in his feet are a problem. Nothing wrong with his…er…other equipment though."

Hidden behind her own fan, Rebecca tittered.

Emma's face turned beet red.

Susan glanced at Patsy but, fortunately, the child was preoccupied with watching the next group of horses.

"We might be interested," Gabriel said, much to Susan's surprise and delight. She doubted her excitement would allow her to get much sleep at the *Pied Bull*.

⟫⟫⟫⟩❧⟨⟪⟪⟪

"FINALLY, MY LUCK has changed," Arthur Coleman hissed.

He quickly pulled the cloth cap lower to hide his face, turning away lest the haughty Susan Crompton and her niece take their attention off the horses parading in the paddock.

Not that there was much chance they'd recognize him. The relentless Jamaican sun had bronzed his skin and bleached his hair. If his father thought he was going to spend the rest of his life in the hellhole his Uncle Nathan referred to as a sugar mill, he was sadly mistaken. Wielding a whip in the sweltering heat was exhausting. One little error in judgment and he was expected to forfeit the Whiteside barony and spend his life dealing with truculent slaves. As if attempting to kidnap the Farnworth brat was such an enormous crime. And, if his henwitted sister thought one of her brood would inherit… "I think not," he muttered.

It hadn't been easy to get away from the plantation. His uncle kept a closer eye on him than on his slaves. However, all the white men who worked as overseers on the plantation took advantage of slave women, so Arthur had followed their example. He had to admit he was fond of one or two of the women he bedded, especially the ones who fought him before surrendering.

His uncle warned him about the black magic practices the slaves carried on. Arthur thought it was all bunkum until he jokingly suggested one of his women cast a hex on his uncle. Nothing too serious. Just to put him out of action for a few days.

Lo and behold, the man had taken to his bed with a bilious stomach and Arthur had fled.

He'd made his way to Kingston, keeping off the beaten track and feeling more like a runaway slave with each passing day. If running meant enduring a thousand insect bites, raging thirst, intolerable daytime heat and freezing nights, why would any slave want to bother trying to escape? What's more, Arthur didn't have to worry about having a limb hacked off if his uncle caught

45

him.

Signing onto a British ship as a crew member had been easy—his skin was the right color and he spoke English. After weeks of hard labor, weevil-infested hardtack, terrible seasickness, and fending off filthy bearded seamen who ogled him like a piece of meat, Arthur fell to his knees, close to tears when he disembarked on the rain-drenched Liverpool docks. He'd made it home.

He'd hoped to sail into Bristol or, better still, London. He had to make money fast if he was to have any hope of reestablishing himself. Liverpool was too close to Preston, where he was well-known; hence he'd come south to Chester, hoping to win big on a horse race.

That hadn't happened. The pittance earned aboard ship was all but gone. However, having followed Susan and Patsy Crompton, he'd discovered the earl's entire family was in attendance. At the end of the day, he trailed them to the *Pied Bull* where he slept in the stables.

ARRIVING IN PRESTON, Griff breathed a sigh of relief when Frederick guided the carriage into the yard of *The Coach and Four* in the late afternoon. He doubted they would have made it much further. A stable boy hurried off with his bag to secure accommodations while he discussed the wheel problem with the inn's ostler and his footman.

They quickly came to the conclusion the buckled wheel was beyond repair and would have to be replaced. The ostler sent the stable boy off to fetch the wheelwright from the other side of town.

Griff had no option but to retire to the inn's taproom. The place was already crowded with jovial men but he was lucky enough to find a seat at a small table near the rear of the cozy room. He looked up at the oak-beamed ceiling and let out an exasperated breath. Here he was, a wealthy earl in possession of numerous expensive carriages, yet obliged to pass the time among common folks waiting for a new wheel. When he got back to Clifton Heights, he'd have to look into purchasing at least one new vehicle, although what was the point if he spent all his time in London?

He was imbibing his third tankard of ale when the nervous ostler approached, cloth cap in hand, to inform him the wheelwright would only undertake the job at his workshop. "So, yer lordship, I sent yer footman off wit' yer carriage," the fellow explained, all the while scanning the surroundings for an avenue of escape.

Too tired and frustrated to care any longer, Griff nodded his understanding, not surprised when the man's frown relaxed and he scurried off.

"What do you suppose he thought I'd do?" he mused aloud. "Punish him for his initiative?"

He became aware of a sudden lull in the conversation at the table next to his. A well-dressed, elderly gentleman leaned his way. "Sounds like you're having a spot of bother, old chap."

"Buckled wheel," Griff replied, thinking the gent looked vaguely familiar. "I'm stranded here until it can be fixed."

"Far to go, have you?"

Griff wasn't one to discuss his business with strangers, but he had nothing else to do. "Actually, I came from Clifton Heights to see the Earl of Farnworth, but my timing was off. He's taken his family to the races at Chester."

His neighbor slapped his thigh. "Thought I recognized you. You're the Earl of Pendlebury. Allow me to introduce myself. Bertrand Coleman, Baron Whiteside," he said extending a hand. "Farnworth's my neighbor."

"Of course, sir," Griff responded, shaking the baron's hand. "I've seen you in the Lords on occasion."

"My tailor," Whiteside said, cocking his head toward his companion. "Mr. Carr."

Griff offered his hand. "Griffith Halliwell. How do you do?"

"I'm well, sir, and you?" the diminutive man declared, accepting the gesture.

"As well as can be expected," Griff muttered.

Carr preened. "I see by the cut of your clothes you have excellent taste, sir."

The baron chuckled. "Mr. Carr has a first rate establishment here in Preston. Outfits all us titled chaps."

"I'll have to remember that," Griff replied, though he couldn't imagine ever purchasing clothing in Preston—not when he had an excellent tailor in London who was always abreast of the latest fashions, even after Brummell's flight to France.

"So, you say Gabriel and his troops have gone off to the races," Whiteside said. "I didn't know they were interested in that sort of thing."

"I don't know him all that well. Perhaps it's just a day out," Griff suggested with a shrug. However, something about the earl's family taking a sudden interest in thoroughbred racing niggled. He recalled Farnworth looking quite bored when Griff had told him about Pendlebury Stables and his plans to buy another thoroughbred. That memory was bothersome. Had Farnworth relayed the information to Lady Susan? He wouldn't put it past the harridan to...

He suddenly realized Whiteside had asked him a question. It brought him back to the inn. After all, what could a bluestocking do to upset his plans? "I'm sorry, sir, I didn't..."

"You must come to stay at Withins Hall," the baron insisted as he stood. "Can't have you bedding down in this place. The ale is passably good, but I hear the accommodations leave a lot to be desired. My carriage awaits."

"Very good of you, sir. I wasn't looking forward to staying here," he replied, glad of the opportunity for a more comfortable night's rest and perhaps a chance to learn more about the devious Lady Susan Crompton.

Carr offered his hand again, bowed and took his leave.

Griff went to speak to the landlord. He left a message for Frederick, paid for his footman's food and accommodations, then retrieved his bag.

Upon reaching the yard behind the inn, he was surprised to see a young woman dressed in filthy rags pulling on the baron's sleeve. The carriage driver stood at his perch, brandishing his whip and shouting threats at the beggar. Scowling, she loped off as Griff approached.

"Are you all right, sir?" he asked.

"Right as rain," Whiteside replied, though his ruddy complexion had turned ashen. "Only Tillie."

Puzzled, Griff assisted the baron into the carriage and climbed aboard. He'd been importuned by many a beggar in the dodgy parts of London, but couldn't say he knew any of them by name. Things were obviously different here in the north.

PRODUCTIVE CONVERSATIONS

T HE NOISY ATMOSPHERE in the crowded dining room of
Chester's *Pied Bull* echoed Susan's excitement. Punters told
and retold stories of wins and losses. Susan longed to boast of her
winnings, but that was between her and Oscar. Ladies didn't
place wagers. The most pleasing aspect of the windfall was that
she'd picked out winners even before Oscar revealed his choices.
She'd preened with pleasure when he'd told her she had an eye
for good bloodlines.

The landlord ushered them to a reserved table. Throughout
the meal—a wholesome, if overly salty, pigeon pie with mashed
potatoes and parsnips—she and Patsy chatted excitedly about the
races. It was apparent the child was as taken with the sport as
Susan.

Gabriel seemed to have enjoyed the day and confirmed that
he and the retired jockey had agreed on arranging a meeting with
the thoroughbred's owner the next morning. Susan assumed he'd
also won a goodly amount of money.

Bradley wasn't his usual effusive self. They'd hardly seen him
throughout the afternoon; Susan suspected he'd lost money on
his wagers.

Emma remarked she'd found the experience interesting and
fun but uninspiring.

Rebecca was clearly exhausted and looked like she might nod
off into the dish of sponge pudding and custard served as the

sweet.

After they retired to their room, Susan and her niece continued their whispered chattering long after Rebecca had fallen asleep. Susan confided that she'd placed bets through Oscar and won five guineas.

"Five guineas," Patsy exclaimed.

"Shhh," Susan replied. "Our secret."

Patsy's grin was the last thing Susan saw before blowing out the candle.

LOUNGING IN A comfortable leather armchair in Baron Whiteside's study, savoring the aroma of an after-dinner cigar, Griff relaxed and blew out a series of perfect smoke rings. "An excellent meal," he told his host. "I'm grateful not to be stuck at the inn."

"I'm glad of the company, and the opportunity for good conversation," the baron replied.

Having listened to Whiteside's daughter prattle on throughout the meal about one of Handel's lesser-known operas, Griff understood. He hoped his dismay hadn't been obvious each time Anthea Coleman-Springer launched into an off-key rendition of the libretto of the plot she'd explained in great detail.

Anthea's only other topic of conversation was her infant daughter's apparently astonishing vocal ability. Griff was assured the little girl would, in the very near future, be recognized throughout Lancashire as a musical prodigy. He doubted that would turn out to be true if the child was as incapable of hitting a note as her mother.

Anthea's husband, whose given name Griff had already forgotten, hadn't said a word all evening. He sat across from Griff, coughing loudly after attempting unsuccessfully to blow smoke rings.

Bertrand Coleman's pear-shaped wife had beamed at every word her daughter uttered, clapping pudgy hands enthusiastically after each musical interlude. Griff could only assume the woman had a tin ear.

Reluctant to bring up a worrisome topic at the table, Griff decided now was as good a time as any while the ladies were in the drawing room. Still intent on contorting his mouth into ineffectual ring-blowing shapes, Springer didn't appear to be listening. "So, Bertrand, the beggar at the inn. You knew her."

As he'd expected, Springer carried on with his failed mimicry, but the baron stiffened. The brandy he'd been sipping suddenly disappeared in one gulp. "Yes. Tillie," he replied gruffly.

It was the first time Griff had seen the baron with anything other than a jovial expression on his face. Had he been the sort of chap who paid heed to inner, warning voices, he'd have let the matter drop. "I find it unusual. That you would know her name."

"There was a spot of bother," Bertrand replied, his jaw clenched. "She used to be a maid at Thicketford."

Interesting.

Leather squeaked when the baron shifted his weight. "She's an inmate at the poorhouse now."

Again, curiosity got the better of Griff. "And where did she dredge up the temerity to approach you?"

Bertrand heaved a sigh and stared into the bottom of his empty glass. "My son was to blame for her downfall," he said, his voice cracking. "I confess I give her the token coin now and then."

Griff finally heard the alarm bells and remained silent. He'd assumed Anthea was the baron's only child.

Whiteside sipped his brandy. "I had to send Arthur to Jamaica. My brother owns a plantation there. He's getting my son back on the right track, teaching him self-discipline, which I freely admit I failed to do."

Obviously, there was more to this story, and it involved a former member of the Earl of Farnworth's staff. Griff wanted to learn as much as he could about the family at Thicketford Manor but, clearly, the conversation was getting bogged down in shifting sands. He tried another tack. "I met Lady Susan recently."

The temptation to slap some sense into his own head was powerful. Why had he begun with that? He certainly didn't want the topic of the trial to arise.

However, Coleman brightened. "Wonderful girl. Watched her grow up. Thought at one point she and Arthur…well, never mind that. Water under the bridge. I was sorry to see her leave."

"She left?"

"Moved to Somerset. Her late father drove her out. He refused to allow a young woman living under his roof to be involved in, well, anything other than looking for a husband, and sewing."

From what little Griff remembered of the conservative Matthew Crompton at Eton, he'd clearly been a chip off the old block. "But she's back now. For good?"

"Yes. Lives at the dower house with the current earl's mother, Rebecca Waterman."

"Let me get this straight," Griff said, crossing one leg over the other. "Gabriel Smith inherited the earldom and subsequently married the late earl's widow?"

"Emma. Yes. She and Matthew previously had a daughter, Patsy."

Griff startled when his host literally vaulted out of his chair to refill his glass, prompting the notion Patsy had something to do with whatever mischief Arthur had become involved with.

"One thing about Lady Susan," Bertrand declared, brandishing the brandy bottle. "Once she gets her teeth into something, she's like a dog with a bone. Never gives up."

Griff raised his glass, signaling his acceptance of a refill, but he lost track when the baron went off on a tangent about arsenic poisoning and the island of Saint Helena—whatever that had to do with anything.

His emotions were mixed. He shuddered at the possibility

Lady Susan might have sunk her teeth into thoroughbred horse racing. On the other hand, outside the court, he'd noticed she had lovely, even teeth. He'd wager she was attractive when she smiled. Such pearly whites could wreak havoc on a man's body.

Suddenly rendered weak in the knees by an erotic vision of Susan Crompton nibbling his cock, he stubbed out his cigar, downed the brandy in one gulp and begged leave to retire for the night before his arousal split apart his trousers.

A NEW DAY DAWNS

I N CHESTER, SUSAN awoke the next morning feeling refreshed, despite having fallen asleep long after midnight. She'd dreamed of riding a spirited Arabian across desert sands, vibrantly colored skirts up around her thighs, hair flying free as she clung to the bare back of the man holding the reins. When she woke, she couldn't for the life of her recall the identity of the rider, but the ride had been exhilarating. Her pillow was strangely damp. "Must have drooled on the fellow," she muttered with a chuckle. The notion gave rise to a peculiar, though not unpleasant, spasm in a very intimate place.

She, Patsy and Rebecca assisted with each other's *toilette*.

"You seem chipper today," her friend remarked.

"Yes," she replied, though she couldn't explain the strong premonition the day held special promise.

They joined the rest of the family in the dining room for a breakfast of scrambled eggs, toast and coffee.

A scullery lad was clearing away the last of their dishes when Oscar arrived with another gentleman he first introduced to Gabriel as Hugh Cavendish, the master of Heaton Hall.

"A pleasure to meet you, my lord," Cavendish declared, removing his bowler hat and tucking it under his arm. He extended a hand to Gabriel who had come to his feet.

"Likewise," Gabriel replied, accepting the handshake before proceeding to introduce everyone else at the table.

Emma rose after being introduced. "Come along, Patsy. We'll leave the gentlemen to their business."

Her daughter obeyed, though her deep sulk left no doubt she was annoyed.

Rebecca followed.

Susan remained in her seat, despite the puzzled expression on their guest's face.

"Please be seated, Mr. Cavendish," Gabriel said.

Susan offered a silent prayer of thanks for this broad-minded man who'd inherited her late brother's title. Most aristocrats would have insisted she leave, but Gabriel hadn't been born into the aristocracy. Still, he was wise enough not to mention it was she who wanted the horse.

Cavendish glanced at the earl, then at Bradley. He scowled at Susan as he sat. "I don't normally..." he began.

"Lady Susan is a trusted advisor in matters such as these," Gabriel interrupted.

Even Bradley gaped. Susan wished she'd brought her fan to hide the silly grin that threatened to split her face. She took a risk. "Tell us about the horse you wish to sell."

Fidgeting with the brim of the bowler perched on his lap, Cavendish directed his response to Gabriel. "Orion is the grandson of Eclipse." He turned to Susan. "Eclipse was..."

"The greatest thoroughbred that ever lived," she supplied, avoiding looking at Oscar standing behind Cavendish. "Undefeated in eighteen races, including eleven King's Plates."

"Well...er...yes. Good. You're aware then..."

"Name your price," Gabriel said softly.

Cavendish likely couldn't tell, but Susan recognized the almost imperceptible tick that betrayed Gabriel's amusement. "Well...er...in his heyday, Eclipse fetched stud fees of fifty guineas for every...er...mare...he...er...covered. So, I'd say Orion's worth at least two hundred guineas."

Susan's eyes almost popped out of her head. Obviously, debt had stolen the fellow's wits. However, it seemed her presence was perhaps of benefit to the negotiations. Discussing the mechanics of horse breeding in front of a female had clearly thrown the master of Heaton Hall off balance.

"However," Gabriel countered, "initially, before his progeny proved themselves, his services were sold for much less, around ten guineas, I believe."

Susan could have laughed at the confusion on their guest's face. Evidently, Gabriel had gleaned the valuable information from the all-knowing Oscar.

She was sure Emma's husband had also noted the frayed edges of Cavendish's sleeves and the shabby condition of his clothing in general. The man was down on his uppers.

"In addition," Gabriel pointed out. "Your horse has bad feet."

Cavendish's face reddened to an alarming degree. "But he doesn't need his feet to…er…that is to say…"

"Forty guineas," Gabriel said.

Cavendish shook his head. "Tattersalls has guaranteed me more."

"An establishment which, I believe, is in London, many miles to the south."

The horse's owner scowled. "I've gone to the expense of building a special van to haul him there."

"If you include the van, I'll offer you fifty guineas, provided it's built sturdily enough to transport the horse to the Farnworth estate today."

"It is," Cavendish replied, squirming in his seat.

Susan feared for the survival of the bowler in the grip of his twitching fingers.

Gabriel held out his hand. "Are we in agreement?"

Susan held her breath, elated when Cavendish accepted the gesture and declared the deal done.

AT WITHINS HALL the next morning, Griff managed to take care of his own *toilette,* unavoidable since there'd been no offer of a valet. Tying a decent cravat proved to be a torment, so he gave up and went downstairs. It wasn't as if he had anyone to impress in this household.

A footman directed him to the morning room. To his dismay, Springer was seated at the table, a curly-haired child squirming on his lap. "Good morning," he offered, startled when a gravelly voice responded, "Morning."

The infant gaped at her father as if it were the first time she too had heard his voice.

Griff helped himself to ham and coddled eggs from the sideboard. A footman poured his coffee. "No one else about?" he asked.

Springer shook his head. "My wife was up for hours with the baby."

"I not a baby," the pouting child insisted, banging the table with a spoon.

Springer ignored the racket his daughter was making. "Lady Whiteside doesn't usually rise until after ten o'clock and the baron is probably sleeping off last night's bender."

Griff paused his fork halfway to his mouth, tempted to grab the spoon from the infant's grasp. The fellow hadn't spoken a word last night; now, apparently, he had the courage to disparage his in-laws. "I didn't think he'd had much to drink."

"You weren't to know the topic of Arthur is a touchy one. Bertrand drowned his sorrows after you left. Pining for her son is the reason Lady Whiteside can't get herself out of bed. Say, you'll have to teach me how to blow those smoke rings."

His appetite having fled, Griff fumed. He hadn't been the one to bring up Arthur per se. True, he'd inquired about Tillie, but how was he to know where that would lead? He got the feeling the baron needed an understanding ear to listen to his heartbreak. It was doubtful anyone in this house understood his pain, apart from his wife who apparently wasn't dealing well with her own grief. Besides which, Griff would like to teach Springer a thing or two about keeping family business private. Noble families didn't air their dirty laundry in front of complete strangers. "Did you ever meet Arthur?"

"Briefly. He's a bad one. If Bertrand hadn't shipped him off to Jamaica, he'd have dangled from a noose. Kidnapping's a capital offense."

"Jam, jam, want jam," his daughter demanded, banging the table with increased fervor.

"No, my love. Jamaica. Anyway, no skin off my nose," Springer shouted over the din. "Arthur can't set foot in England, so my sons will inherit."

Griff was tempted to remind the crass fellow he'd have to sire boys before he got too comfortable, but the problems of this household weren't his concern. He felt heartily sorry for the baron, a jovial chap brought low by his own son and stuck with Anthea's poor excuse of a husband in the hopes of an heir. The situation strengthened his resolve to remain a confirmed bachelor. The only fly in that ointment was his duty to sire an heir for the earldom of Pendlebury. He owed that much to his parents.

He'd looked forward to spending a pleasant day at Withins Hall but, now, he itched to get away. "Perhaps I can borrow a horse. I should go into Preston to see about my carriage."

"Help yourself to whichever one you want," Springer replied.

Griff ought to take proper leave of the baron, though he intended to return before dark. "You'll relay my whereabouts to your father-in-law?" he asked.

"Of course."

As the racket and the child's strident yelling continued, Griff drank the last of his coffee and left, annoyingly sure Springer would forget to pass the message to the baron.

GABRIEL SENT EMMA, Patsy and Rebecca home from Chester in the carriage, having been assured by Cavendish the van he'd constructed was roadworthy.

Susan took Gabriel's arm as they followed the master of Heaton Hall to an area of sprawling stables not far from the racetrack. Oscar and Bradley made their way to the rear of the inn and retrieved the horses ridden from Thicketford Manor the previous day.

Cavendish dragged open the enormous door of one building and ushered Susan and Gabriel inside. It wasn't the first time she had entered a stable. The odors were familiar—leather, hay, manure. However, she found herself looking down the length of a long gallery, the likes of which she'd never seen before. There must have been twenty stalls, each housing a horse, but she was immediately drawn to a glossy chestnut about halfway down the gallery. "Orion," she whispered.

Cavendish eyed her curiously. "That's him."

"He's a beauty," Oscar declared as he joined them, leaving Bradley outside with the Farnworth horses. "Come see, my lord."

Susan was grateful for the strength of Gabriel's arm as they approached the thoroughbred. Emotion swirled in her heart; she didn't know whether to weep or laugh out loud. Orion snorted when she reached up to touch him, but she felt no fear.

"He likes you, Lady Susan," Oscar remarked.

She nodded. *Likes* didn't begin to describe it. She shared an affinity with this magnificent creature—and he felt it too. She would never be able to describe what passed between her and the horse as she stroked him. If he proved to be worthless as a stud, she still had to have him.

As if sensing her amazement, Gabriel patted her arm and released her.

Reluctantly, she removed her hand from the horse and stepped aside as Cavendish swung open the half-door and pushed the suddenly agitated horse further back into the stall.

Gabriel winked at her. "I'll just check him out. Make sure he is a…"

"Oh, he's a stallion, all right," Oscar exclaimed. "As you can see."

Susan feared her knees might buckle. It wasn't the length of the horse's *equipment* that stole the breath from her lungs. It was the erotic dream that suddenly broke—the unknown rider she'd drooled on was none other than the hateful Griffith Halliwell.

Lightheaded, she became vaguely aware Gabriel was waving a promissory note under Cavendish's nose. "The van?" he asked.

"Behind the stables," the fellow replied grabbing the note.

Oscar closed and secured the half-door.

Susan watched the men leave, but she remained rooted to the spot. She looked into Orion's huge, mysterious eyes. The horse flared his nostrils, as if to say, "I'm not the only beautiful creature you crave."

THE DAY UNFOLDS

L EAVING WITHINS HALL, Griff enjoyed the easy six-mile ride into Preston and soon forgot his irritation with Springer and his undisciplined brat. He didn't have to worry overmuch about controlling the docile gelding chosen by a stable lad. The beast knew the way.

Scanning the landscape, he filled his lungs with air that was definitely fresher than in London, though a few giant chimneys belching smoke on the far horizon to the west hinted at the rapid industrialization of the county.

The fields were different from those in the south—rockier and rugged; more difficult to farm productively, he would think. His father had always said northerners were a hardy bunch. The recollection of his sire's pride in his Lancashire roots brought a lump to his throat.

Awash in memories of his beloved parents, he came to a bridge spanning a river. "Is this the Ribble?" he shouted to a lad fishing on the bank.

"Nay, sir, 'tis the Darwen. Ribble's further on. Thee can't miss it if thee's bound for town."

He tossed the boy a farthing and was soon riding alongside a much wider river, which he eventually crossed, whereupon he discovered he'd arrived in Preston. As a passenger in Whiteside's carriage the previous day, he hadn't paid attention to the road. Thus, he had no notion how to locate the inn where he hoped to find Frederick, nor the wheelwright's workshop.

A little further on, he encountered a wide thoroughfare. Glancing to the left, he noticed a sign declaring the corner shop to be the premises of Carr and Sons.

The tailor he'd met at the inn seemed friendly and anxious to please. He would be a good source of information as to which direction to take, and might even know how to tie a decent cravat.

⇒⟫⟪⟸

ASTRIDE GABRIEL'S HORSE, Susan cast a dubious eye on the contraption into which Orion had eventually allowed himself to be led. It had taken a good deal of coaxing on Oscar's part to convince the stallion. The retired jockey had wisely kept away from Orion's deadly back legs. The same couldn't be said for Cavendish who was lucky the stallion hadn't unmanned him. He'd put on a brave face, for Susan's benefit no doubt, but she'd wager he'd be sporting a livid bruise before the morrow dawned.

"Don't worry," Gabriel said from his perch on the driver's seat of the van. "I saw similar vehicles during the Napoleonic wars. Your horse will be safe."

Apparently satisfied his own horse was securely harnessed to the van's traces, Bradley climbed up to join Gabriel. "Folks will think we're gypsies," he said with a chuckle.

Susan considered her own appearance. No matter how she tried to arrange it, her gown refused to cover her ankles. It reminded her of…good grief!

However, there was no side saddle available and she couldn't imagine riding for four hours seated in one. She preferred to ride astride, though her clothing on this occasion was totally unsuitable.

Gypsies indeed!

Impatient to be off, she waved to Oscar and set her horse in motion.

"We'll have to take it more slowly," Gabriel shouted.

She slowed her pace. At this rate it would be dark before they reached Thicketford Manor.

As the miles crawled by, her mind wandered. She'd embarked on this horse racing odyssey as a way to get under Griffith Halliwell's skin, though she wasn't certain exactly how that plan was supposed to unfold. Now, she'd fallen madly in love with a thoroughbred stallion and couldn't get the rogue of an earl out of her mind. It was a most distressing state of affairs for a woman who prided herself on her clear thinking.

The solution to her dilemma came so suddenly, she scolded herself for not thinking of it before. If she set her cap at Halliwell, he'd run as far and as fast as he could. He'd hie back to London and his fancy women. Fascination would turn to disgust and she'd have no trouble cleansing him from her thoughts.

AWAKENED LONG BEFORE dawn by the activity in the inn's stables, Arthur dogged his prey's movements again, intrigued when Susan and the earl appeared to be negotiating for a horse with a chap who accompanied them to a large stables near the racetrack.

He knew fortune was smiling on him when he watched his quarry depart with the stallion loaded into a strange-looking horse-drawn vehicle, the earl taking the reins. Susan rode away astride, of course. For as long as he'd known her, the woman hadn't comported herself as befitted a member of the nobility.

It appeared they were headed home to Thicketford Manor, though Arthur doubted the vehicle would make it all that way.

Going north into Lancashire was risky, but this was too good an opportunity to miss. He'd wager the earl intended to use the horse for breeding. Arthur salivated, envisioning the outrageous stud fees he could charge if the horse belonged to him. Withins Hall was the perfect place for a stud farm. Of course, his father would never allow it. However, Bertrand Coleman was elderly. He wouldn't live forever. And accidents could happen.

Arthur wondered if Tillie was still in the area. She'd proven to be a pathetically useless accomplice in his last endeavor. Thanks to her, he'd ended up in Jamaica. However, the twit did know how to please a man in bed, and a good romp was definitely long overdue. Of course, he'd have to make her pay for letting him down. His cock saluted the prospect of the many ways he might exact punishment.

Whistling jauntily, he retreated to the *Pied Bull*, pondering how he was going to get to Preston.

ALL IN ALL, Griff considered the day a waste of time. The visit to Mr. Carr's establishment had proven to be the one bright spot. Not only had he come away with a perfectly tied new cravat, Carr had measured him for a number of frock coats, breeches and undergarments which were to be delivered to Clifton Heights within a fortnight. It meant delaying his return to London, but installing a new estate manager would also take some time. Carr had confirmed his thoughts about the Earl of Farnworth's stalwart character. "Indeed, his whole family is to be admired," the tailor insisted.

Griff couldn't help himself. "Even Lady Susan? I hear…"

"Unconventional, for sure," Carr interrupted, "but she's a true Lancashire lass—honest, loyal and true."

A treasured memory of Griff's mother sprang to mind. Originally from Wales, she'd readily adapted to Lancashire. Folks had said the same thing about her, although no one could ever accuse the conventional Alice Halliwell of being a bluestocking.

He'd admired his mother's perceptive nature, and wondered now if there were intellectual pursuits she'd forsaken in order to be the model wife of an earl. Much as Griff loved his jovial father, he couldn't imagine him encouraging his wife's interest in anything other than playing the role of a dutiful countess—an extension of himself, if you will. The realization he'd never really known if his mother was truly happy tightened Griff's throat.

When he finally found the wheelwright's workshop, he was disappointed to learn the work on his carriage wasn't finished. However, the exterior looked much cleaner. "You've done a good job," he told the wheelwright.

"Not I," the fellow replied. "The missus. Did the inside too. Smelled like a chicken coop."

Not willing to get into an explanation for the stink, he reiterated his thanks, paid above the estimate for the work and left instructions with Frederick to drive to Withins Hall once repairs were completed.

Not anxious to return for another round with Springer, he dropped into *The Coach and Four* for a quick bite.

The hearty plateful of bangers and mash was delicious, and three glasses of dark ale went down well. Normally, he would have accepted the invitation from a blonde serving wench to visit her upstairs room. With his mind on Susan Crompton, he wasn't in the mood for a meaningless romp, though the lass was well endowed in all the right places. He must be ailing for something he'd picked up from the noxious air in the court, or the feathers in the carriage, or…

He left the sulking chit a hefty tip and retrieved his horse. When he reached the gates of Withins Hall a short while later, he debated taking a short detour to Thicketford Manor. It was getting on for dusk and the earl was probably home by now. He could drop in to arrange a meeting for the morrow.

A LATE VISIT

AFTER THE SEEMINGLY endless carriage ride home to Thicketford Manor, Emma, Patsy and Rebecca collapsed into deep armchairs in the drawing room. Rebecca stated a preference to wait for Susan's arrival before proceeding to the dower house. Amelia brought Rafe from the nursery and Emma cradled her sleeping son in her arms.

"He fretted all the time you were gone," the nanny lamented.

"I suppose it's to be expected," Emma replied, feeling guilty. "That's the first time since he was born both his parents have been absent for so long."

"He certainly missed you," Amelia confirmed.

"Now I'm here, he's fallen asleep," Emma whispered, kissing her babe's sweet-smelling forehead.

In the silence broken only by the loud ticking of the Perigal clock on the white marble mantelpiece, Emma held her babe to her breast and lapsed into memories of her first husband. If Matthew had lived, he'd have insisted his children be raised in the nursery by a nanny and governess. It was how his parents had raised him and Susan. Noblemen and women didn't concern themselves with the messy, day-to-day business of rearing children. It was probably the reason Matthew had found it difficult to show emotion. Only Susan had refused to buckle down to her stuffy, overbearing father.

Emma uttered a silent prayer of thanks. She'd been blessed to fall in love with and marry her late husband's successor. Gabriel Smith might be an earl, but he was also a man who doted on his infant son and showered love on Patsy, though she was another man's child. Born into the landed gentry, Gabe eschewed many of the antiquated beliefs bred into the aristocracy.

She wasn't sure what roused her from a pleasant doze. Perhaps it was Rebecca's soft snoring, or the weight of Patsy's head leaning against her arm. Half-asleep, it came to her the butler had entered the room. "What is it, Frame?"

"A visitor, my lady."

"At this hour?" she asked lazily, reluctant to move.

"He apologizes for the lateness of his arrival, but the Earl of Pendlebury requests a brief meeting with his lordship."

Jolted completely awake by the turmoil suddenly roiling in her belly, Emma tried to determine the best course of action. Sparks might fly if Susan and the Earl of Pendlebury were to unexpectedly meet each other, especially with a thoroughbred racehorse thrown into the mix.

However, she couldn't very well turn a fellow earl away at the door; he must have traveled quite a distance.

The ever-efficient Amelia appeared. "I'll take Rafe," she whispered, lifting the baby from Emma's arms.

"I'll get Miss Ince to put Patsy to bed," Rebecca said with a yawn as she rose.

Within a minute, Emma was alone with Frame; the decision whether to allow Pendlebury entry had been taken out of her hands.

"Shall I show the earl in?" the butler asked. "And bring tea?"

"Something stronger," she countered. "Brandy, perhaps."

SHIFTING HIS WEIGHT from one foot to the other, Griff loitered in the opulent foyer of Thicketford Manor, convinced he wasn't going to be received. It was his own fault for calling so late in the day but being turned away would still be an insult. Perhaps the Earl of Farnworth had learned of Griff's lascivious thoughts concerning his blonde countess.

His spirits lifted a little when a young woman carrying a sleeping infant appeared. An older woman followed, leading a bleary-eyed child by the hand. The group climbed the central staircase and were soon gone from sight.

Potts' double reappeared, crossed the foyer and entered another room from which he emerged minutes later bearing a silver tray with several crystal decanters and glasses. All this was accomplished in silence. Clearly, the crystal knew what was expected of it.

The older woman eventually descended the staircase, nodded at him and re-entered what he assumed was the drawing room.

His impatience mounting, Griff paced. On the verge of taking his leave, he realized the butler stood nearby. He hadn't heard the fellow approach and couldn't help but be reminded yet again of Potts. Thicketford Manor might still prove to be a place where he'd obtain guidance about the management of his northern properties. The gleaming foyer smelled of lemon polish and wealth, unlike Clifton Heights.

"If you'll follow me, my lord," the butler intoned.

Upon entering the drawing room, he was dismayed to find only the countess and the older woman he'd seen earlier. It was a relief Lady Susan was absent, but where was the earl?

The countess' pursed lips indicated she remembered their last meeting outside the court. He wondered if Lady Susan had shared his flippant remarks. Of course, he hadn't known the identity of the blonde at the time. "Thank you for agreeing to see me," he said formally, ready to bestow a gentlemanly kiss of greeting on her ladyship's knuckles.

"My husband is not at home," she replied, both fists clenched at her sides. "May I present Mrs. Waterman, my husband's mother."

He bowed, though she evidently wasn't a person of rank. "Mrs. Waterman."

"My lord earl," the unsmiling mother-in-law replied with a nod.

"Please take a seat," Lady Farnworth said. "Can I offer you brandy?"

The distinctly unfriendly tone of voice made it clear she hoped he would decline both offers. He got the feeling the countess was nervous—surely he hadn't made such a bad impression outside the court. Wishing with all his heart he had waited until the morrow to call, Griff soldiered on. "As you know, I'm in the area on a...er...legal matter."

Cursing himself for a complete fool, he cleared his throat and tried again. "While I'm in Lancashire, I was hoping to meet with your husband. I'm in need of advice regarding the management of my..."

"Mummy, mummy!"

Startled by the interruption, Griff swiveled his head to the doorway at the same moment the countess sprang forward like a horse out of the starting gate. A bright-eyed little girl clad in night attire stood in the doorway.

"Mummy," she repeated. "I was watching through my window. Daddy and Aunty Susan are home with the new racehorse."

WELCOME HOME, ORION

SUSAN WAS SO exhausted, she was afraid her legs would buckle once she got off the horse. An hour into the endless ride from Chester, she'd given up trying to protect the bare skin of her calves from the chilly air.

The journey had shredded her nerves. They'd been forced to make frequent stops to water the horses and to calm the snorting Orion. It was a miracle his powerful back legs hadn't splintered the rear door of the wooden box.

Bradley had gone off to rouse the stable lads and Gabriel was unhitching his tired horse from the van.

It seemed unlikely anyone was coming to Susan's aid. The alternative was to slide to the ground. Plucking up the courage to lift her leg over the horse's rump, she stopped short when she became aware of a man staring at her.

A shiver of recognition raced through her body, though it was difficult to see in the dimly lit stable yard.

It can't be.

But it was. The absentee earl who didn't give a fig about anything except horses was somehow at Thicketford Manor.

"Allow me," Pendlebury said, his gaze lingering over her bare calves as he reached up to grasp her waist.

The only coherent thought in her head was that if she didn't accept his help, she'd likely crumple in a heap on the cobblestones. She gripped his shoulders as he hauled her off the horse.

As she feared, her trembling legs turned to jelly and she collapsed against him.

An errant thought occurred as his warmth seeped into her cold limbs. This was the plan, wasn't it? Make him think she was impressed with the broad chest, the powerful thighs braced against hers, the musky aroma of expensive cologne and…

"You needn't bat your eyelashes at me, Lady Susan Crompton," he said, a smirk of amusement spoiling the appeal of tempting lips…

Stop it.

"I was not batting," she insisted, pushing him away. She swayed, instantly missing the strength of his support.

"Pendlebury," Gabriel declared, thankfully taking hold of Susan's elbow when he arrived on the scene. "I thought I recognized you."

"Farnworth," the earl replied, extending a hand. "Forgive my dropping in unannounced. I'm staying with Whiteside and wanted to discuss a few matters with you." He cocked his head toward the van as Gabriel shook his hand. "I see you're busy. Perhaps I should come back on the morrow?"

Light flooded the yard as agitated stable boys arrived to set wall torches ablaze. One led away the weary horses that had traveled all the way from Chester.

Griff followed when Gabriel escorted Susan to the rear of the van. "It's no bother. In fact, we might need your expertise. Lady Susan bought a racehorse in Chester, but coaxing him out of this contraption could prove challenging. He hasn't enjoyed the journey."

Susan derived enormous satisfaction from Pendlebury's worried frown. If he clenched his jaw any tighter it might snap.

"A racehorse?" he asked.

"Yes," Gabriel replied. "Not to race, however. Orion has foot problems, apparently."

GRIFF STARED AT the irritating grin on Susan Crompton's face, struggling to deny what he suddenly knew to be true. She'd bought his Godolphin Barb—the horse he'd counted on to add the ultimate cachet to Pendlebury Stables; the stallion whose ancestry would ensure Griffith Halliwell could boast of having the Prince Regent as a patron.

To think, he'd been so easily aroused by bare calves, lush breasts pressed against his chest, and disheveled raven locks. Susan Crompton looked like a wild gypsy with her skirts tucked up—

Cease!

She was devious, and clearly out to retaliate for his perceived failure to take care of his tenants.

Well, he would show her—just as soon as he got his arousal under control.

His worst fears were confirmed when the remaining stable lads lowered the rear door of the van. He'd never set eyes on the stallion Richard Tattersall had undertaken to procure, but he recognized Eclipse's bloodlines in the magnificent chestnut beast snorting to be free of his confinement.

Almost paralyzed by anger, he resolved to deal with Susan Crompton later. His first concern had to be the horse. The animal was clearly in distress. "He's been in there too long," he spat, shrugging off his frock coat and rolling up his sleeves. He entered the van, edging past the deadly back legs.

"Be careful," Susan cried.

Cooing soothing sounds, Griff maneuvered past a powerful shoulder, then stroked the stallion's long forehead, breathing again when the horse eventually calmed. "The silly woman is concerned I might hurt you," he whispered. "Obviously, she doesn't know me at all."

Irritated he found Susan's low opinion of him bothersome, he untied the rope and gently coaxed the horse to move backwards out of the van.

SUSAN WAS CONCERNED for the horse, but became fixated on the way Halliwell purposefully rolled up his sleeves. Clearly, his tailor had no need to add padding. His shoulders really were as broad as they seemed. No padding there. The silk waistcoat was form-fitted to his body, emphasizing a trim waist and…

The errant thoughts fled and her heart leaped into her throat when Halliwell ventured into the van. She abhorred the way he treated his tenants, but didn't wish him ill. Entering a confined space with a very unhappy horse took courage. One kick from those deadly hooves, and…

She was trembling uncontrollably and close to tears by the time he'd coaxed the agitated stallion into the yard.

Compelled by a need to calm her racing heart, she took hold of the halter, rested her cheek against the horse and whispered, "Welcome home, Orion."

It was impossible to ignore the man standing beside her who held the opposite strap of the halter. The resentment pouring off him was palpable. However, something else flickered in the dark eyes. "I assume you know a valuable stud needs special care," he said with undisguised mockery.

Susan the Bluestocking might have retorted with some sarcastic comeback, but she couldn't fault the way he'd treated her horse with love and a sure hand. She had no doubt his expertise had saved the animal from injury. "Thank you," she whispered, biting back the apology she should perhaps have offered.

LOVE HER AND LEAVE HER

RIDING BACK TO Withins Hall, Griff inhaled the cool night air. It would be a mistake to allow his anger to cloud his thoughts. He had to plan, and planning meant reining in his temper.

He'd secured a breakfast appointment with the earl and his estate manager for the following morning. Hopefully, discussions about improving things at Clifton Heights would prove fruitful.

However, another, more vital goal had come to the fore. If he wanted to retrieve Orion—and he most certainly did—he'd have to win the redoubtable Susan Crompton to his side.

It would be no easy task. She hated him but, as the wrought iron gates of Withins came into view, he chuckled. If there was one thing he excelled at, it was wooing women. Even the most reluctant eventually succumbed to his considerable charm. He'd yet to meet the chit who wasn't impressed with his physique and his slow seduction.

He'd have to be careful not to show his true feelings, but Susan wouldn't be the first woman he'd bedded for whom he felt nothing. Sexual congress was a purely physical pleasure. It was dangerous to give a female power over one's emotions. A man had to guard his heart. The deaths of his beloved parents had almost destroyed him.

Once he'd convinced Lady Susan that Orion would be much better off at Pendlebury Stables than stuck in a rural Lancashire backwater, he'd *love her and leave her*, as the saying went.

As he dismounted and handed the reins to a stable boy, the notion was irritatingly troubling. Bedding wealthy widows who didn't care a hoot about the *ton's* opinion was one thing; deliberately leading Susan Crompton up the proverbial garden path was quite another.

Even in the north, far from wagging London tongues, a woman's reputation could be irretrievably ruined.

It wouldn't be easy, but he was confident he could eventually coax Susan into his bed. The prospect was annoyingly more appealing than it ought to be and he never shied away from a challenge.

However, he would earn her everlasting hatred if he stole her maidenhead then abandoned her. His cock saluted the vision of Susan writhing beneath him, her cheeks flushed with pleasure as she screamed his name. At the same time, chills ran up and down his spine—fury would be unleashed when she realized he'd tricked her. He would also lose the Earl of Farnworth's regard, even earn the enmity of a worthy peer. Bertrand Coleman wouldn't be impressed with such behavior either.

He gritted his teeth as Whiteside's butler ushered him into the ornate foyer of Withins Hall. The irritating Susan Crompton had him tied in knots.

"To make matters worse," he mumbled as he mounted the stairs to his chamber, "she genuinely loves Orion." He chuckled. "She was more concerned about the bloody horse than she was about me." Given the fate of his hapless tenant weavers, he perhaps deserved her scorn, but her disdain pricked his male pride.

AFRAID SHE MIGHT collapse from exhaustion and the turmoil in her heart, Susan appreciated Emma's hug as she entered

Thicketford Manor.

Sulking, Patsy stood beside her mother, arms folded. "I wanted to stroke Orion."

Susan put an arm around her niece's shoulders. "The poor thing wasn't feeling very happy. Tomorrow, he'll be more settled."

She hoped that would prove to be the case. After all, she knew nothing about the care of thoroughbred horses.

"The earl was brave," Patsy declared as they headed for the drawing room.

Susan agreed. Entering the narrow van could have resulted in a catastrophic injury. She couldn't deny Pendlebury's bold confidence had calmed the frenzied horse. It was fortuitous he'd happened along. Gabriel and Bradley were both courageous men who'd distinguished themselves at Waterloo, but she doubted they'd have willingly ventured into the van.

Even the Thicketford ostler seemed intimidated by the stallion. Pendlebury had sensed that too. He'd hurried to the stables and dispensed instructions to the grooms. His love of horses seemed genuine.

"Why don't you and Rebecca stay here overnight?" Emma suggested. "It's too late to walk to the dower house and you both look done in."

Susan agreed. The thought of getting back on a horse and riding home couldn't be borne, but she would miss her own bed and Rebecca didn't like having her routine disrupted.

Patsy ran to greet her stepfather when he entered, Frame not far behind.

"What are you doing out of bed, young lady?" Gabriel asked, hoisting her to settle on his hip.

"I wanted to see the horse," she whined, snaking her arms around his neck.

"You'll have to wait until tomorrow. The Earl of Pendlebury has promised to return to give us some pointers on feeding and so on."

Apparently mollified, she kissed his cheek and slid down to the floor. "Goodnight."

Everyone wished her the same before she scooted back to the stairs where Miss Ince waited.

"I'm starving," Gabriel declared. "Any chance of a bite from the kitchen?" he asked Frame.

"I'll see to it, my lord," the butler replied. "For Lady Susan and Mrs. Waterman as well?"

"Yes," Susan replied, suddenly deeming it vital she be at Thicketford Manor when Pendlebury called. After all, she wanted to learn as much as she could about racehorses—and implement her plan to flirt. "I think we should stay the night and I'm hungry too."

"Nothing for me," Rebecca replied. "We ate on the way home."

Susan half-expected the earl's mother to insist they return to the dower house. She was pleasantly surprised when Rebecca agreed to stay.

Emma rose. "I'll get Mrs. Maple to prepare your rooms," she said. "It's good you'll be here when Pendlebury arrives."

Susan preferred not to ponder further on why that would be a good thing, nor did she understand the reason for Emma's knowing smile as she left the drawing room. Was it possible her friend suspected her plan to toy with the rogue earl's affections?

LET THE GAMES BEGIN

T HE NEXT DAY, feeling a little like Daniel entering the lions' den, Griff took a deep breath as Frame led him into the morning room at Thicketford Manor.

The noisy chatter abruptly ceased as Earl Gabriel stood, shook his hand, reintroduced everyone at the table, and bade him sit.

"Lady Emma, Lady Susan, Mrs. Waterman, and Miss Crompton, good morning to you," Griff said, bowing politely to each female before he took a chair. Patsy giggled at the formal address.

It was important to set Susan Crompton's low opinion of him straight. He was an earl after all. He may have inherited the title years before he'd expected to, but his father had nevertheless groomed him from boyhood.

The memory of his beloved father washed over him, tightening the knot in his chest. Perhaps he hadn't yet lived up to his sire's expectations.

"Good morning, my lord," Susan said, her tone unexpectedly friendly. "I didn't realize you are acquainted with Baron Whiteside."

"Yes," he replied. It wasn't an outright lie. He and Bertrand were acquainted. "And please, my name is Griffith."

I'll coax her into calling me Griff later, when we're more…

It suddenly struck him he'd never allowed any of his paramours to call him Griff. Such a thing would be too personal, too intimate. Unthinkable. "You're fortunate to have a good neighbor," he said, tucking in to the plate of bacon and eggs served by a liveried footman.

"Whiteside's a good chap," his host replied.

"Unlike his son," Patsy declared, her pretty features spoiled by a grimace.

"Now, Patsy," her mother chided. "All that's in the past, and Arthur has paid for his sins."

Griff kept chewing, convinced now his suspicion that the kidnapping had involved Patsy was correct.

He stopped chewing when his glance fell on Susan. She was doing it again. Fluttering her eyelashes. The plan to seduce her might be easier than he'd thought. He feared he might choke on a piece of bacon that went down the wrong way when the minx said, "So, Griffith, I'm anxious to learn from an expert how to start a stud farm."

He guzzled the glass of water Emma passed to him. "Er…" he gasped, his eyes darting around the table. It seemed no one else was shocked by Susan's inappropriate proposal. "I'd hoped to have a private discussion with the earl about improving the management of my estate," he offered as a way out.

"And so you shall," the earl replied. "It's Gabriel, by the way."

"Gabriel," he acknowledged, risking another forkful of fried egg. The food was wholesome, the eggs cooked just the way he liked them, the buttered toast perfect, the coffee strong. As he cleaned his plate, he realized with satisfaction he had truly enjoyed his breakfast for the first time in days. But it wasn't simply because of the food. The members of the family who resided at Thicketford Manor were congenial and friendly, notwithstanding the confrontation at the trial.

The prospect of using guile to regain Orion suddenly didn't sit well in his gut.

"Do you plan to take action to mitigate your tenants' convictions, Griffith?" Susan asked with a false smile, quickly ridding him of bothersome scruples.

"Yes, Susan," he replied sweetly, pleased when his failure to use her title banished the smile. "As a matter of fact, I was thinking of seeking out the justices later today. Would you like to accompany me? It can't hurt if we both plead their case."

SUSAN HESITATED, TRYING to decide if Griffith Halliwell was up to something. Was he playing his own game, or was he falling for her feminine wiles? Although, she hadn't really used any yet. Not that she knew much about feminine wiles when it came to men. Did she even possess such skills?

Having decided the welfare of the weavers had to be her priority, she looked into expectant green eyes. "I'd like to accompany you, but it's rather a long way."

"Not to worry," he replied with what seemed a genuine smile. "My carriage is being repaired in Preston. Hopefully, it will be ready today and we can travel in comfort. If the distance proves too much, you can stay overnight at Clifton Heights and return on the morrow."

Susan felt obliged to protest the impropriety of such a suggestion, but Pendlebury carried on. "Perhaps Lady Emma might come with us."

That raised Susan's hackles. Surely he didn't intend to persist in his flirtation with Emma? And she couldn't very well begin her campaign to flirt with Halliwell if Emma was present.

"I must decline," Emma replied. "I already feel guilty about the time spent apart from my infant son while we were in Chester."

Susan was relieved but worried the opportunity to speak on behalf of the weavers was slipping away.

Rebecca came to her rescue. "I'd like to accompany you. It's a cause I too firmly believe in."

"The ladies can perhaps give me pointers about Clifton

Heights," Halliwell offered, bringing a big smile to Rebecca's face. "I admit I've neglected the place."

"It's as well you and Susan will have a chaperone with you," Emma murmured nervously.

Halliwell raised an eyebrow. "Don't worry," he replied with a disturbing chuckle. "We'll all be on our best behavior, won't we, Susan?"

The intensity of his emerald gaze sent very peculiar but not unpleasant sensations spiraling into Susan's womb. She glanced down quickly, mortified to see her tingling nipples putting on quite a show. "Yes, of course," she replied, filled with a ludicrous sense of regret that she didn't know the first thing about misbehaving with a man.

⋙⋘

GRIFF WANTED TO crow and strut like a rooster. One seemingly innocent comment accompanied by a lascivious glance was all it had taken to get Lady Susan hot and bothered.

Mind you, the pebbled nipples and the way she squirmed in her seat were rather titivating—too much so, he realized when his groin tightened and familiar urges stirred at the base of his spine. Who would have thought a prim and proper bluestocking could be aroused so relatively easily? Or that she'd hold any appeal for him? It was almost a pity Rebecca Waterman was coming with them.

He sipped the last of his coffee, willing his erection to subside before he stood.

Unfortunately, Gabriel was already on his feet. "We'll repair to the library for our discussions. Blair is waiting."

Left with no choice, Griff stood, holding his napkin against his body until he could turn away from the table. "Lead on," he replied jovially, tossing the linen back onto his chair.

He had to get his male urges under control, though he'd had

little experience reining them in before. However, this was a game he couldn't afford to lose. He mustn't let Susan get the upper hand; that might prove more difficult than he'd anticipated if he allowed himself to become emotionally involved.

The notion sent chills racing across his nape. He didn't even like brunettes, nor olive-skinned women, though he had to concede Susan's raven locks and gypsy coloring made for a potent combination.

RACK AND RUIN

G RIFF FOLLOWED HIS host, thankful his interest in Susan was abating. The enormous mahogany desk in one corner of the small library indicated the earl used this space as a study. Floor-to-ceiling shelves were crammed with a wide variety of books, some leather-bound and weighty. He could imagine Susan spending many enjoyable hours in this well-stocked library.

Where had that thought come from? He had to get her off his mind and concentrate on the urgent matter of Clifton Heights.

A man rose from his seat in front of the desk and offered his hand. "William Blair, my lord earl," he said, his smile genuine.

Griff accepted the handshake. "Mr. Blair. I appreciate your taking the time to enlighten me," he replied.

"Please, sit," Gabriel said, indicating a chair next to his manager while he took a seat behind the desk.

"I'm not sure how I can be of help," Blair said, clearly comfortable opening the discussion—a sign Gabriel trusted him.

Griff hesitated. He'd be obliged to explain that the main reason Clifton Heights had fallen into disrepair was his own lack of oversight. "I'm unhappy with my estate manager," he began.

Blair rested an ankle atop his thigh, very much at ease.

Gabriel steepled his fingers.

"The staff he hires are useless, and the man seems to spend most of his time at the village pub."

"Ye're speaking of the household servants?" Blair asked.

"Yes, maids, footmen, the housekeeper, cooks, and so on."

"To be frank, my lord, I don't manage those aspects of the manor. Frame is in charge of the personnel in this house—more of a majordomo, ye might say. What ye need is a competent man such as he to organize yer household."

"I have a butler who could do that," Griff conceded. "In fact, he was the butler at Clifton Heights for many years."

"And now?" Gabriel asked.

"He takes care of my London townhouse," Griff replied. "I moved to the capital and took him with me."

"I see," Blair said, uncrossing his legs. "Since ye're absent most of the time, ye need trustworthy people. It's a tall order for an estate the size of thine."

Griff didn't detect censure, nor did he fault the man's skepticism. As the newly-minted earl, he'd thought nothing of fleeing to London and trusting his ancestral home to the safekeeping of a man who'd turned out to be untrustworthy.

"I believe ye also own a farm down south, my lord?" Blair asked.

"Not really a farm. Pendlebury Stables. I breed horses."

"And ye have a manager there who is taking care of things in yer absence?"

"Yes," Griff replied. "Tom Glazebrook."

Blair raised an eyebrow. "Now there's a good Lancashire name."

"Indeed," Griff agreed, suddenly feeling even more uncomfortable. "He was the ostler at Clifton Heights. Competent chap. What he doesn't know about horses isn't worth knowing."

"So, you took him with you as well," Gabriel said quietly, tapping his steepled fingers together. "And you trust him."

Griff felt like he'd been sucker-punched in the ribs. He was beginning to realize he'd gutted Clifton in favor of getting himself established in London. Now, he was reaping the consequences and his ancestral home was going to rack and ruin.

For the first time, he wondered if Potts and Glazebrook were truly happy in London.

"What about the home farm at Clifton?" Gabriel asked.

Griff racked his brain for the name of the fellow who managed the home farm—to no avail. "Er…that seems to run well. Mostly sheep."

"Seems to me ye need an overseer," Blair said. "I can recommend Harry Rogerson, my lord. He works with me here, one of my gamekeepers. I can vouch for his competence and honesty."

"Would he be willing to relocate to Clifton?"

"Rogerson's looking to advance himself. I think he might."

"I'll approach him, if you wish," Gabriel offered.

Griff nodded. "I'd appreciate that. As for a butler…"

"I can ask Frame to join us."

Griff hesitated. He should have consulted Potts first. His butler was sure to know someone suitable. "Perhaps another time. I have to be on my way to Withins Hall. Hopefully, the new wheel has been fitted and my carriage returned."

"You'll come back for your ladies?" Gabriel asked.

"I will," he replied, not sure what to make of his fellow earl's cryptic smile.

SEATED BESIDE REBECCA, Susan waited impatiently in the drawing room. Her friend startled when she bolted out of her seat as soon as Frame informed them the Earl of Pendlebury's carriage had arrived. Not certain of the reason for the butterflies flitting about in her stomach, she rose, smoothed down the skirts of her gown, made sure her hairpins were all still in place and went out to greet the earl in the foyer.

She wished Griffith Halliwell wasn't so annoyingly handsome. Convincing him she found him attractive shouldn't be difficult. Women reportedly fell at his feet, so he must be used to it. Hopefully, he was too conceited to distinguish between real affection and false flattery.

He greeted them both, though his eyes locked with Susan's. "Ladies," he crooned.

She refused to look away, despite the loud pulse thudding in her ears. "My lord earl," she gushed, offering her hand.

She conceded the kiss he bussed on her knuckles was well done. His moist lips were quite…

Snatching her hand from his warm grasp, she finally dragged her gaze away from his green eyes. Surely she hadn't seen amusement lurking there?

Frame assisted Rebecca with her cloak, but Halliwell took Susan's cloak and furled it around her shoulders. "I'm a fortunate man. Two lovely companions," he declared, fastening the cloak under her chin. "A visit to the court isn't usually an excursion to look forward to, is it?"

With her chin tilted up, Susan had no choice but to look into the green depths. He was baiting her, but she couldn't seem to get words past the lump in her throat. "But…"

"Come now, Lady Susan," he crooned. "Surely you're not worried about gossip? After all, who could fault three persons of noble intent embarking on a humanitarian mission? Your reputation for championing the oppressed is well known."

Susan suspected he might be toying with her, but it was too late to renege on her promise to go with him. She wanted desperately to do what she could for the weavers, even if it meant enduring Halliwell's company for a few hours in a carriage. "Very well," she said. "I suppose there's no harm in it."

MALEVOLENCE

ARTHUR COLEMAN DISMOUNTED a mile or two from Thicket-ford Manor, tempted to abandon the mule he'd stolen from the *Pied Bull*. The poor excuse for a horse wouldn't make it much further. However, it might fetch a bob or two if he could sell it to a glue factory.

Pulling on the beast's reins, he neared the impressive wrought iron gates of the Farnworth estate and decided to test his luck. It was doubtful the old gatekeeper would recognize him. Indeed, he couldn't recall ever meeting the fellow face-to-face, and a baron's son wouldn't sport a cloth cap and be dressed in worn homespun.

Pulling down the neb to further hide his face, he greeted the old gent. "By 'eck, who lives 'ere in this grand place?" he asked, quite pleased with his imitation of the local dialect as he gestured expansively to the gates.

The gatekeeper narrowed his eyes at the weary mule. "Yon nag's on 'is last legs."

Arthur seethed. He could have told the fool that, but he held on to his temper. "Must be some rich toff lives 'ere."

"This 'ere's the estate of the Earl of Farnworth and no place for one such as thee to loiter. Bugger off."

Tempted to punch the old codger in the ribs, Arthur was distracted when a carriage approached from within the estate. He stepped aside as the gatekeeper shuffled to open the gates.

He refused to turn away when Susan Crompton looked down her aristocratic nose through the window of the carriage. He almost wished she'd recognize him and spew her outrage, but she'd apparently looked right through him. It was of limited satisfaction when she turned to speak to the gentleman traveling with her. He didn't recognize the other female passenger.

The vehicle had seen better days. The coat of arms on the side needed repainting. The owner must be down on his uppers. Not surprising really; what wealthy gent would marry Susan Crompton? He assumed the chap was her husband since they sat side by side. If not, the older woman was doing a poor job of chaperoning.

"Yon mon's the earl, then?" he asked the gatekeeper, though he knew the gent wasn't Farnworth.

"Not that it's any of thy business, but that was Lady Susan Crompton, accompanied by the Earl of Pendlebury, and Mrs. Waterman, mother of the Earl of Farnworth," he replied, his chest thrust out as if announcing attendees at a ball. "Now, be off with thee."

"Keep yer 'air on," he replied. "I'm going. Better things to do than waste time with thee. One last thing. Canst ye tell me if Tillie still works 'ere?"

The old man spat into the dust. "Tillie! Nah! Probably in the poorhouse by this. What would thee want with the likes of 'er?"

"Just an old acquaintance," he replied before sauntering off.

INSIDE THE CARRIAGE, Susan glared at Rebecca. Why hadn't the woman taken the seat beside her instead of obliging Halliwell to do so? Despite the heat pouring off the man's body, she shivered, her unease deepening when he took hold of her hand. "Don't worry," he purred. "You're safe with me."

Looking into teasing green eyes, she doubted that was true,

but she must remember to be pleasant. "I'm not worried," she lied, hesitant to tell him the real reason for her disquiet. "I feel like someone just walked over my grave."

That remark finally tore Rebecca's attention away from the passing scenery.

She should have rebuffed Halliwell when he leaned closer and put an arm around her shoulders, but his warmth was comforting and Rebecca had returned her gaze to the seemingly fascinating countryside.

"Like you've seen a ghost?" he said, sounding genuinely concerned.

"More like a premonition something bad is going to happen," she murmured, feeling rather ridiculous. She believed in facts, not superstitious nonsense. "Silly, really."

"Not at all," he replied, withdrawing his arm. "I once had a similar premonition."

The wistful sincerity in his voice made her curious. "And did it come true?"

He averted his eyes to look out the window. "Yes," he said hoarsely. "My parents were killed in a carriage accident."

Susan's heart broke for him. He might be a rogue and a reprobate, but to lose one's parents so tragically... "I'm sorry," she murmured. "Were you close?"

He remained silent for a long while, his attention seemingly still on the scenery, obviously not wanting her to see his inner turmoil. His silence, however, was answer enough.

Rebecca jumped into the conversation. "I don't know if you'd call it a premonition, but I knew in my heart that my two eldest boys had died at Trafalgar, even before we received official word."

"I'm so sorry, dear lady," Halliwell replied with sincerity. "It's difficult to lose loved ones."

"I miss my parents and my brother too," Susan said softly. "Although my father and I didn't get along."

"Let me guess," Halliwell quipped, the flippant arrogance

back in his tone. "He thought a woman's place was in a man's bed, not in a library."

Blushing fiercely, Rebecca leaned her head against the side of the carriage and closed her eyes. It wasn't long before she was snoring softly.

Susan bristled. Her father would never have expressed his opinion in such blunt and coarse terms; Halliwell had voiced his own view of women. "My father did not approve of my thirst for learning," she allowed.

He turned his unsettling gaze on her. "Is that why you bought Orion? Because you thirst to learn more about thorough-breds?" he asked, his eyes hooded.

She gritted her teeth, not sure what was behind the bitterness she detected. Her plan to make him think she was attracted to him would flounder if she confessed she'd intended to spite him. "No, I bought Orion because I fell in love with the sport of kings as soon as I entered the grounds at Chester."

His puzzled frown mirrored her own surprise at the truth of her words. "I know exactly what you mean," he said. "Except, for me, it's the wonder of watching an elegant foal take its first steps. I enjoy wagering on the outcome of a race, but I relish the beauty and grace of the horses themselves, not the winning or losing."

"I enjoyed winning, though," she retorted, wondering why on earth she'd revealed that she'd wagered money.

He arched a brow. "You picked winners?"

"I have an eye for bloodlines," she preened, echoing Oscar's praise.

She felt strangely bereft when his eyes darkened and he clenched his jaw. "Is that the only reason you bought Orion?"

"What other reason could there be?" she asked nervously, avoiding his gaze.

"Because you knew I had already made arrangements to buy him."

She closed her eyes, her stomach suddenly in knots. He wouldn't believe her if she denied it. And she'd thought her plan to make him think she liked him was going so very well.

As they continued their journey in silence, her jumbled thoughts drifted back to the grubby laborer she'd seen loitering outside Thicketford's gates. There was something about him she couldn't quite put her finger on, but she'd sensed malevolence, and now things had gone awry.

AN INQUIRING MIND

GRIFF WAS ANGRY with himself. Why had he revealed Orion was supposed to be his horse? Now, if he pursued his plan to convince Susan he had feelings for her, she'd think he was somehow finagling to get the stallion back. And she'd be right.

He was going to have to put on a masterful performance to prove his affection was genuine. It wouldn't be the first time he'd lied his way into a woman's heart, but the bed partners he normally pursued weren't known for their intellect.

That notion triggered a wry smile. A female's brain wasn't what interested him. Admittedly, he had what some might consider a prodigious sexual appetite, but he was a young man, after all. He needed women who were wanton, lusty, playful—and, of course, well-endowed physically.

Mind you, Susan qualified as far as the latter was concerned. But he'd always insisted on another criterion, hadn't he? What was it? Oh, yes. She had to be blonde, naturally. He'd never made an exception. Not that he could recall.

He took a deep breath, resolved to keep his eye on the prize. "I take it you were not aware of my connection to Orion?" he asked, pleased he'd managed to keep his tone civil.

"No. I honestly was not. I knew you had plans to purchase a thoroughbred Arabian at Tattersalls. I was so angry with you, I wracked my brain to come up with a plan to buy it from under your nose. But it never occurred to me your horse would be in

Chester. I simply fell in love with Orion as soon as I saw him."

He found himself believing her, and couldn't fault her honesty, but the reason she was being so forthright puzzled him. She seemed to have softened her attitude toward him. Was his infallible charm working on the indomitable Lady Susan? He hoped so, because his plan to offer to buy Orion fizzled when she spoke of her love for the stallion. He knew only too well the power of an emotional attachment to a horse.

Perhaps he should cut his losses and return to London.

"We will need guidance," Susan said softly.

"Guidance?" he echoed, ignoring a warning bell going off in the back of his head when she did that eyelash fluttering thing and sighed, "We plan to set up a stud farm at Farnworth. You know. To charge fees for…er…"

Did she seriously think he didn't know the purpose of a stud farm? He had to admit, though, her blush stirred his male interest.

He cleared his throat, annoyed he'd even noticed she was blushing. "I can certainly advise you," he declared, abandoning all thoughts of returning to London in the near future.

Apart from the occasional polite remark about the state of the road or the look of the weather, Susan and her companions completed the journey to the court in silence.

Normally a good conversationalist, she couldn't think of a single thing to say and Rebecca seemed determined to pretend she'd fallen asleep. Susan came to the conclusion she was rubbish at this game between males and females.

She'd never been in a confined space with a man for such a long period of time. Gabriel and her late brother didn't count, of course. Griffith Halliwell certainly didn't fit into the category of relative—or married man.

His cologne was pleasant, unlike any she'd encountered before. Not overpowering, just…intriguing.

She risked a furtive glance at his beautifully manicured hands resting atop buff breeches that clung to well-muscled thighs. It came as something of a shock she'd never considered how much larger a male hand was than her own. His were darker than hers, though his skin was fair. And who knew men had a dusting of hair on the backs of their fingers?

The carriage became stiflingly hot when errant musings wandered to the color of the hair at his groin, assuming men grew hair there. They must, mustn't they?

She had a vague memory of asking her mother why she didn't have the same appendage as her brother when they were little children. She knew the answer now, no thanks to her evasive parent.

Was it possible the noticeable swelling at the apex of Halliwell's powerful thighs was the same male appendage? If so, it must grow with time, which made sense since a woman's breasts became larger.

A memory of Orion's endowments in that regard came to mind. She doubted a foal would be born with such an organ. It would make walking difficult for a young animal.

Chuckling inwardly, she averted her curious gaze quickly when Halliwell took his attention off the scenery and glanced at her. She retrieved the fan from her reticule. She'd always had an inquiring mind but cerebral questions had never caused her to overheat so markedly.

It came as a relief when they arrived at the court, though it was a good thing Halliwell offered his strong hand as she alit from the carriage because she was feeling decidedly peculiar.

GRIFF OUGHT TO have been amused by Susan's surreptitious perusal of his person, but he found it annoyingly arousing, hence the unfortunate bulge at his groin—which she had definitely noticed if the persistent blushes and fan fluttering were any indication. For a bluestocking, Susan was a surprisingly practiced flirt.

She was clearly falling under his spell. He built on his progress by elbowing Frederick out of the way and assisting Susan to alight. Rebecca Waterman appeared to be sound asleep, so he was about to suggest they not disturb her.

Alas! All for naught. "Locked," Frederick announced after trying the main door.

Further attempts to gain entry proved futile. The court was, in effect, sealed up tighter than a drum. An ancient, bespectacled watchman eventually appeared and informed them the justices had embarked on their usual circuit around Lancashire—interrupted by the special session for the trial of "them poor weavers."

Uncertain what to do next, Griff raked a hand through his hair. Susan's lips tightened into an unattractive pout.

He itched to suggest they repair straightaway to Clifton Heights, but that might scare her off and ruin the sympathetic persona he was trying to cultivate.

"Do you have a barrister?" she suddenly asked.

"Solicitor, yes. Rowbotham of Rowbotham, Bootle and Radcliffe. Their offices are not far from here."

Her eyes widened. "He's our family solicitor as well. We should ask his opinion."

A GLIMMER OF HOPE

W HEN SUSAN ENTERED his office in the company of Griffith Halliwell, Aloysius Rowbotham's whiskered jowls ballooned. He removed his steel-rimmed glasses and held them up to the skylight.

She suppressed the urge to chuckle, noting Halliwell's wry smile. The solicitor's reaction wasn't surprising. She and the earl did make an odd couple—not that they were a couple—and Rowbotham was clearly taken aback.

Having been kept waiting in the outer office for a full half-hour for no good reason she could discern, Susan wasn't in a mood to waste time; much to Rebecca's justified disgust, the solicitor's nervous clerk hadn't even offered a cup of tea. The straight-backed, wooden chairs were decidedly uncomfortable and too close together. It had been deuced difficult to keep her thigh from touching Halliwell's. However, deciding, for once, to abide by society's expectations, she held on to her temper and deferred to her male companion to explain their presence.

Apparently reassured he wasn't hallucinating, Rowbotham shook hands with Halliwell. He then made a half-hearted attempt to lift his sizable frame in order to execute a bow in Susan's direction. When he collapsed back into the chair, dust motes danced, settling eventually atop the thin layer already coating the file boxes piled on his desk.

Rowbotham bade them sit, then declared, "I assume you've

come to discuss what can be done for your unfortunate tenants."

Halliwell looked as surprised as Susan felt at this opening gambit, but he let the solicitor talk.

"Not to worry, old chap. As you suggested, I've been in touch with the Home Secretary, through the appropriate channels, of course. I may be jumping the gun, but I'm fairly certain the sentences will be commuted."

The confusion left Halliwell's face, but Susan floundered. She could scarcely believe the selfish earl had already set an appeal in motion. "Commuted?" she echoed.

Rowbotham explained. "It seems the Home Office is dealing with quite a backlash. Between you and me, there's a rumor the Prince Regent himself deemed the judgment too harsh."

Susan's hopes rose. "So, are the men to be pardoned, the sentences quashed?"

Rowbotham's rheumy eyes peered at her over the rim of his spectacles. "Dear lady, of course not," he said with an indulgent smile. "They'll probably get ten years hard labor."

Outrage tightened Susan's throat. A deafening pulse throbbed in her ears. She opened her mouth to speak, distracted when Halliwell put his hand on her arm.

"It's better news than I expected, Susan," he said softly. "At least they will be able to reunite with their families one day."

Bees buzzing in her head, she stared at his long, elegant fingers—an unexpected anchor keeping her afloat in a maelstrom of emotions. It was still a gross miscarriage of justice, but he was right.

She resolved to do what she could to help the weavers' wives and children, though she wasn't sure how that could be accomplished. It would mean trespassing on another earl's jurisdiction. Gabriel's standing among his peers in the Lords might be damaged.

"Ten years is a long time for a family to be without a breadwinner," she murmured.

A spark of hope flickered to life when Halliwell said, "I suggest you and I share the news with my tenants and do what we can."

⟫⟫⟫❧⟪⟪⟪

As THEY LEFT Rowbotham's offices, Griff wished the words unsaid. The hostile atmosphere at Clifton Heights was bad enough. The tenants on his lands wouldn't welcome him warmly. It might be dangerous, and Susan would be there to witness the melee.

On the other hand, things might go better if the tenants saw him with the woman who had championed their cause.

He wasn't sure how she felt about his suggestion, though she boarded the carriage without hesitation. As she preceded him, he couldn't help but notice her very appealing bottom. Indeed, it was all he could do not to place his hand on her hip–just to assist her inside, mind you. She'd probably slap him. Perhaps he should add a pleasing *derrière* to his list of required feminine attributes.

Again, Rebecca Waterman obligingly chose to sit across from her friend. It was hard to tell if Susan's glare meant she was pleased he would have to sit beside her, or not.

Once they were all inside, Frederick closed the door and put the step back in place. The carriage rocked as he mounted to the driver's bench.

Preoccupied with trying to decide where to direct his footman, Griff was shocked when Susan put a hand on his arm and asked, "Do you think it's wise?"

Griff the Rake should be delighted she'd touched him willingly, but the unexpected gesture was more arousing than was good for his self-control. His thoughts muddled, he pondered her meaning. "You're not still worried about your reputation, are you?"

He realized his mistake when she withdrew her hand and narrowed her eyes. "I am not a frivolous woman of the London *ton* who cares about her reputation. It's well known I am a bluestocking who isn't interested in the marriage mart. My concern was for your safety. I cannot imagine you are held in high esteem by your tenants."

She'd scolded him like a child who'd misbehaved in the schoolroom, yet there was something undeniably arousing about the anger blazing in those gray eyes. Was she truly concerned for his welfare? Or was it an act?

For some unfathomable reason, her assertion that she wasn't interested in marriage struck him as deeply unfortunate. Susan was a highly principled woman who would be intensely loyal to the man she married. It was an admirable quality he would want in a wife—if he ever married. Which he never would. Until the earldom needed an heir.

But, the woman stirring up these maudlin feelings had stolen his horse, and he'd best not forget it. He took hold of her gloved hand and brushed a kiss on her knuckles. "I appreciate your concern on my behalf," he crooned, summoning his best rakish voice. "Perhaps the wisest course of action is to repair first to Clifton Heights and send a message to my tenants that we intend to visit on the morrow with good news."

IN HER ELEMENT

"Your gates seem to be in a state of disrepair," Susan remarked when Halliwell's carriage reached Clifton Heights. She'd sensed his apprehension growing as they neared his ancestral home. That alone should have warned her to keep her mouth shut. The firm set of his jaw revealed his annoyance and embarrassment that the gates were hanging off their hinges like drunken sailors.

"Hence the need for a new estate manager," he replied tersely.

The driver proceeded slowly but the carriage lurched each time the wheels encountered a pothole. Susan held on to the strap, finally accepting it was inevitable she and Halliwell would be thrown against each other. She forced a smile, pretending she was enjoying the frequent contact. It was actually a good thing he was there, otherwise she'd have been bumped and bruised.

Wait! That didn't make sense. If he wasn't here…

The nonsensical conundrum was forgotten when she finally espied the house. Larger and more grandiose than Thicketford Manor, the edifice had obviously been built to showcase the wealth of its owners. The soaring pillars holding up the *porte-cochère* spoke of power and dependability, but the plaster was peeling badly. The years hadn't been kind and the only word that sprang to Susan's mind was *monstrosity*.

It reminded her of renderings she'd seen of recently discovered Indian temples smothered by jungle vegetation. Ivy and morning glory clearly ruled here, and not the decorative kind.

It would take enormous amounts of labor and money to restore it to its former splendor, but the effort would be well worth it.

However, this time, she paid heed to the anger radiating from her companion and kept silent, as did the gaping Rebecca.

"It's seen better days," he allowed. "And I warn you, the interior isn't much of an improvement."

It was tempting to retort that this kind of ruination could only come about as the result of neglect, but the resignation in his voice told Susan he'd already acknowledged that fact.

"Hopefully," he said as he offered his hand to help her alight, "the chap recommended by your Mr. Blair can start putting things to rights."

Perhaps emboldened by the strength of his hand, she didn't let go once she stepped down. She'd held her peace long enough. "But you should be here to oversee the improvements. You must love this grand house."

"I used to," he said with a sigh, the bleakness in his gaze touching her heart.

The revelation of his parents' untimely demise highlighted that there was more to his abandonment of his responsibilities at Clifton Heights than she'd realized.

Accustomed to Frame's efficiency, Susan was embarrassed for Halliwell when he was obliged to knock more than once on his own front door to gain admittance. When a butler finally appeared, he seemed not to instantly recognize his master. His hesitation in acknowledging them with a perfunctory bow was intolerable.

"Andrews," Halliwell hissed by way of introduction as he ushered Susan and Rebecca inside. "My butler. Another symptom of the problem, as you see."

Judging by the scowl on Andrews' ill-shaven face, Susan could readily see he was not a trained butler. He'd made no effort to greet them or take cloaks and gloves.

She had just untied the laces of her cloak when Halliwell abruptly unfurled it from her shoulders and practically shoved it at Andrews. "See that chambers are prepared for Lady Susan and Mrs. Waterman," he said as he repeated the performance with Rebecca's garment. "The ladies and I will take tea in the drawing room."

Andrews eyed Susan with disdain, clearly assuming she was no lady.

"Lady Susan Crompton," she declared with as much snobbery as she could infuse into her voice. "Of the Farnworth Cromptons."

It was unclear if the name meant anything to the servant, but at least he averted his cheeky gaze.

Following Halliwell's lead, she slowly peeled off her gloves and held them out for the butler to take. She wasn't surprised the scowling fellow couldn't meet her gaze as he bundled up all the outwear and strode off.

Susan took the opportunity to look around the huge foyer. Many of the statues were missing limbs that probably weren't supposed to be missing. Cracks had spread like spiders' webs across the plastered walls and ceiling. Dust motes hung in the air, some clinging to long, stringy cobwebs. The odor of damp was pervasive. Most of the candelabra were without candles. Dead roses lay curled up in tarnished bowls long since gone dry.

Shock paled Rebecca's countenance.

How Halliwell ran his household was none of Susan's business, yet she couldn't keep silent. The neglect was heartbreaking. "This must have been a grand house at one time."

His arm tensed as he escorted her into the drawing room. "It was, when my parents were alive. My mother loved this house."

"You miss them," she replied as she sat on a sofa that had seen better days. The striped fabric had faded to a degree that it was impossible to discern the original colors. Stuffing poked through several slits in the padded arms. She tried valiantly not to let him see she'd noticed.

Rebecca opted for an upholstered armchair that looked to be in slightly better repair.

"I found it impossible to live here after they died," Halliwell admitted.

Susan suspected he hadn't confessed that to anyone before. "You were lonely."

He narrowed his eyes. "Actually, I found I preferred the life in London."

She'd seen a glimpse of the grief-stricken young man he must have been, but his clenched jaw made it clear he already regretted letting his visitors see his vulnerability. Perhaps it was time to move to a safer topic. "And you embarked on breeding horses."

EVERY MUSCLE IN Griff's body tensed. He'd let down his guard. It was dangerous to forget the rules of this game. No emotional involvement. Susan must never think she'd reached his heart.

In truth, seeing the wretched state of his home through her eyes made it seem even worse. He'd deliberately ignored deficiencies he was noticing now. "I'll speak to the housekeeper about replacing the candles," he said lamely.

She worried her bottom lip, clearly of a mind to voice an opinion. That shouldn't surprise him. On the other hand, she was trying valiantly to overlook the state of the sofa—another shortcoming he hadn't noticed. "I could speak to her, if you wish," she offered. "Sometimes, a woman's requests carry more weight with staff."

He ought to reject the offer. Only the mistress of the house normally instructed servants. However, neither Andrews nor Mrs. Brass had paid heed to his orders. He'd like to see them ignore the redoubtable Susan Crompton's "requests"! "I couldn't impose," he replied, knowing full well she would insist.

"I insist," she declared, squaring her shoulders. "It seems to me your staff is shirking its duties."

He hid his amusement. She was in her element. Reminding people of their duty was her forte! In fact, with her breasts thrust out, she looked rather like he imagined Boadicea before a battle. Strong, determined, magnificent in her fury. The vision stirred surprisingly strong interest in his sac. He ought to rein in his body's reaction, although it might make his feigned attraction seem more real to her.

SHOWDOWN

R EBECCA CHATTERED NERVOUSLY as they waited and waited for breakfast to be served the following morning. Eyeing the empty sideboard in the morning room, Susan couldn't contain her annoyance when Halliwell entered. By the looks of things, he'd tied his own cravat and the beige frock coat only emphasized his pallor. He looked like he'd slept as badly as she had, though she'd wager he hadn't dreamed of galloping across desert sands, hair flying free…

"Before you ask," she declared, determined to drag her thoughts away from the recurring erotic dreams of Griffith Halliwell. "The mattress is lumpy. There was no water in the ewer, and the linens haven't been aired in…forever!"

Rebecca nodded her agreement.

"And good morning to you too," their host replied with a wry smirk that somehow made him even more boyishly handsome. The morning stubble on his dimpled chin only enhanced his rakish charm.

Rubbish!

"Really, Halliwell," she blustered, wishing she had a fan.

He held up his hands in surrender. "I know, I know. It's intolerable. And, please, call me Griff."

He was making an effort to be nice, but did she want to be on such familiar terms with him? "No breakfast yet, Griff," she muttered, crumpling her napkin as she stood. "I'm off to the kitchen."

Having no idea how to find said kitchen, she was relieved when he rose. "I'll accompany you," he said. "Though I don't recall ever visiting Cook's lair before."

Exasperation threatened to boil over as she strode out of the morning room, once more wondering how it had come about that men ruled the world.

HAVING FINALLY LOCATED the servants' staircase, and acknowledged Susan's justified outrage over the dilapidated condition of the risers, banisters and plastered walls, Griff was further angered to find Fothersgill sitting at the large wooden table in the kitchen.

Clearly taken off guard, the fellow stood too quickly for Griff to shove his face into the remains of the hearty cooked breakfast he'd been enjoying.

"My lord," he rasped. "I didn't realize…"

"Of course you didn't," Griff roared, grabbing hold of Fothersgill's lapels. "Perhaps if you spent more time doing your job…"

It was tempting to use his fists and throw the man out on his ear, but he became aware a silence had fallen. The cook, the housekeeper, the butler and Lady Susan Crompton all stood with mouths agape. He'd never been a violent man, but this was outside of enough. Still, an earl had to be dignified. Hadn't his father drummed that into his head?

Susan's calm, authoritative voice broke the silence. "Why has his lordship's breakfast not yet been served?" she asked the cook.

Apparently struck dumb by the steely tone of the question, the rotund, red-faced woman scurried to the pantry.

His outrage abating, Griff let go of Fothersgill's coat.

Susan turned to Andrews. "It's a butler's responsibility to keep the household staff on their toes."

"Yes, my lady," he allowed, though his sulk deepened.

Susan clearly didn't care for his demeanor. "We'll talk further," she warned. "As for you," she said, turning to Mrs. Brass, "if you are the housekeeper, you should be ashamed of the state of the guest bedrooms. Find fresh linens and see to it at once."

By the time only Fothersgill remained to be dealt with, Griff's anger had subsided and he accepted what had to be done. "You're dismissed. Be off the premises within the hour."

He proffered an arm to Susan, wondering, as he escorted her from the kitchen, if he'd truly invited her to call him Griff.

WAITING FOR THE long-awaited breakfast to be served in the morning room, Rebecca continued her meaningless chatter. Susan sat across from her silent host, regretting the impulse that had driven her to act as if she were the lady of the manor. Halliwell had a right to be offended, though he'd encouraged her to call him Griff, which must mean—truly she had no idea what it meant. No man had ever invited her to address him with such familiarity. It was as if he considered her a friend. Did she want to be friends with such an irresponsible man? Perhaps honey might achieve what marching weavers could not. "I apologize, my lord," she began. "It wasn't my place..."

"Not at all," he replied, shaking his head. "You did what I should have done long ago."

Rebecca stopped talking. The silent minutes crawled by.

Halliwell played with his fork, squaring his shoulders when a scowling Andrews ushered in a footman Susan recognized.

"This is Frederick," Halliwell explained. "I brought him with me from London."

Frederick proceeded to unload plates of food from his tray. Appetizing aromas filled the air. Protocol demanded the butler remain to oversee the footman, but he disappeared without excusing himself, leaving Frederick to serve the meals.

Susan couldn't keep quiet. "Where do you think Andrews is off to in such a hurry, Frederick?" she asked, hoping the London footman's loyalty lay with his master.

Blushing surprisingly deeply for such a large, gruff-looking fellow, Frederick glanced at Halliwell, cleared his throat and said, "I believe he intends to meet with Mr. Fothersgill, my lady."

A furious frown distorted Halliwell's handsome features as he threw down his napkin. "We'll see about that," he blustered. "Please excuse me, Susan, Mrs. Waterman."

She picked up her knife and fork after he and the footman left, insanely pleased he hadn't used her title.

FOTHERSGILL AND ANDREWS did their best to recover from the shock of Griff's clearly unexpected arrival in the staff kitchen.

However, they couldn't hide the burlap sack fast enough.

The fleeting realization that he'd been a complete fool flitted through Griff's brain. He'd seen the butler with the sack and thought nothing of it. He grabbed the sack and slowly untied the twine, quite enjoying the fear creeping into the two men's eyes. Inside were several items from the drawing room—silver candlesticks, a small bronze statuette of some Greek god his father had bought, and various other knick-knacks. What infuriated him the most was the discovery of an antique porcelain figurine, the last birthday gift he'd given his mother before the accident. She'd adored the vibrant red skirts and jaunty plumed hat of the pretty French shepherdess, and been reduced to tears by the little lamb she carried in her arms. He closed the bag and clutched the top so tightly his fingers turned white.

"Frederick," he hissed. "Escort these thieves from the premises."

Grinning, the burly footman grabbed the collars of both cringing men and nigh on lifted them off their feet.

"If you ever show your faces here or in the village again," he warned, unable to continue when his throat constricted.

He stood alone for several minutes, confident they'd consider themselves lucky not to be hauled before a magistrate. However, he couldn't return to the morning room until the trembling stopped and his breathing slowed. He acknowledged Susan was right—for too long, he'd chosen to ignore problems that were right under his nose.

THE WATCHMAN

ARTHUR COLEMAN COULDN'T deny he was nervous venturing into the grimy slums of Ancoats. However, the Watchman's notorious Red Bandana gang ruled this seedy area of Manchester. Arthur would need blunt and connections if the thoroughbred caper was to be successful. There was no better partner than the Watchman to assist with such an endeavor. He'd have ways of getting rid of Arthur's father that wouldn't raise questions.

However, the gangland kingpin might not be happy to see him. He'd settled his previous debt to the unpleasant fellow by consigning Tillie to work in one of his brothels. If she was an inmate in the Preston poorhouse, she must have escaped. "Trust the bitch to screw up my plans yet again," he muttered to the mule.

His gut clenched when four toughs armed with coshes loomed out of the shadows of a narrow street and blocked his way. Shorn heads and the splash of red at their throats were a clear sign they were members of the gang he sought.

He reined the beast to a halt but didn't dismount. On foot, he'd have no chance to escape a beating. Swallowing his fear, he narrowed his eyes. "I've come to see the Watchman," he said, pitching his voice lower.

Edging closer, they made no reply.

"I've a proposition for him," he continued as cold sweat trickled down his spine.

In Jamaica, he'd learned to smell a slave's fear. These animals no doubt possessed the same instinct. "A money-making proposition," he added.

He tightened his white-knuckled grip on the reins and urged the animal forward when they stepped aside and beckoned him into the shadows.

He obeyed when gruffly told to dismount, deeming it wise not to protest the blindfold. Prodded in the back by a cosh, he took tentative steps forward. Stumbling along, turning right, then left, then right, he began to think he'd never find his mule again—if he was even given the option to leave. The sniggering thugs behind him were clearly enjoying his predicament. A vivid flash of memory had him back in the sugar mill. Only, this time, he was the mouse and not the cat.

At length, he was shoved into a dwelling—probably the kitchen judging by the overwhelming odor of fried food, burned grease and human waste.

Somewhere in the house, a woman screeched at a wailing babe.

He blinked when the bandana was untied and he found himself the object of the Watchman's predatory gaze.

Arthur's first thought was to babble his admiration of what the gang boss had achieved. For a young man of maybe twenty years to build such an empire…

However, the Watchman knew the extent of his powers of intimidation without Arthur telling him. He opted instead to extend his hand. "Well met once more," he rasped, instantly regretting a gesture that hinted at social superiority.

A tic toyed with the Watchman's upper lip. He slowly curled his fingers into the long tresses of a doe-eyed girl kneeling at his feet and pulled her head back. Arthur's cock reacted predictably to the adolescent breasts that popped out of her ragged frock. He shifted his weight, beyond aroused when the Watchman lowered his head and greedily suckled a nipple. The girl didn't complain though she was clearly in discomfort. The message wasn't lost on

Arthur.

"I came with a proposition," he said, wishing the fellow would at least invite him to sit before his trembling knees buckled. On second thought, the Watchman sprawled in the only chair in the dingy place.

"First, we'll discuss the wench," the gang boss growled.

"Of course," Arthur agreed, once more cursing the day he'd dallied with Tillie.

An hour later, blindfolded again, he left the disgusting place, thankful for an escort back to his mule.

He was satisfied with the Watchman's plan for stealing the horse and getting rid of his father. He'd have preferred not to involve Tillie in the scheme, but the gang boss insisted he wanted her back. Mounted on the mule, he patted the satchel slung around his body. The Watchman hadn't advanced him as much as he'd asked for, but it was better than nothing. Once the stud fees came rolling in, he'd be a rich man, though he'd been obliged to agree to a smaller share of the profits than he'd anticipated.

TILLIE EMERGED FROM the parish poorhouse, lifted her chin and inhaled deeply. The sun's weak rays did little to chase away the chill but even a hint of sunshine was a reassurance she was still alive.

Clutching the penny doled out reluctantly by the spiteful woman employed as matron of St. John's Parish Almshouse, she shrank deeper into the meager shawl deemed adequate by the Poor Law commissioners and set forth to make the most of the one day a week she was allowed to venture into town.

Much as she looked forward to a few hours of relative freedom, it was tempting to retreat back into the wretched poorhouse when she heard an all too familiar voice calling her name.

Instead, she summoned what little dignity she had left and accosted Arthur Coleman. "Don't call me that," she hissed, hands braced on hips. "I'm Matilda."

The fiend responsible for her miserable fate had the gall to smirk. "My word! Gone all posh, I see."

Common sense told her to get as far away from Arthur as she could, but where would she go? "No. I used my full name so your cronies in Manchester wouldn't find me if they came looking."

"It was brave of you to escape," he said softly, touching his fingers to her cheek.

She tried really hard to hold back the tears and stay angry with him. "I ended up in that awful brothel thanks to you."

"I know," he crooned, opening his arms, "and I'm sorry. But what else was I to do? They'd have killed me if I hadn't handed you over. And you did muff up your part of the plot to kidnap the Crompton girl."

That wasn't precisely the way Tillie remembered the fiasco—how was she to know the Earl of Farnworth's valet would show up with a rifle? However, Arthur's reappearance was perhaps a godsend. She needed a patron if she was ever to escape the poorhouse. Ignoring a faint alarm bell ringing in the back of her head, she went into his embrace, warmed by the memory of the erotic delights they'd shared. "You 'ave to take better care of me, Arthur," she murmured.

"I will, dear girl," he promised. "I have a plan to make us rich."

Tillie liked the sound of riches. Then she'd have a thing or two to say to the holier-than-thou mistress of St. John's Parish Almshouse. "I missed you," she cooed, grinding her mons against the hard maleness that proved he still loved her. "You've been 'iding somewhere tropical."

Raking a sun-bronzed hand through golden hair, he revealed he'd been working for the East India Company.

"Oooh," she replied, cupping her hand around a lovely arousal nestled in excitingly coarse trousers. "I've 'eard they get up to all kinds of naughty things in India."

"I can't wait to show you," he growled, linking her arm.

She went with him willingly, feeling like a proper lady on the arm of a baron's son.

VISITING TENANTS

R EASONABLY IN CONTROL of his anger over Orion and the thefts at Clifton Heights, Griff acceded to Susan's suggestion they go on horseback to visit his tenants instead of taking the carriage. Even cleaned and with the wheel fixed, the vehicle wasn't up to his parents' standards. It suddenly seemed important to live up to their expectations. He doubted Susan had made the proposal for the same reasons. She was right again that he'd appear less like the haughty lord of the manor arriving on horseback.

This was the trouble with bluestockings. Very often, they were so annoyingly right. Suggestions from interfering females usually rubbed him the wrong way, even if they were good ones. He supposed he was getting used to Susan's habit of speaking her mind. It was part of her personality.

He shouldn't have been surprised when she turned up her nose at the first mare he picked out for her. She reluctantly agreed to use the lady's saddle only after he pointed out the tenants would be scandalized if she rode astride. The argument reminded him of the night she'd ridden into the stable yard at Thicketford Manor from Chester, hair windblown, skirts up around her thighs—a gypsy. He cleared his throat when the erotic memory stirred his male interest.

He should have left well alone and allowed the groom to assist her to mount. Instead, he compounded his problem by setting his hands about her waist without so much as a by-your-leave.

Her squeal of surprise as she grasped his shoulders was gratifying, not to mention arousing. He'd soon have her eating out of the palm of his hand if the dazed look in her eyes was any indication.

ADMITTEDLY, THE SHOCK of finding Griff's big hands spanning her waist took Susan aback. It was a good thing his broad shoulders provided an anchor. However, she took the unexpected gesture as proof he was falling under her spell, though exactly what she'd done to enchant him remained a mystery. She'd complained loudly about the state of his household, overstepped with his servants and made a fuss about his choice of a horse for her to ride. Mind you, Emma always said Gabriel overlooked her faults because he loved her.

Love! No, she didn't want Griff Halliwell to fall in love with her. She stifled an involuntary snort. As if that would ever happen! He was too self-centered to care about another person. The unavoidable truth of it made her feel inexplicably sad. If he ever did give his heart…

She corralled her wayward musings, wondering about the pretty porcelain figurine he'd reverently placed on the mantel upon his return from the servants' quarters. Jaw clenched, he'd advised her of what had transpired with Andrews and the estate manager. She'd wisely not pried into the details, though it had taken restraint not to remark it was the kind of thing one might expect of servants left to their own devices.

As they left Clifton Heights, he still seemed to be in a mood not to engage in conversation; she resolved to speak only if called upon once they reached the village where most of the cottages were apparently located.

Surveying the rural landscape not unlike that surrounding Thicketford Manor, it came to her she was enjoying riding in the company of a gentleman. Perhaps a compliment would be in order. "You sit a horse very well," she said, instantly sorry she'd mentioned a part of his anatomy a lady never cast eyes upon. She startled when he swiveled his head to pierce her with his emerald gaze.

"Why, Lady Susan," he replied with a chuckle. "I do believe you just paid me a compliment."

SUSAN REACTED PREDICTABLY to Griff's teasing. That was one thing he liked about her. It was easy to make her blush, probably because she wasn't equipped with the arsenal of seduction skills most women of his acquaintance possessed. He'd wager she had very little experience bantering with men—arguing, yes; flirting, no. She was an innocent when it came to the opposite sex.

He quashed the arousing notion when the village came in sight. His ultimate goal was to convince her to part with Orion, not to get himself hot and bothered.

He and Susan quickly found themselves surrounded by a scowling crowd, mostly women and ragged urchins, though there was a hint of puzzlement on several faces when they realized who had accompanied him.

He thought back to the times, as a child, he'd accompanied his parents into the village, usually to distribute alms on holidays and Holy Days. The atmosphere was decidedly different. There'd been gratitude and respect on the tenants' faces then. He straightened his shoulders, acknowledging he had to do better. He was still his father's son. "Lady Susan Crompton and I have come to inform you Fothersgill is no longer in charge of managing the Pendlebury estate."

Susan's arched brows reflected his own surprise. He hadn't

intended to mention her name, nor had it come to him until that moment that Fothersgill was likely the source of many of the tenants' problems as well as his own. If the man had kept him informed…

Still, ultimately, these people were his responsibility. Encouraged by a few tentative nods and grunts of approval, he soldiered on. "A replacement—Rogerson's his name—will be arriving soon," he announced. "There is some good news regarding the harsh sentences handed down last week. It's probable your menfolk won't be transported."

"Will my man be coming home then?" one woman shouted.

He wished he had better news and the crowd sensed his hesitation. The angry scowls were back.

"Lord Pendlebury has secured a guarantee of a prison sentence," Susan declared. "It is still harsh and unjust, but the earl and I will do all we can to lessen your burdens."

Her assurances stunned everyone into silence, including Griff. He should have been affronted. These were his people. However, for a fleeting moment, she'd reminded him of his mother. He wondered if the tenants saw the same noble demeanor.

Susan's wide-eyed gaze jolted him out of his reverie. She'd opened the opportunity for him to utter the same reassurances. "Yes," he said. "Rogerson will see to the distribution of whatever you need to survive until your men can come home."

"What about the plight of the weavers?" someone shouted. "We've no work."

It was a grim reality—one Griff had been woefully ignorant of until Susan brought it to his attention. He couldn't shy away from his responsibility now. "I don't have a great deal of sway in the House of Lords," he admitted. "But I'll do what I can to petition on your behalf."

"As will the Earl of Farnworth," Susan added.

It wasn't much to offer, but Griff sensed the hostility ebbing—until a stern-faced woman who probably outweighed him by several stone elbowed her way to the front of the crowd.

"Will ye and yer lady come in for a cup of tea?" she asked, gesturing to a thatched dwelling in need of whitewash. "'Twould be an honor, yer lordship."

The simple truth was humbling. All these hardy northern folks needed was a sympathetic ear. He didn't have the heart to tell the crowd Lady Susan wasn't his lady. "We'd be delighted," he replied.

GETTING TO WORK

"IT WAS AN eye-opening experience," Susan told Rebecca after she and the earl returned to Clifton Heights. "I'm very glad Griff accepted the invitation to take tea with his tenant."

"So, it's Griff now, is it?" Rebecca asked with a smile.

Susan tensed. "Yes. He asked me to call him that. It means nothing. He even allowed Mr. and Mrs. Fazakerly to address him as Pendlebury, which amazed me, to be honest."

"I'm still astonished he took tea with his tenants," Rebecca replied. "Where has he rushed off to now?"

"To his study. He'll join us after he's attended to urgent correspondence. He seemed genuinely shocked by what he learned of the weavers' plight."

"Before he comes, tell me about the cottage."

"Small, cozy, but in need of significant repairs that Mrs. Fazakerly didn't hesitate to point out."

"I'll wager that ruffled his feathers."

"Actually, no. He promised to send Rogerson to make a list of the most urgent repairs needed by all the villagers. He apologized for the lamentable state of the cottages. He could do no less after seeing the problems for himself—rotted thatch, cracked walls, broken windows, no source of safe drinking water."

"Sounds like he's turned over a new leaf."

Susan's throat tightened. Could a negligent landowner change his tune overnight? Had she succeeded in opening his eyes to the realities of the workers' lives? Or had he merely made expedient promises he had no intention of keeping?

She hoped he was a man of his word because she was beginning to like him. However, a leopard couldn't change its spots. She'd hate to think she was drawn to a rogue who had no genuine wish to change his rakish ways. However, she had to remind herself she wanted to drive him back to his dissolute life in London. Didn't she?

Rebecca's fidgeting returned her confused thoughts to the drawing room. "You seem anxious."

Her friend blushed. "I have to confess to wandering about this huge house while you were gone. There is enormous potential here. Will Halliwell be affronted if I share some suggestions?"

GRIFF COULDN'T AVOID overhearing Mrs. Waterman's question as he entered the drawing room. "I promise you I shan't be upset," he assured her. Susan had shared with him her friend's talent for decor.

He brandished the letters he'd written. "I'm sending for Potts, my London butler," he explained, not yet ready to reveal the recipient of the second missive. "Of course, I normally hand correspondence over to my butler to post. With Andrews gone, I'll have to depend on Frederick to take these into Manchester and put them aboard the Royal Mail coach."

"I hope you don't mind, my lord," Rebecca said. "I had a chance to speak to your remaining staff."

"Not at all. I'm interested in improving things. And please call me Pendlebury."

"The cook and the maids are glad to see the back of the two men you fired," she said. "The extent of their…well, you'll find out soon enough, I suppose. However, I'm not sure you want to keep Mrs. Brass as your housekeeper. She's impertinent."

He chuckled inwardly at the notion the mild-mannered Mrs. Waterman would find anyone impertinent, but perhaps she had a point. "One of the things that struck me during our visit to the village was the way Mrs. Fazakerly didn't hesitate to criticize me."

He held up his hand when Susan opened her mouth to rebut him. "However, I never once considered her impertinent—just a plain-speaking Lancashire lass ready to express a few home truths. And she couldn't say enough good things about my parents, particularly my mother."

Susan nodded. "They were obviously well thought of."

Griff bristled. The weaver's wife's complaints had under-scored his failure as a landowner and peer of the realm. He was ready to face up to his deficiencies and make amends, but it bothered him Susan had been right all along about his shortcom-ings. The child-like craving for an opinionated bluestocking to think well of him was surely beneath his dignity.

He strove to turn the conversation back to the staffing prob-lem. "Potts will soon get things organized. He was the butler here for years and knows everyone in these parts. As for the repairs needed to this house…"

"I have some ideas," Mrs. Waterman offered.

"And I've dealt with tradesmen in Preston and Manchester on behalf of Thicketford Manor," Susan added, her eyes bright with enthusiasm.

He suddenly liked the idea of Susan spending a few days at Clifton. It would afford him opportunities to convince her to turn Orion over to him. "I'd appreciate your insights, ladies," he declared.

A NEW MAN

ARTHUR BRUSHED BITS of straw off his homespun trousers and retrieved his cap from behind the bales of hay. Setting her disheveled clothing to rights, Tillie was still pouting about having to return to the poorhouse, though she'd become more amenable to the idea now he'd tupped her in the stables behind *The Coach and Four*.

"Promise you'll come for me," she whined.

If it wasn't for the amazingly hot sex, and the fact the Watchman wanted her back, he'd have left her to rot in the institution. "Of course, but you must see I can't arrive at Withins Hall with you in tow. I have to first convince my father the time spent in India has reformed me."

"I like the naughty things you learned in India," she cooed, fluttering her eyelashes.

He didn't let on he'd taken to smacking his bed partners in Jamaica. A man had to be firm with his slaves. Who knew Tillie would find a sore bottom arousing? "Off you go," he insisted, bussing a kiss on her forehead before he became too preoccupied with the notion of reddening her tempting backside again.

He waited until she was out of sight before stuffing the cap into his jacket pocket and setting off down Friargate to the local tailoring shop.

Carr's unctuous smile faded when he saw who had entered his establishment. He wrinkled his nose, horror blossoming on his face as he eyed Arthur's working-class clothing.

Arthur bristled, itching to plant his fist on the man's nose. A shopkeeper looking down on a baron's son! One day, he'd teach the supercilious midget a lesson in respect for one's betters. "I've recently returned from India, Mr. Carr," he declared, "and, as you see, I'm in need of more suitable raiment than these shipboard rags."

Carr had the effrontery to narrow his eyes.

"If it's payment you're worried about, my father has an account here. One you value highly, I'm sure."

Arthur could almost see the wheels turning in Carr's head. One word of dissatisfaction from a titled customer and he'd be ruined.

"Will you require your purchases to be delivered to Withins Hall, sir?" the tailor asked.

Arthur breathed again. There'd be no necessity to spend any of the coin the Watchman had given him in this pitiful shop.

"Most of them, yes. However, I'd like to leave here with whatever you can provide in terms of ready-made."

Arthur didn't need to see Carr's wide-eyed shock to know he'd committed an unpardonable offense. No gentleman would ever contemplate buying clothes off the rack! Unthinkable. However, he couldn't turn up at Withins Hall dressed as he was.

"Certainly," Carr replied, apparently having decided to swallow his pride. "Let me see what we have in your size."

An hour later, Arthur stepped out of the shop feeling like a new man. The linen shirt wasn't of the finest quality but Carr insisted it was all he had. The blue woolen frock coat was a mite snug across the back and the buff breeches were a size too small. Still, nothing amiss with a fellow flaunting his endowments, so to speak. Carr had prattled on about the importance of a perfectly tied cravat and had spent at least fifteen minutes ensuring Arthur left his shop with an acceptable neckcloth.

The outfit would suffice to make a good first impression until the other clothing he'd ordered arrived. Tucking the brown paper parcel containing his old clothes under his arm, he set off down the street to follow Carr's recommendation of Timpson's for new boots. Thence, his last stop before Withins Hall would be the stables behind the inn. While romping with Tillie, he'd noticed a gelding that would be much more suitable than his mule for a grand homecoming.

LATER THAT AFTERNOON, Arthur leaped from the gelding's back, took the front steps of Withins Hall two at a time and lifted the door knocker. The sonorous echo added to the euphoria humming through his veins. It was damned good to be home where he belonged.

He thrust the package of his laborer's togs at the gaping butler who answered the door and nigh on collided with Anthea and her husband in the foyer.

As he should have expected, his sister swooned and his brother-in-law scowled. A chap might be justified in thinking Springer would be used to Anthea's histrionics by now. It appeared she still thought of herself as Handel's tragic operatic heroine. Some things never changed.

Arthur hesitated when his father appeared on the scene, no doubt drawn by Anthea's performance and the frantic maidservant fussing over her moaning mistress.

When the color drained from the baron's face and he pressed a hand to his chest, looking as if he might crumple alongside his daughter, it occurred to Arthur he may not have to resort to using members of the Red Bandana gang. If Whiteside suffered a fatal apoplexy, Arthur could be baron before the night was out.

However, his father's eyes didn't roll back in his head. His ruddy complexion restored, he stayed upright and narrowed his gaze at his son. "Arthur? What the blazes are you doing here, Boy?"

It took enormous effort, but Arthur adopted a contrite pose, deciding at the last moment that falling to his knees might be a bit much. "Father, I've learned my lesson and I'm here to beg your forgiveness."

Tears welled in the old man's eyes. He opened his arms wide. "Welcome home, Son," he rasped.

Arthur went into his embrace, confident he'd won the first round. Whatever obstacles lay in the path of redemption, his father loved him too much to allow them to triumph.

JOHN SPRINGER WASN'T fooled by his brother-in-law's act of contrition. He'd played the role of dutiful husband and son-in-law for too long not to recognize a fellow imposter.

Tempted as he was to shove the maid's smelling salts up his melodramatic wife's nose, he helped her rise, all the while cooing endearments.

Clearly, the baron believed Arthur's masterful performance. Could he not see the wretch was wearing someone else's clothing? A new plan was necessary or the foolish old man might decide to reinstate Arthur's claim to the title. John had endured too much to allow that to happen.

FEELING AT HOME

"I CAN SCARCELY believe you've only been here a fortnight," Susan whispered to Potts as she and Griff conducted their inspection of recent hires at Clifton Heights. A crew of properly liveried servants stood in an orderly line in the newly painted foyer.

"Still much to do, my lady," the butler replied with a sigh.

His unsmiling response didn't surprise her. Like Frame, Potts would never admit to being completely satisfied with the household arrangements.

Appalled by the state of the house upon his arrival from London, the butler had immediately set about finding suitable staff. Many of the workers he'd recruited had been employed at Clifton before and seemed happy to be back when Griff acknowledged remembering them.

Resplendent in a mob cap, black crepe dress and starched apron, Mrs. Fazakerly looked the very picture of a competent housekeeper. Her husband had been put to work in the stables. The tenants were not Potts' first choice, but he'd apparently ceded to Griff's request the couple be given employment. It was understood they were "on trial", but Susan had a good feeling about the outcome. She was also pleased Griff had agreed to give employment in the kitchens to some of the children of the condemned men.

Gangs of painters, plasterers and carpenters were still busy throughout the house and probably would be for some weeks.

Susan had thoroughly enjoyed working with Rebecca, sharing ideas for refurbishing Clifton's stately rooms. It was indeed gratifying to see the house reborn, as it were.

However, it was the change in Griff that gave her the most pleasure. He was clearly delighted to see his ancestral home gradually being restored to its former glory. His frequent smiles led her to hope they'd left their enmity behind and become friends. It was true the feelings his smile evoked were more wanton than friendly, but that simply made it easier to play the flirt.

"This house is growing on me," she admitted to Rebecca as they took tea in the freshly wallpapered drawing room one afternoon. She'd begun to look forward to the daily ritual. Griffith Halliwell was proving to be an excellent conversationalist with a keen sense of humor. He'd kept them amused with all kinds of tales, including one about a nobleman betting on a race between two raindrops on a window pane. He appeared to enjoy discussing current events—a topic men normally reserved for visits to their gentlemen's clubs.

Rebecca raised a brow as she sipped her tea. "Clifton Heights suits you."

Heat that had nothing to do with the hot beverage rose in Susan's face. She'd tried valiantly to hide the burgeoning feeling of belonging at Clifton but, clearly, her friend had taken note of the way she swanned about like the lady of the manor. "It's a grand house," she agreed, stroking the rich brocaded texture of the reupholstered sofa. "Any woman would be fortunate to call it home."

"And you've taken a liking to the earl, as well," Rebecca asserted.

"What if I've discovered qualities I didn't suspect he had?" Susan retorted. "That doesn't mean..."

She closed her mouth abruptly when Griff sauntered into the room. For a big man, he moved with athletic grace. He was definitely at home in his own skin. "I've heard they have something called punkah fans to cool rooms in tropical climes," she mused aloud in an effort to distract attention from her blushes. "This room gets stuffy and could benefit from such a contraption."

"I believe we'd need a eunuch to make it work," Griff replied, bestowing one of the mischievous smiles that never failed to make Susan's nipples tingle.

Rebecca slurped her tea in a most unladylike manner, clearly amused by the unpardonable mention of anything to do with male body parts, or lack thereof.

"Tea?" Susan asked, doubtful she'd be able to hold the teapot steady enough to pour a cup without spilling into the saucer. Not for the first time, she pondered what it was about him that triggered wanton sensations. Broad shoulders, a ruggedly handsome face and arrogant masculinity normally left her cold.

"Allow me," Rebecca said, coming to her rescue when Griff nodded.

He wasn't one of those dandies who stuck out his pinkie in an affected manner when drinking from a cup. Most men of Susan's acquaintance, even Earl Gabriel, never seemed to know quite what to do with a china teacup and saucer. Griff, on the other hand, balanced the saucer on one thigh, managing to return the cup to its cradle after taking a sip—all with unerring accuracy, though he didn't even glance at the saucer. Susan became fixated on his thighs, spread as they were to accommodate the balancing act. It wasn't a gentlemanly way to sit since it inevitably drew the eye to…

"We really must think of a way to cool this room," she insisted, fanning herself with her hand.

"You seem to be the only person feeling the heat," Griff replied with a chuckle.

She averted her eyes from his teasing gaze. The bounder knew she found him attractive. If she were being honest with herself, what she was beginning to feel for Griff Halliwell went far beyond mere attraction.

"Have you ever bred horses here?" Rebecca asked, thankfully steering the conversation in another direction.

"At one time," Griff replied. "Clifton has the space and the facilities, but I've invested a lot in moving to Pendlebury Stables."

"You prefer the big city," Rebecca said.

Susan would have thought he'd be anxious to head south again. She was surprised when he hesitated in response. "Before you ladies got started on fixing up this house, I would have said I did feel more at home in London. However, now…"

Susan had to be careful not to fall into the temptation of thinking his enjoyment of her company was perhaps the reason he lingered in Lancashire. It was more likely a desire to get his hands on Orion that was keeping him at Clifton Heights. "Perhaps you could give us a tour of the facilities here," she suggested. "That way, we can have some idea of what's needed for our stud enterprise at Thicketford Manor."

"Excellent idea," he exclaimed, seemingly unperturbed by her determination to keep Orion in the north. "I'll arrange it with Rogerson for the morrow."

He rose and handed his cup and saucer to Rebecca. "This evening, after dinner, I suggest we baptize the billiards table they delivered yesterday."

Susan's heart raced. He could have no way of knowing she'd been playing billiards since she'd lived with Hannah in Somerset. Her mentor had ridiculed the notion that ladies of breeding didn't indulge in the sport.

"I couldn't possibly play," Rebecca exclaimed. "I'll leave it to the two of you."

Susan hoped Griff didn't notice her friend's naughty wink.

WAVING AWAY FREDERICK who hurried to assist him, Griff pushed his chair back from the table and contemplated the two women who'd joined him for dinner that evening.

The refurbishment of the dining room was still a work in progress but the space already felt more inviting without the old-fashioned Queen Anne sideboard. Susan could hardly contain her impatience for the arrival of the newly ordered satinwood furniture designed by Sheraton. Her enthusiasm for the house reminded him of how much he'd loved the place of his birth before tragedy struck. He felt at home here again, although he could never move back north and live alone. He was too gregarious and outgoing to cope with loneliness.

As his dinner companions chatted about this and that, it came to him he hadn't enjoyed meals as much for quite some time. Before his move to the capital, dining alone in this cavernous room had aggravated his grief. Life in London was fuller in terms of things to do and places to go, but he ate by himself most evenings if he didn't dine at his club.

He'd never consciously avoided inviting his mistresses to join him for meals, but he couldn't imagine the dinner table conversations being as lively and intelligent as sparring with Susan and Rebecca. Edwina Waxenby, for example, was prone to prattle on about the pitiful quality of Lady So-and-so's lemon tarts. She relished passing on the latest scandalous rumor running rampant through the *ton*. Since Griff wasn't in the marriage mart, he avoided balls and had no interest in the *on dits* that flowed from such events. Unfortunately, they formed the basis for Edwina's conversational arsenal. Not that they'd done much talking during their trysts but he'd been obliged to feign interest in a great deal of nonsense during the admittedly tedious seduction. And it had all been for naught when he learned of her horror of horses.

There was perhaps something to be said for making education more widely available to women. Most of his fellow peers would disagree, although Gabriel Smith was a forward thinker in that regard.

He got to his feet when Mrs. Waterman beckoned Frederick

to assist with her chair. "I think I'll retire," she said, bestowing a kiss on Susan's cheek. "This house is wearing me out."

Griff took her hand when she offered it and bussed a kiss. "I appreciate everything you've done, Mrs. Waterman. Clifton Heights is fortunate you came to stay."

She nodded modestly and bade them both goodnight.

Griff helped Susan rise from her chair. "Still up for the noble game of billiards?" he asked, anticipating showing off his prowess by teaching her something she didn't know.

"Indeed," she replied with entirely too much enthusiasm for his liking.

GAMES

"WE PLAY WITH three balls and, as you see, there are six pockets," Griff explained. "These flat walls are to keep the balls from falling off,' he added, running his hand over a side rail of the new billiards table.

Feigning amazement, Susan widened her eyes.

"They are called 'banks'," he continued, peeling off his frock coat. The waistcoat hugged his body like a glove, the black silk a stark contrast with the brilliant white of his shirtsleeves. "I suppose like the banks of a river."

Susan couldn't see the correlation but held her tongue, too fixated on his broad back and tapered hips to consider it as he examined a number of cues in the wall rack before choosing one and handing it to her.

"The balls can bounce off the rails, so you can deliberately aim at them. That's called a 'bank shot'."

"Perhaps you could demonstrate," she replied, sensing he was itching to show off.

She took a step back when he leaned over the table and lined his cue up to strike a ball. The new position gave her an excellent view of his backside, rendered all the more appealing by the tight breeches. She found herself more interested in his physical endowments than in the result of his shot which rebounded off four banks before knocking another ball into one of the pockets. "I see," she said. "Clever."

"You can put spin on the ball, like so."

She knew very well how to make a ball behave with the use of spin, so, this time, she concentrated on his long legs. She suppressed the compulsion to giggle at the smug look on his face when he turned to grin at her after sinking another ball. She hadn't giggled since—well, ever. Lady Susan Crompton wasn't a frivolous woman who giggled.

"Englishmen visiting the United States showed Americans how the use of spin can make the billiard ball behave differently depending on what type and amount of spin you apply," he said. "That explains why it is called 'English' in America but we call it 'side'."

Blushing slightly as if he realized he'd been lecturing, he smoothed a hand over the green baize. "In London, I heard of experiments to replace the wooden tops with slate, but those tables are impossible to find. This surface is flat now because it's new but, eventually, the wood will warp like the old one. Lancashire's damp climate almost guarantees it."

"Slate sounds like a good idea," she replied. "And Wales has a lot of slate quarries. Perhaps there's money to be made."

Griff rubbed his knuckles along the evening stubble shadowing the chiseled lines of his chin. "It would make the table much heavier, of course, but you could be right."

Shoving aside the urge to touch her fingertips to the prickly beginnings of his beard, she struggled to organize her scattered thoughts. "And people rarely move their billiards tables once they are installed in a room specially designed for the game, like this one."

"The legs would have to be reinforced," he remarked, obviously warming to the idea. "I should look into slate quarries. I confess to not knowing much about them."

Susan couldn't resist. "The Chetham Library is the place I usually go when I'm researching new opportunities."

A vision of marching into the male dominated Chetham Library on Griff's arm filled her head. The old codgers would faint!

She gripped the cue when his smile fled. "They allow women in the Chetham Library?" he asked, incredulity evident in his wide eyes.

Enough was enough. Suddenly tired of the charade, she leaned over the table, lined up her shot and sank the third ball.

His response wasn't what she expected. Most men would be irritated she had led them on. Griff laughed heartily. "You've played before, I take it. Either that, or you're an exceptionally fast learner."

His rich laughter and the hint of seduction in his voice sent chills racing up her spine. Her most private place suddenly felt embarrassingly damp, the gown too tight across her breasts. "I like to learn new things," she cooed, in a sultry voice she didn't recognize.

"A wager then?" he suggested.

Astonishment warred with a desire to best him. For a man to risk losing to a woman in any endeavor was unheard of. However, her beleaguered mind was busy recalling something Rebecca had once told her. She'd dismissed the rumor that rakes played a game with their mistresses known as strip billiards. It was too shocking to contemplate.

"What did you have in mind?" she asked, irrationally disappointed when he replied, "I propose a guinea to the winner."

In the end, it was a close game, and she might have gone to bed victorious if she'd spent more time lining up her shots and less on mentally stripping Griff Halliwell down to his skin.

"AFTER CAPABILITY BROWN designed the original house and the layout of the gardens, it's said he declared this room to be his favorite." It sounded pompous to Griff's own ears but, if he stopped expounding on the decor of his chamber, he'd have to examine his motives for bringing Susan into his bedroom.

After last evening's game of billiards, continuing to deny he was aroused by Susan Crompton seemed pointless. He'd played the game with numerous mistresses, but simply as a way to get them out of their clothes. He'd been sorely tempted to suggest they play for similar stakes last evening. Trouble was, he got the feeling the feisty bluestocking would have agreed. Perversely, he wanted to be the one to peel away the layers that concealed the real Susan Crompton. She was an enigma and solving the riddle was becoming an obsession.

When he'd first suggested over breakfast that she and Mrs. Waterman apply their talents to the lord's chamber, she'd hesitated, eyeing him with the unsettling gray gaze that seemed to look right through him. Rebecca had flat-out refused but, astonishingly, Susan had agreed.

So, here they stood, either side of the enormous bed he'd never shared with anyone. After the accident, it had taken months to pluck up the courage to move into the lord's suite of rooms. He'd never been tempted to bring a female into the chamber, or even into the house. Using his parents' bed for meaningless sexual adventures would have been sacrilegious. Potts' justifiable silent censure would have been too much to bear.

He closed his eyes, willing away the lunatic notion Susan belonged in this chamber. Looking everywhere but at the bed, he felt like an awkward adolescent.

He'd tried hard over the past fortnight to deny his growing attraction. The plan was to use his irresistible powers of seduction to convince her to part with Orion. However, he was increasingly afraid he'd have difficulty controlling his male urges if he embarked on a liaison with her. She'd somehow gotten under his skin. The opinionated bluestocking with the stern countenance had metamorphosed into a charming and beautiful temptress. Or had the task of breathing new life into Clifton Heights revealed the real Susan Crompton?

There was no prospect of a future for them, and he wasn't

ready for a long-term commitment, though, eventually, he'd have to produce an heir. Insistent as his cock was that he should bed her, he'd come to accept that Susan wasn't the type of woman he could dally with—nor, amazingly, did he wish to ruin her.

He preferred life in London, although Clifton Heights didn't seem as lonely now. Susan, Rebecca and Potts had chased away the emptiness. Even Mrs. Fazakerly had wrought miracles with the enormous task of banishing years of dust and grime. Newly arrived from the Farnworth estate, Rogerson had immediately impressed Griff with his suggestions for improving management of the estate. Mr. Fazakerly reported the new manager had made a good impression on the tenants during his first visit to the village.

"I would recommend any color, except green," Susan said, jolting him back to the bedroom.

Still trying to keep his mind off the bed, Griff wasn't sure what she was talking about. "Pardon?" he replied.

"Green," she repeated. "Paints and wallpapers of that color are made with arsenic. We discovered that when we believed Gabe…"

Griff concentrated on her lips. She was explaining something about poisonous wallpaper—he must have misheard! But those lips looked so kissable. One kiss couldn't hurt, could it?

"Oh," she exclaimed when he suddenly strode to her side of the bed and put his arms around her waist.

The unexpected desire lurking in the depths of wide gray eyes pushed him over the edge. Still, the second before his lips touched hers, he cursed himself for a fool. Even if she had feelings for him, she was too straitlaced to do anything about it.

His body mocked his assumption when she molded her body to his. Emboldened, he nibbled her lower lip, his heart and loins taken completely by surprise when she did the same to him.

NEVER HAVING KISSED a man before, Susan was embarrassingly unsure what to do when Griff nibbled her lip. However, his nibbling gave rise to pleasant sensations in her lady parts. It seemed only logical to return the favor.

He growled deep in his throat, which lessened her anxiety. He liked the nibbling.

An inner voice whispered that kissing Griff Halliwell was a mistake. Men like him only wanted one thing from a woman, a fact borne out by the way he put his hands on her bottom and gathered her to his hard body.

However, the warmth of his tongue that she had somehow allowed into her mouth was quite distracting, and didn't feel wrong at all. She liked it when the tips of their tongues toyed with each other.

In fact, the entire experience of being kissed while held in strong, possessive arms was much more pleasant than she'd have believed possible. Of course, this experience wasn't the kind of thing a woman could research.

She conjured a vision of the shock on the Chetham Library docent's face if she announced she wished to research kissing. Amusing though it was, this errant musing fled when Griff's hand wandered to her breast. His thumb stroked her nipple, highlighting another gap in her knowledge. Who knew nipples were so intimately connected to an even more private area of a woman's body?

That was her last coherent thought before her mind switched off and she surrendered to the wave of intoxicating sensations running rampant through her body. She let Griff breathe for her, savoring the rich taste of fine brandy as a hint of his cologne stole up her nose.

A voice whispered she should object if he coaxed her to his bed. However, when they broke apart, she saw the same confusion in his eyes that she felt. He dropped his hands as if suddenly realizing he'd picked up a red hot coal. "Forgive me," he rasped, his shoulders tense. "I shouldn't have."

She opened her mouth to assure him his kiss was the most wonderful thing she'd ever experienced, but he assumed the mask of indifference she'd seen in the court.

Wounded that he had used her so callously, she allowed outrage to twist her own features. "You, sir, are a cad."

Smiling smugly, he proffered his arm. "Once a rake, always a rake," he sighed. "Shall we?"

INVITATION

I N THICKETFORD MANOR'S morning room, Emma dabbed her lips with a napkin after finishing a breakfast of buttered toast and gooseberry preserves. "You know," she said to her husband, hoping to distract him from the morning newspaper. "You've been the Earl of Farnworth for well over a year, but we've never hosted any kind of celebration here."

Gabe put aside *The Times*. "What about our wedding breakfast?"

"True, but the guests were mostly close friends and relatives. I was thinking more along the lines of Baron Whiteside's musicale. We could invite the cream of Lancashire society."

Gabe rolled his eyes. "Don't remind me of that ordeal. Besides, then we'd be obliged to ask Anthea and her mother to perform and I have no wish to endure that again."

So far, the conversation was going in the direction Emma had hoped. She, Gabe and Susan had laughed themselves silly after finally escaping Withins Hall following Anthea's performance, but sitting through it without laughing had been torture. She certainly didn't want to organize a musicale. "Perhaps a ball instead?" she asked innocently.

"A ball," Patsy exclaimed, her wide eyes bright. "Like in London."

Emma was surprised she'd managed to distract her always-hungry daughter from her breakfast, but Patsy's enthusiasm might prove useful.

Narrowing his eyes, Gabe folded his newspaper. "What are you up to? I'll wager your late husband never hosted a ball at Thicketford Manor. Nor his parents before him."

"Daddy didn't dance," Patsy said wistfully.

It was a source of regret for Emma that her daughter had only vaguely sad memories of her late father. "You're right about Matthew, but his mother loved giving balls here in her younger days. In fact, the occasions were famous throughout the county for their extravagance and gaiety."

"Hard to imagine," he replied, "and I'm not sure I like the sound of extravagance with the economy in its present state."

"Nor I," she agreed truthfully. "We could set our own tone. Elegant simplicity. We have a beautiful ballroom upstairs that hasn't been used in years. I think it's our duty to invite the local gentry. They'd appreciate an opportunity to get to know you better. It can only help garner support for whatever you hope to achieve in the Lords. And we can let everyone know about Orion and the proposed breeding program."

Gabe rubbed his chin. "Your last point is a good one," he conceded. "When do you propose we hold this ball?"

"In a fortnight, perhaps?"

"That's not long to make preparations."

"It won't take much to get the ballroom ready. Musicians should be relatively easy to find. The invitations will take some time, but Baron Whiteside will be of help in that regard."

"Who else is going to assist you? With Susan and my mother away at Clifton Heights…"

Emma waved a dismissive hand. "Don't worry. I'll send a letter, inviting Pendlebury. That should bring them home."

"I miss Aunty Susan and Grandmama Rebecca," Patsy lamented. "Why have they stayed at Clifton Heights so long?"

"Eat your oatmeal," Emma chided.

Gabe rolled his eyes. "I was right. You are up to something. But, seriously…Susan and Pendlebury?"

Patsy snorted. "They can't stand each other."

Not wishing to get into a discussion that might result in her fragile intuition faltering, Emma stood. "I'll get the missive in today's post."

Feeling a little guilty she hadn't told her husband the complete truth, she sought out James Footman and handed him a sealed note she'd penned the previous evening. "Find Conrad and tell him to drive you to Clifton Heights. I'd like my letter delivered to Lady Susan this afternoon."

THE MORNING AFTER the fiasco in his bedroom, Griff wasn't surprised when Mrs. Waterman informed him Susan had asked for a breakfast tray to be sent to her room. "I'm a little out of sorts myself," he told her—the understatement of the decade!

Every mouthful of his mixed grill tasted like paper. In an effort to make sense of his shameful behavior the previous night, he replayed his actions in his mind.

What had he been thinking, kissing a woman he wasn't even attracted to? That blatant lie worsened the pressure on his temples. Susan boasted few of the attributes he usually looked for in a bedmate and she had personality traits he usually avoided like the plague—but he craved her. He'd nigh on exploded in his breeches when her nipple pebbled in response to his touch. Griff Halliwell, the notorious rake, brought to his knees by a bluestocking. It was probably her first kiss, but the moaning, the tongue mating, the way she'd melted into him...he couldn't recall ever being so inflamed by a woman.

Then, clearly unhinged by the sexual turmoil roiling in his loins, he'd insulted her by making light of the whole thing. Better that, he supposed, than dragging her into his bed and plunging his greedy shaft into her heat.

Sweating, he shoved away his half-eaten breakfast.

"Perhaps it's something you and Susan ate that has you both feeling poorly," Rebecca remarked.

Irritated by the hint of sarcasm in her voice, he made his excuses and set off to find Rogerson. A day spent riding around the estate would clear his head and give him a chance to confirm Clifton Heights had adequate facilities to set up a small breeding operation. He'd originally planned to transport Orion to London once he got the stallion in his clutches. However, the difficulties involved were daunting and the horse might not survive such a journey. He shuddered to think of the condition Orion might have been in if he'd been shipped to Tattersalls in the van as originally planned. Susan had done him a bloody favor!

Looking to the future, if Orion sired foals worthy of his bloodlines, it would be an easier matter to get them to his stables in London, although there was probably a sizable market for purebred horses in the increasingly wealthy northern counties. Susan had been right in that regard as well, which was of no consolation. Confound the woman and her brilliant ideas.

SUSAN HAD ALWAYS been a decisive person. The idea of hiding in her room at Clifton Heights was ridiculous. She was a woman who tackled problems head on.

However, the problem of Griff Halliwell was too overwhelming to even contemplate.

Her path in life had been mapped out years ago. She'd always seen herself as a doting spinster aunt, respected far and wide for her intellect and dedication to causes that mattered—like her mentor, Hannah More.

Griff's kiss rendered that future lonely and barren. After her father's rejection, she'd clad herself in the armor of a nonconformist—a bluestocking who laughed in the face of societal censure. A woman who didn't need or want a husband and family. She had Emma and Gabriel and Patsy and Rafe and Rebecca.

Griff had pierced the armor. It beggared belief that a man she didn't even like…

She scoffed at the lie. God help her, she craved the rogue. She'd fallen so easily into his trap. Clearly, a man like Griff would never be genuinely interested in her. Orion was the prize he sought. He was probably laughing smugly at her response to his kisses. Her breasts swelled just thinking about his touch.

Gritting her teeth, she steeled herself for a confrontation and entered the dining room.

She was both relieved and stupidly disappointed to learn from Rebecca that Griff had gone riding and wasn't expected back until later in the afternoon.

SATISFIED WITH THE afternoon's thorough inspection of the Pendlebury estate, Griff thanked his new manager as they dismounted in the stables. "So, you agree we could fence off an area in the lower fields that would be suitable for the actual breeding."

"Yes, my lord," Rogerson replied. "The stables are more than adequate to accommodate your clients' mares. However, I confess I'm not the man to oversee such an enterprise."

Griff handed the reins to a groom. "No worries. I've written to my chap in London. If Glazebrook wants to move back to Lancashire, the job's his. If not, we'll find someone, I'm sure."

"He's from here, is he, my lord?"

"Indeed. I took Tom with me when I moved to London, but I suspect he's still a Lancashire lad at heart."

The crunch of carriage wheels on the drive distracted Griff's attention from whatever reply Rogerson was about to offer. He took his leave and hurried to the house, dismayed to see the

Farnworth coat of arms on the side of the black carriage grinding to a halt. He'd apparently alienated Susan sufficiently for her to send for a vehicle to take her home.

As he bounded up the steps, it occurred to him that scenario was impossible. She'd hardly had time to get word to Thicketford Manor so quickly.

Potts greeted him at the open door, eyeing the bewigged footman in Farnworth livery who followed up the steps.

The fellow bowed. "James Footman, my lord. The Earl and Countess of Farnworth sent me with a message for Lady Susan."

Griff breathed more easily—unless his fellow earl meant to chastise Susan for staying too long at Clifton Heights.

"You may wait in the foyer," Potts instructed him. "I'll fetch Lady Susan."

Griff preceded the footman into the house, his heart doing a strange flip when he saw Susan striding into the foyer. *Never a shrinking violet* was his first thought. Resilience, curiosity and courage were traits he'd never thought to admire in a woman but grudgingly admitted they were aspects of Susan's character that appealed to him. He ought to have faced her earlier and discussed what had happened instead of running away from a confrontation. But then, what would he have said? To his relief, she bestowed a weak smile on him before acknowledging the visitor. Her puzzled frown indicated she hadn't expected anyone from Thicketford Manor.

James Footman handed her a note. "I'm to await your response, my lady," he said politely.

Griff breathed again when her face brightened as she read the missive.

"Gabriel and Emma plan to host a ball," she explained to Mrs. Waterman who'd followed close behind.

"Splendid," her friend exclaimed.

"But it's to be in two or three weeks," Susan added. "Emma needs our help with planning."

Griff's spirits plummeted. She would probably leave that very afternoon. The house would feel empty and lifeless once more. It might be months before he had a chance to see her again. That prospect bothered him more than the difficulties her departure presented in terms of securing Orion. Perhaps he should return to London forthwith, forget the horse, forget Susan, forget Clifton Heights.

"They've extended an invitation to you, of course, Pendle-bury," Susan said.

It may have been his imagination, but the hint of breathless anticipation in her voice convinced him he'd never get Susan Crompton out of his system. "Decent of them," he replied, trying not to sound too much like a schoolboy promised a special outing.

INDECISION

"THIS DEVELOPMENT MEANS Rebecca and I must leave Clifton Heights, Lord Pendlebury," Susan said, the use of his title sour on her lips.

His arched brows told her he'd noticed the retreat into formality. And was there a hint of disappointment in his green eyes?

Conscious of Rebecca, James Footman and the all-seeing Potts standing close at hand, she bit back the longing to confess she didn't want to leave. Born with an innate compulsion to always get to the bottom of things, the prospect of leaving matters as they were didn't sit well. If Griff's sexual advances were prompted solely by self-interest and he felt nothing for her, then so be it. If his feelings were genuine…

For once in her life, she faced a quandary for which there seemed to be no solution. Logic insisted Griff was an inveterate rake, but there was no logical explanation for her attraction to him.

"Of course," he replied coldly. "With your permission, I might follow. I've been anxious to see how Orion is getting on in his new home."

Susan floundered in a quagmire of conflicting emotions. He was coming to Thicketford Manor. She didn't have to bid him farewell. But Orion was the lure, not her. "Of course," she replied. "We'll appreciate your input into starting up our stud farm."

"I'm sure I'll be welcomed at Withins Hall if it's too much to have me underfoot while preparations for the ball are underway."

Again, Susan's thoughts see-sawed. It would be better if he stayed with the baron, wouldn't it? Then she might quickly rid herself of the constant need to see him, and give her full attention to the ball. "Emma won't hear of it," she declared. "You must stay at Thicketford."

AN HOUR AFTER seeing the ladies off in the Farnworth carriage, Griff dithered in the foyer of Clifton Heights. His valise was packed and loaded aboard the carriage waiting outside. Frederick had served as his valet and helped him shave and change out of his riding clothes. The versatile footman now stood ready to drive him to Thicketford Manor. If he didn't depart soon, it would be dark before he arrived. Still, he couldn't make up his mind if he should go or not.

He'd be better off staying at Clifton Heights, far away from Lady Susan Crompton. However, the house was full of laborers and reeked of fresh paint and plaster. Besides, he missed her already, damn it.

He was genuinely interested in Orion's welfare, but worried seeing the horse again might resurrect the compulsion to get his hands on the stallion. And why on earth did Susan's opinion of him suddenly seem more important than owning Orion?

He glanced around the newly refurbished foyer. His mother would be pleased with the changes Susan had made. She'd no doubt also be happy to see him settled, with a wife and family of his own.

The prospect of marriage had always sent shivers racing up and down his spine. Now, God help him, his errant thoughts kept wandering to planning a future with Susan. He was even contemplating moving back north.

Jaw clenched, he yanked open the front door before Potts had a chance to open it for him, ran down the steps, jumped into the carriage and ordered Frederick to drive him to Withins Hall.

In the course of the two-hour journey, he began to wonder when he'd started chewing his fingernails. "This love business is getting out of hand," he muttered, pulling on his leather gloves.

Love! Ridiculous! He could concede he might be in lust with Susan Crompton, but love?

By the time Frederick knocked on the door of Withins Hall, night had fallen. Standing behind his footman, Griff prepared his apology for arriving late, unannounced and uninvited.

He was taken aback when a scowling young man he hadn't met before opened the door. His ill-fitting clothes—tawdry, off the rack stuff by the looks of it—indicated clearly he wasn't a butler.

"Griffith Halliwell, Earl of…"

"The baron's not at home," the fellow said rudely.

"Nevertheless, he and I…"

He gritted his teeth when the door slammed in his face.

The anger contorting Frederick's chiseled features mirrored his own. "I never saw the like, my lord," his footman declared, fists clenched.

However, banging on the door and demanding to see the baron, or Springer at least, was out of the question. "Nothing for it but to proceed to Thicketford Manor," he said, hoping a similar welcome didn't await them there.

⧯

SUSAN KEPT TELLING herself it was of no importance if Griff didn't follow her to Thicketford Manor. "He may come, and he may not," she told Emma, trying to sound nonchalant about it as the footmen cleared away the last of the dinner plates.

"He'll come," Rebecca insisted.

"What makes you so sure, Mother?" Gabriel asked, an unmistakable teasing glint in his wide eyes.

"Just a feeling I have," Rebecca replied sweetly, avoiding Susan's glare.

"He'll come to see Orion," Patsy declared, aggravating Susan's inner turmoil.

Out of the mouths of babes…

"It is getting rather late for a visitor to arrive," Emma conceded. "Perhaps he'll come tomorrow. The guest room is ready, whatever the case."

A polite cough announced Frame's arrival in the dining room. "The Earl of Pendlebury apologizes for the late arrival, my lord," he told Gabriel.

"Told you," Patsy declared, sliding off her chair. "May I be excused?"

She rushed off without waiting for permission, her exuberance jolting Wellington from his nap beneath the table. Barking and growling, the poodle followed Patsy into the foyer where he was soon joined by Princess and their entire yapping brood.

Gabriel and Emma left the dining room to greet their guest.

Paralyzed by the sheer joy flooding her body, Susan feared her knees might buckle if she attempted to rise. She longed to throw herself into the arms of the man she'd missed terribly in the few short hours they'd been apart. Instead, she met Rebecca's smug gaze. "What?" she demanded.

"Nothing, my dear," her friend replied. "Aren't you going to greet the earl?"

Left with no alternative, Susan stood and flounced out of the dining room.

The foyer buzzed with noisy activity. Yapping poodles scampered about underfoot, rendering Frame uncharacteristically nonplussed; Gabriel shook Griff's hand, bidding him welcome; Emma exhorted Patsy to take charge of her dogs; Patsy tugged Griff's sleeve, peppering him with all kinds of questions about horses.

Susan studied Griff, elated when he shifted his gaze to her. She couldn't hide her joy that he'd come. And neither could he.

WELCOME TO THICKETFORD

G RIFF'S INNER TURMOIL drained away when he saw Susan staring at him. Amid the noisy chaos in the foyer of Thicketford Manor, they were the only two people. She made no effort to hide her pleasure at his arrival. Nor could he deny he was glad to see her again though they'd been apart only a few hours. The woman whose very existence should raise his hackles had suddenly become important to his heart's contentment.

The butler's loud cough alerted him to the fact the din had subsided and everyone was staring at him. "Er…I sincerely apologize, Farnworth," he told his fellow earl. "I've come uninvited, unannounced and very late."

"Nonsense," Gabriel's wife replied. "We've been expecting you."

"Yes," Susan confirmed. "I explained you would be setting off from Clifton Heights shortly after me and Rebecca."

A titled gentleman had a right to expect this kind of warm welcome at a noble household, and it was a far cry from the insult he'd been offered at Withins Hall. The heartwarming greetings at the Farnworth mansion was clearly genuine. Well, the butler was standoffish, but that was to be expected. Like Potts, Frame would likely faint dead away if asked to crack a smile. Griff decided not to spoil the jovial atmosphere with mention of the rude stranger at Withins Hall.

"You've come in the nick of time," Farnworth said, clapping a hand on his shoulder. "As the only male in the family, I never get the chance to withdraw to the library for a glass of brandy and male camaraderie while the ladies do whatever ladies do when left to their own devices after dinner."

Brandy sounded tempting, but Griff hadn't eaten since breakfast.

To his surprise, Susan linked her arm with his. "I suspect Griff hasn't had a chance to dine yet," she said.

Patsy asked him something about Orion. Mrs. Waterman arrived on the scene and greeted him warmly. Frame corralled the dogs with Frederick's help. Emma sent a maid off to the kitchens to procure food for him. Gabriel gave assurances the butler would provide his footman with a bed in the servants' wing.

Griff must have uttered all the appropriate responses but was only vaguely aware of the people around him. Not only was Susan back to using his nickname, she'd taken his arm as if it were the natural thing to do, as if they belonged together. The press of her breast against his bicep was highly arousing and slightly terrifying.

⤜⤜⤜⤛⤛⤛

A WOMAN OF strong convictions, Susan had never second-guessed her actions. Everything she did was based on rational thought. Linking arms with Griff, pressing her breast to his upper arm, and acting as though they were more than close friends was therefore perplexing to say the least. Next, she'd be back to fluttering her eyelashes at him. Not that she ever had.

"Do you have something in your eye, Susan?" Griff asked as they entered the dining room.

"No," she replied, disentangling her arm from his, reassured her gushing welcome had been prompted by nothing more than a desire to make him believe she cared for him. Which she most definitely did not. Just because his kiss was the most…

"I expect you'll want to see Orion in the morning, Lord Pendlebury," Emma remarked.

"Why can't we do that tonight?" Patsy whined.

"Because it's past time you were in bed," Gabriel replied. "Please bid everyone goodnight and off you go."

Pouting, Patsy did as he asked.

"She'd have put up a fuss if I'd sent her to bed," Emma said with a smile after her daughter left. "But she always listens to my husband."

Polite conversation ensued, but Susan's thoughts wandered. Emma and Gabriel had always made her feel part of their family. Yet, she wasn't. Suddenly, being the maiden aunt to their children wasn't as appealing as it used to be. Passing on her love of learning to little ones of her own would fill her life with purpose.

A footman arrived with a plate of food for their guest. She watched him tuck in, thinking how wonderful it would be if…

Rebecca began to describe to Emma some of the improvements to Clifton Heights they'd suggested. Caught up in visions of little girls with Griff's smile and intriguing eyes, Susan paid scant attention, merely smiling like a contented cat when required.

She bristled when she realized the earls were discussing Orion. She should have paid closer attention. Surely, Griff hadn't said the breeding facilities at Clifton Heights were better than those at Thicketford Manor?

Gabriel was nodding. Had he agreed?

This was exactly the kind of male arrogance she despised. She might have expected it from Halliwell, but Gabriel? How dare they exclude her from their discussions?

"Ready for a brandy?" Gabriel asked his guest as he stood.

"Indeed," Halliwell replied, dabbing his mouth with a napkin.

They departed for the library before Susan had a chance to shove aside the memory of kissing those full lips.

"MY APOLOGIES AGAIN for the late arrival, Farnworth," Griff told his host as his weary body settled into the red leather armchair.

"Think nothing of it," his fellow earl replied, handing him a glass of brandy. "And I prefer to be called Gabriel."

"My thanks," he said, raising his glass. "Here's to Orion."

The excellent brandy warmed Griff's throat, but he detected a note of hesitancy in Gabriel's voice as he echoed the toast. As he might have expected from the plain-speaking Earl of Farnworth, the reason was soon forthcoming.

"I hear what you're saying about moving Orion to Clifton Heights, but you must remember the stallion actually belongs to Susan. She'll have the last word."

"Of course," Griff agreed, still confused by Susan's reaction when he'd arrived. He was used to being able to classify women without any difficulty—some were mistress material, others not.

Susan was impossible to pigeon-hole. He acknowledged he definitely wanted her in his bed, but she would never agree to be his mistress. Nor would he be comfortable suggesting it. However, the women who fell into the non-mistress category were unappealing and usually boring. Life with Susan would never be boring.

He took another sip of brandy, alarmed by the direction his thoughts had taken. Was it possible he was contemplating spending his life with her?

"I'm glad to see you and Susan getting along," Gabriel said, interrupting his musings.

"Yes," Griff replied, wondering about the hint of curiosity in the remark. "She and your mother have been a tremendous help with the house. I just hope she'll at least consider the proposal to move Orion."

"I've always found her to be a reasonable woman," Gabriel replied, after draining his brandy.

Griff might have agreed had it not been for the way Susan had responded to his advances—not how he'd expected, and definitely not rational. The same could be said for the fire she'd lit in his loins. "What's the old saying?" he asked with a chuckle. "The heart has its reasons that have nothing to do with reason."

Gabriel narrowed his eyes. "I don't want to see Lady Susan hurt," he warned. "She's a much-loved member of this family."

Griff squared his shoulders. "I understand. I was referring to her love for the horse," he lied.

In an effort to relieve the unwelcome silence that ensued, he said, "By the by, I called at Withins Hall on my way here. Just to say hello to Whiteside."

"He's well, I trust."

Having embarked on the tale, Griff couldn't stop now. "Actually, I was rather rudely turned away by a young man I didn't meet on my last visit there."

Gabriel's jaw clenched as he leaned forward in his chair. "Springer, the son-in-law perhaps?"

Griff suddenly recalled the baron's son had been involved in a crime against the Farnworth household. "Er, no. I met Springer. This man was about the same age. He looked like he'd spent time in the tropics. India, perhaps."

He startled when Gabriel stood abruptly. "Forgive me," he said. "I must speak with my wife. Frame will show you to your chamber. Help yourself to more brandy, if you wish."

And with that, he was gone.

CONTEMPLATING CHANGES

After tossing and turning most of the night, a yawning Susan came downstairs for breakfast the next day determined to be more circumspect and ladylike in her response to whatever was proposed for Orion. She was a reasonable person, after all, although the irrational temptation to sneak along the dark landing and confront Griff in his chamber last night had been overwhelming. Yes, confrontation had definitely been her intent. Why else would a respectable woman visit a man's bedchamber?

Preoccupied with these confusing thoughts, she startled when both earls rose to greet her in the morning room.

Determined as her intellect was to treat the visiting earl with cool disdain, she couldn't deny the joy flooding her body. His smile was just so damnably appealing, his broad shoulders so annoyingly broad. "Good morning," she began, the quiver in her voice obvious even to her. And why was Emma looking so smug?

"Are we going to see Orion now that Aunty Susan is here?" Patsy asked as Susan sat.

"Patience, young lady," Gabriel replied.

"I'm as anxious as you to see him again, Patsy," Griff said. "And you've been close by, whereas I've been at Clifton Heights."

"But I haven't been allowed near his stall," Patsy pointed out.

"Well," Susan said. "You'll be welcome to come with us this morning."

Emma frowned. "I thought you and Rebecca and I might get

started on planning the ball this morning."

Susan was torn. She noted the disappointment in Emma's voice and wanted to help with the ball in any way she could, but it was imperative she protect her interests as far as the horse was concerned. She couldn't explain the deep attachment she felt for the animal. Griff would have a fight on his hands if he thought to take the stallion away.

GRIFF'S THOUGHTS WERE muddled. He'd spent a restless night contemplating wandering the halls of Thicketford Manor—a ludicrous notion that would have resulted in a terrible scene in the unlikely event he'd even been able to locate Susan's chamber.

Her arrival in the morning room had instantly resurrected the unwelcome erection he'd been willing away since waking. He genuinely wanted to see Orion again and truly believed Clifton Heights was a better location for a stud farm. However, the fire in Susan's eyes left no doubt she'd be devastated if the horse was taken away.

The fact he was considering the establishment of a stud farm in the north was perhaps a sign he was losing his mind. Yet, he couldn't deny the enthusiasm bubbling in his gut for such a venture. He'd received no reply from Tom Glazebrook, though he sensed the man would willingly return to Lancashire.

Even the possibility of leaving London and moving back into Clifton Heights didn't give rise to the usual knot of dread in his belly, although the enormous place would still be lonely, unless...

"I'm sure a quick visit to the stables won't infringe too much on Susan's time," Gabriel said, earning a sigh of relief from the lady in question and a frown from his wife.

"On another note," Gabriel continued, cautiously eyeing Patsy. "I'd like to meet later to learn more about the stranger who turned Griffith away from Withins Hall last night."

Emma didn't seem surprised by his remark, but Susan's wide-eyed gaze swiveled to Griff. "You went to Withins before coming here?" she asked, unmistakable pique in her voice.

"Just to pay my respects to the baron," he lied, gobsmacked by her obvious annoyance he hadn't made a beeline for Thicketford Manor.

⸭⸭⸭≪≪≪

STUPIDLY HURT GRIFF hadn't been as anxious to see her as she'd hoped, Susan was equally perplexed by mention of a rude stranger at Withins Hall. She had a terrible premonition—confirmed by the warning in Gabriel's eyes—it could be Arthur.

Had the wretch crawled out from whichever rock he'd been hiding under?

However, such a discussion couldn't take place in front of Patsy. The child had barely recovered from the trauma of the attempted kidnapping.

Impatient to be off to the stables, Susan stood. "Let's go, Patsy," she declared. "Orion awaits."

Her niece leaped out of her chair. The men got to their feet and, within five minutes, the four of them arrived at the door to the stables.

"I think you'll be pleased," Gabriel told Griff. "Our ostler is still intimidated by the stallion, but Blair and our farm manager made certain your directions about feeding, grooming and exercise were followed. They've soaked his feet in warm water, as you instructed."

Excitement tightened Susan's throat when the ostler led Orion out of the stables.

She stood motionless, unbidden tears welling as she watched Griff run an expert hand over the sleek chestnut stallion and inspect every inch of the horse. The animal stood stock still, clearly trusting Griff. It struck her like a blow to the belly she might be in danger of losing both the magnificent creatures she loved.

"HE'S IN FINE fettle," Griff declared. "You've done well," he told the ostler who beamed a toothless grin in reply.

He didn't know what to make of Susan's reaction to seeing the horse again. She seemed to be in a trance. He could only assume the tears were caused by joy. He knew how she felt. His heart recognized an unspoken bond between himself and the stallion. He loved horses, but this magnificent creature was special—one in a million. He knew without a doubt it was his destiny to ensure Orion's bloodlines continued.

He was also coming to realize there was an equally strong and undeniable alchemy between him and Susan. However, the situation was volatile. He sensed she was as confused about their relationship as he was. Dithering uncharacteristically as to the best course of action, he breathed again when Gabriel suggested, "It's a lovely day. Susan, why don't you and Griffith take Orion for a walk to the dower house?"

"I would like to see the house," Griff said when Susan hesitated, looking like a rabbit caught in a snare. "The exercise will do Orion good and give you a chance to get reacquainted."

The last suggestion seemed to resonate.

"I'd like that," she confessed, stroking the horse's nose. "But you should lead him."

Accepting the concession as a good omen, Griff took the rope attached to the halter and proffered an arm. "My lady," he said with a polite nod, pleased and not a little aroused when she linked her arm with his.

They walked in silence for a few minutes, Orion following like a docile puppy.

"Tell me about the dower house," he said in an effort to start the conversation off with something innocuous.

She turned wide eyes on him. The anger burning in those gray depths was a clear sign he'd erred.

"You do know it's where my father died?" she asked, her lovely lips pressed in a thin line.

Griff hadn't known that, but people died all the time, and he'd understood Susan and her father didn't get along. "No. I asked because you live there and…"

Her frown eased. "I apologize," she said. "The dower house can be a touchy subject. You'll see it has been restored. There was a fire."

Griff got the uneasy feeling there was more to the tale than she wanted to tell him. For once, he paid heed to his intuition and said nothing.

"My father set the fire deliberately," she said softly. "It's common knowledge he died in the flames. Mad as a hatter."

Saddened by the sorrow in her voice, he longed to let go of the rope and take her into his embrace. "That must have been a dreadful time. I'm sorry. I had no idea."

She inhaled deeply. "It was hardest on Matthew. As the new earl, he suddenly found himself facing a scandal. People tend to get nervous if they think members of the local aristocracy have gone off their head."

"It's possible I was dealing with my parents' accident at the time," he suggested. "I admit I was oblivious to just about everything going on around me."

"It's the reason you moved to London, isn't it?" she asked.

"Yes, Clifton Heights was too much. I was lonely."

He realized he'd never admitted that to anyone before.

"I expect you're anxious to get back to the city."

Now, it was his turn to fill his lungs and hope he didn't spoil the fragile moment of friendship. "Actually, I've been toying with the idea of moving back."

She came to halt and looked into his eyes. "What about Pendlebury Stables?"

"Clifton Heights is well equipped to be a profitable stud farm. It's close to Manchester and within easy reach of several wealthy estates."

Eyes narrowed, she remained silent, so he carried on. "Lancashire is destined to become increasingly industrialized, resulting in enormous wealth for others besides the nobility. These new titans of industry may not be noblemen but they'll feel pressure to act as if they are. The sport of kings will grow in popularity; owning a winning thoroughbred will be a status symbol."

To his relief, she didn't pull her arm away. He hoped that meant she was considering his reasonable arguments.

"You intend to bring your operation north?" she asked after they'd walked a little further.

This was the point of no return. He heard the doubt in her voice. Orion snorted and he hoped the animal's warm breath on his nape augured well. "Yes, and I would like permission to add your horse to the string of stallions. Orion will be the jewel in the crown."

He suddenly realized they'd reached the dower house. "Impressive," he declared, struggling not to appear impatient with her silence.

"I can show you the interior, if you wish," she said, confirming once more he should always expect the unexpected from Susan.

"I'd be honored," he replied truthfully, suspecting few, if any, gentlemen had ever been invited into Susan's home.

He tied Orion's rope to a nearby tree and followed her to the front door.

"You'll recognize Rebecca's influence," she said as a wide-eyed butler let them into the foyer.

"The Earl of Pendlebury," she explained to the servant.

"Jenkinson, my lord, at your service."

Griff handed his hat to the haughty fellow who'd clearly been trained by Frame, though a glint of surprise twinkled in Jenkinson's eyes.

Ignoring her butler, Susan proceeded to describe the provenance of several works of art on display in the expansive foyer.

"You're avoiding answering my proposal," he said.

He followed when she stuck her chin in the air and flounced off into what turned out to be a drawing room.

"Please sit," she said curtly.

"I'd prefer to stand," he replied.

"So you can throttle me if I say no?" she asked with a wry smile.

Hope rekindled, he took a risk. "I want to touch that lovely neck of yours, but choking would be the last thing on my mind."

Her smile fled. "You simply want me to believe you are attracted to me so I'll give in to your request. You must realize how hard it would be to let Orion go. I know your home isn't at the other end of the country, but..."

She stopped abruptly when he took hold of her hands and said, "Then come to live at Clifton Heights."

PLEASURE

I T WAS AS well Griff had hold of her hands else Susan might have slapped him soundly, or swooned, overcome by the same shock she saw in his eyes. "That's a highly improper suggestion," she managed from her dry throat, though she loved Clifton Heights and would be happy to make her home there, if…

"Not if you agree to be my wife," he said.

Dumbfounded, Susan stared at him. There was sincerity in his voice and no hint of mockery in his gaze. But this was Griffith Halliwell proposing marriage, a rogue well-known for his rakehell lifestyle. She had always based decisions on logic and none of this made sense. "You must really want my horse," she said, immediately regretting the insult when disappointment darkened his eyes.

"This has nothing to do with Orion," he growled. "Even if you deny me the animal, I still want you. Perhaps it's the prospect of marriage to me that has upset you."

Her heart in knots, she sought the security of the settee. "No," she confessed as she sat. "I'm drawn to you—in every way."

She startled when he went down on one knee. "Lady Susan Crompton, will you do me the honor of becoming my wife?"

He'd uttered no words of love, but she couldn't deny her feelings for him. What was the alternative? A life without sparring with Griff Halliwell. The bleak prospect tightened her throat.

Perhaps in time… "I accept," she whispered.

Grinning from ear to ear, he rose from his knees, his lips pursed ready to kiss her. They startled when a light tap at the door heralded Jenkinson's arrival. The butler's mouth fell open when he espied the compromising scene, but he recovered quickly. "Would you like tea served, my lady?"

The tongue wagging would soon begin in the servants' quarters, but Griff came to the rescue. "Please inform the staff that Lady Susan and I are engaged to be married."

Jenkinson's wide eyes betrayed his surprise—most of the servants surely never expected their bluestocking mistress to marry—but the butler's smile was genuine. "May I humbly express my congratulations to you both, my lord."

"You may," Griff replied, "and we'd like to be left undisturbed until we ring for you."

Susan couldn't see Griff's face but, judging by the glint of amusement in Jenkinson's eyes, she suspected some message understood only by males of the species passed between the two men.

Her suspicions were proven correct when Griff launched himself at her before the door had even clicked closed.

Elated to discover this beautiful man evidently found her attractive, she surrendered to his kiss, happily suckling his tongue as wanton cravings rampaged through her body.

THE RATIONAL SIDE of Griff's brain insisted on an explanation. *What in blazes had he done? Had he actually asked Susan to marry him? Was he mad?*

However, reason stood no chance against the craving to taste this feisty woman, to touch every part of her tempting body, to make her his. If the only way to have her was for them to wed, then so be it. He'd be obliged to marry sooner or later.

His heart acknowledged there was more to it than simple

expediency. He admitted inwardly he'd been happy during the two weeks they'd spent together at Clifton Heights—happier than he'd been in many a year. With Susan in residence, the house had felt like a home again.

Swept along on a river of thoughts and emotions, he savored the growled response of the woman beneath him on the settee when he cupped her breast and played with the rigid nipple.

The tantalizing aroma of female arousal stole up his nostrils. It was humbling that a woman who mistrusted men wanted him. Susan wasn't a person to give her love lightly. Nor was she the sort a man could betray—strangely, he was contentedly comfortable with the prospect of fidelity.

He wanted Susan more than he'd ever wanted anything in his life, but he might alienate her if he attempted to take her on the settee in her drawing room. That kind of behavior belonged to the old Griff. "I want you, Susan," he rasped, lost in the gray depths full of longing. "This isn't the time or place to make you mine, but let me pleasure you."

Susan's life had been full of pleasing things. Campaigning against slavery brought righteous satisfaction. She loved reading, both novels and weighty tomes. She relished intelligent conversations with friends and family over a good cup of tea. Emma's children were a source of delight. Even Patsy's poodles could sometimes be counted on to brighten a dull day. She lived in a comfortable house, refurbished and modernized after the fire. Orion was a newly discovered passion.

She lacked for nothing. Or she'd thought so, until Griff Halliwell came into her life. His kiss gave rise to previously unknown sexual cravings. His deep voice promising pleasure thrummed through her body. She'd always been proud of being a woman who wanted more out of life than society was often willing to give. Now, life had brought her a man who would teach her what being a woman was really all about.

She lay on the settee, intoxicated by the desire in his emerald gaze. He wanted her—Susan the unlovable bluestocking held power over a man. All her life, she'd resented male domination—but giving herself to Griff wouldn't mean surrender. It would complete her.

She knew a moment's hesitation when he knelt beside the settee and pushed her skirts up to reveal her pantaloons.

"Trust me," he whispered. "You'll enjoy it."

He was right. She had to trust him if they were to be married. "I want you to touch me," she replied in a sultry voice she barely recognized.

Smiling, he took her hand and placed it on his most intimate maleness. Masculine heat penetrated the wool of his breeches. Desire blossomed inside her, causing an embarrassing gush of liquid just as he gently, almost reverently, pushed her skirts to her hips.

She was mortified. He couldn't fail to notice the moisture when he spread her legs, parted the tops of her pantaloons and gazed at a part of her body she'd never seen.

She stopped breathing when he lowered his head and swiped his tongue over a very sensitive spot. His member pulsed beneath her hand.

"You're delicious," he growled, "so very wet for me."

"I didn't know…" she tried, awed by the sight of his head between her legs.

"Let me show you," he replied. "Lay back and relax."

She obeyed, though relaxing was out of the question when he lapped like a cat laps up cream. He purred, the vibration of his lips only adding to the sensual delights running rampant through her body.

Whimpers became full-throated moans when he inserted a finger inside her pulsing sheath. In and out, with his tongue all the while suckling.

She wasn't sure at what point she began playing with her own nipples, frustrated by the gown.

He growled his delight when he noticed what she was doing. She realized she was in the hands of an expert when her breasts were quickly and efficiently bared to his view and he suckled a nipple.

The urge to whine that she wanted his mouth on her womanhood and her nipples at the same time melted away when he simplified things. "Squeeze your nipples," he commanded before returning his fingers and tongue to their task.

She complied, wailing when a wave of rapture swamped her from the tips of her toes to the top of her head.

Griff's grunt of satisfaction penetrated the haze of euphoria. "Beautiful," he rasped.

As she returned to earth, it came to her she'd always believed it was a good idea to learn new things from an expert.

PROTECTOR

L YING ON HIS stomach in the wide meadow between the copse at the edge of the Whiteside estate and Farnworth lands, Arthur was confident the long grass hid him from view.

He'd spent most of the afternoon in the uncomfortable position, his father's telescope trained on the stables behind Thicketford Manor. Well, that wasn't strictly true. He'd taken a couple of breaks to let off steam with Tillie, but she'd since fallen asleep.

The sex at least made up for a complete failure to spot the thoroughbred. If it wasn't in the stables, where was the animal?

He was about to shake Tillie awake and pack his telescope away when he saw two people approaching the stables—with a horse trailing behind.

Excitement bubbled when he put the telescope to his eye again and focused on the magnificent chestnut stallion he'd watched the earl buy in Chester. "Soon, you'll be mine," he muttered, furious when he made out the identity of the man and woman, "What have we here? Lady Susan Muck and her fancy man."

Tillie sat up beside him and stretched. "Who?" she asked with a yawn.

"Stay low," he hissed, clamping his free hand on her thrusting breasts and giving her a shove.

He snarled at the sight of Susan staring up at her companion like a lovesick puppy. They were holding hands, for God's sake. Both Crompton women sickened him. First, Emma had spurned him when he did the gentlemanly thing by suggesting a liaison after her first husband's death. Then, she'd had the nerve to marry a soldier. Now, Susan had latched on to some earl. A baron's son clearly wasn't good enough. Even when they were children living on neighboring estates, she'd considered herself superior.

"Can we go soon?" Tillie whined. "I 'ave to get back before they lock the doors."

He collapsed the telescope, tucked it in the waistband of his trousers and got to his knees. "You go first, on all fours until we reach the trees. Like a dog."

She took up the position, smiling at him over her shoulder. "You just want to see my bottom wiggle."

"I do," he replied with a grin. "And when we're safely in the copse, I'll conduct a closer inspection."

"To make sure it's still red?" she asked with a giggle.

"Exactly," he growled, his cock already anticipating seeing the imprint of his hand on her backside. The folly in the grounds of Withins Hall would be the ideal place. It was on the way back to the house. He could enjoy one last fucking then send Tillie off across country to the main road.

Cold dread replaced the anticipation in his gut when they entered the folly. Two of the Watchman's henchmen stood in the shadows, arms folded across burly chests.

Tillie shrank behind him, clinging to his arm. "Who are they?" she whispered.

Not wanting to reveal his promise to consign her back to the brothel, he eased himself out of her manic grip. "Off you go. I'll send for you when the time is right."

He breathed again when she obeyed.

"Enjoy yer afternoon, did ye?" one of the toughs taunted.

Arthur gritted his teeth. These men would think nothing of snapping his neck like a twig, but the notion they'd watched him and Tillie made his blood boil. "She's a passable lay," he replied with a forced grin. "What are you chaps doing here?"

"The Watchman sent us to keep an eye on ye and his coin. He wants the horse put to stud right quick."

"I have a plan," Arthur lied, hoping they couldn't detect the tremor in his voice. "So, it's good you are here to assist. But you will ruin everything if you are seen. You must lie low until I need you."

The taller of the two nodded. "Don't worry about us. The Watchman's getting impatient and ye wouldn't want him to lose his temper."

"No, indeed," Arthur agreed wholeheartedly.

Thankful they'd done nothing beyond issue a warning, he left the folly, relieved Tillie was nowhere in sight.

TILLIE MINGLED WITH the crowd of destitute women returning to the poorhouse, hoping the beady-eyed matron standing on guard at the door wouldn't see the grass stains on her skirts. Even if she did, and jumped to the inevitable conclusion, Tillie didn't care. The crotchety crone had probably never known the thrill of sexual congress with a powerful man like Arthur. The memory of the afternoon's naughty delights caused a spasm in her lady parts.

So what if her bottom stung like the devil? If it gave Arthur pleasure to smack her, she would bear the pain. When he inherited his father's title and she became his baroness, she'd insist he make sure the cruel matron was sacked.

Joining the queue for her meager share of the slop the alms-house commissioners provided as sustenance, she wrinkled her nose against the smells emanating from her fellow inmates. From the distinct odor of sex, she'd wager several had been obliged to spread their legs in some back alley. At least her protector had never insulted her by offering money in exchange for her favors.

He was right when he said he couldn't be seen on the road to Preston, so she'd happily walked the six miles back to the poorhouse. Somehow, the trek had seemed longer than the walk to Withins Hall, but then she'd been anxious to meet her lover earlier in the day. Now, she was worn out.

She took solace in Arthur's promise that he'd soon be able to come out of hiding. Then she'd bathe every day in steaming hot, perfumed bathwater instead of scrubbing down with lye soap once a week. Arthur didn't like the smell of lye soap.

Everything would work out once he'd made sure his father had squared things with the Earl of Farnworth. She remembered her former employer as a reasonable man. Surely he was over the upset of the kidnapping attempt by now?

What the horse had to do with anything, she wasn't sure, but Arthur seemed convinced the solution to their problems lay with the animal. He'd refused to let her use his precious telescope but, even without it, she could tell the stallion was a fearsome beast. Arthur had undoubtedly been joking when he casually mentioned she'd have to ride the horse. He'd always been a tease.

"Lady Matilda on a horse," she muttered with a chuckle, gritting her teeth when the matron glared at her and bellowed for silence.

Just a few more days and she'd be free of this hellhole.

GRIFF HAD MIXED feelings about accompanying Gabriel to Withins Hall. He'd taken a liking to Baron Whiteside. The jovial fellow had welcomed him into his home and treated him well. The unfortunate incident with the rude young man who'd turned him away was perhaps a simple misunderstanding.

However, as they set off from Thicketford Manor, Gabriel's uncharacteristically stern demeanor confirmed Griff's suspicions. His fellow earl suspected Arthur Coleman had returned from wherever he'd been hiding.

Gabriel Smith wasn't a vindictive man but there was no hint of compassion in his steely gaze. If Arthur had indeed returned, he couldn't expect forgiveness from Lord Farnworth.

Griff sympathized. He'd been apprised of the full details of Arthur's crime and his flight to the Caribbean. If someone ever tried to kidnap a child of his…

The notion stirred pleasant memories of his tryst with Susan earlier in the day. The enticing prospect of filling her delectable body with his child was arousing. Who'd have thought it? The rakehell Griffith Halliwell eager to become a father!

"I'm sorry to drag you into this," Gabriel said, jolting him out of his reverie. "It's important there be a reputable witness to any conversation I might have with the baron."

"Of course," he replied, wondering if this was the right time to share his plans to marry Susan. They'd returned hand in hand from the dower house, a fact that must have reached Farnworth's ears. "I suppose you've realized Susan and I plan to wed. I like Baron Whiteside and I pity his predicament, but family always comes first in my book."

"I hope that's true," Gabriel replied, his tone holding a hint of warning. "I consider myself Lady Susan's protector."

"I would expect no less of you," Griff replied. "However, that will be my role once we marry."

Gabriel extended a hand as the carriage rolled to a halt. "Forgive me. I'm preoccupied. I wish you both every happiness. Now, let's get this over with. I sent a footman ahead, so Bertrand knows we are coming."

Griff accepted the gesture and they climbed out of the carriage.

EAVESDROPPING

HIS INNARDS STILL in turmoil after the encounter with the thugs from Manchester, Arthur scanned the servants' entry at the rear of Withins Hall. His father had ordered him not to leave the house until things were sorted out with Farnworth. Thus, he could hardly enter the front foyer. The back door was actually more convenient, coming as he was from the far fields.

All in all, he was satisfied with his afternoon. Tillie had helped relieve some of the tedium. Small wonder the Watchman wanted her back. She'd be an asset to any brothel. He pitied the poor sods who paid prostitutes in some filthy back alley for what he enjoyed for free. Initially, he'd been angered to learn the toughs had watched but, on second thought, it was amusingly arousing to think they'd probably taken matters into their own hands.

Tillie wasn't the brightest star in the universe—had she truly expected him to let her use his father's telescope? Anyone with half a brain would realize he couldn't take her back to Preston. He'd make his grand reappearance soon enough, once he'd convinced his father he was truly repentant.

Calmer now, he made his way stealthily through the servants' quarters, which seemed to be deserted. He really needed a bath but, so far, only his immediate family and the snooty butler were aware of his homecoming, so he couldn't summon scullery lads to fill the tub.

Resigned to climbing the back staircase that led from the

foyer to the bedchambers, he paused, the hairs at his nape bristling when the rap of the front door knocker echoed through the house. Holding his breath, he gripped the rough wood of the rickety banister and listened. The butler allowed the visitors immediate entry. Evidently, they were expected. Arthur heard male voices and the sound of booted feet crossing the tiled floor to the drawing room. Then, his father's voice. "Farnworth, Pendlebury, come in, come in. Brandy?"

Jaw clenched, Arthur backtracked to the passageway behind the drawing room and pressed an ear to the wall. A lot was riding on his father convincing their neighbor of his son's reformed character. It was a good sign he'd invited Farnworth, but the old fool had better not let him down.

✦

GRIFF ACCEPTED THE brandy glass from Bertrand and took a seat in one of the upholstered chairs. Gabriel declined the offer of brandy and stated a preference to remain standing.

"What can I do for you chaps?" their host asked, more than a hint of nervousness in his voice.

"I'm here on behalf of my wife," Gabriel began. "She plans to host a ball at Thicketford Manor and will need your help with a list of appropriate people to invite."

Griff hid his initial surprise when he realized Gabriel's tactic. Why come out with heavy guns blazing when you can lull your enemy into letting down his guard? He was beginning to see why the former soldier had made a success of running an earldom he'd never expected to inherit.

"Of course, dear boy," Whiteside replied with a broad smile, clearly more at ease. "I'll get Anthea to send over a list."

"Much obliged," Gabriel said. "Perhaps I'll have that brandy now."

Bertrand extricated himself from his deep armchair. "Coming

right up."

"Griff tells me he was turned away from your home by a rude individual. It wasn't Arthur by any chance, was it?"

The crystal decanter in Bertrand's hand rattled against the glass as he poured. He turned to offer the brandy to Gabriel, his face ashen. Griff knew the elderly man's reply would be a lie.

"Arthur? This is the first I'm hearing of it. I do apologize. I wasn't informed you'd called. No, Arthur's still in the tropics. Although, now you mention it, his Uncle Nathan assures me the boy has turned over a new leaf. He longs to come home and right the wrong he perpetrated."

"And how does he propose to do that?" Gabriel asked.

Bertrand slumped into his chair and took a hefty swig from his glass. "Make amends, I suppose. What would you suggest?"

Gabriel put a booted foot on the ledge of the hearth. "Let me make my position clear. Your son terrorized members of my family. You decided to allow him to escape and I don't blame you for that. However, if Arthur ever sets foot in England, I'll have no choice but to pursue charges against him."

Bertrand stared into his empty glass as the silent minutes ticked by. "I understand," he said finally. "I realize I might have lost everything if you had pursued the matter of my helping him escape, but you didn't."

Gabriel offered the baron his hand. "You're a good neighbor, and I prefer we continue our friendly relations. However, I cannot allow Arthur to live so close to my family."

"No," Bertrand agreed. "I'll explain things to him in a letter. I'm certain he'll understand. From what Nathan tells me, my son likes the hot climate."

Left with no doubt it was indeed Arthur who'd turned him away and sensing the baron was at his wits' end, Griff stood. "We can see ourselves out."

Their host merely nodded as Griff and Gabriel took their leave.

"SPINELESS," ARTHUR HISSED, his forehead pressed to the flaking plaster. *"My son likes the hot climate,"* he mimicked. "Your son despised the relentless heat, you old crow. Going to write me a letter, are you?"

He clenched his fists. What was he supposed to do now? Hide in Withins Hall forever?

He pressed his fingertips to throbbing temples. "Think, man. Think of a way to get rid of dear Papa."

He had to get his hands on a copy of the will. Once Arthur was declared Baron Whiteside, Farnworth and Springer could go to hell.

Inhaling deeply, he tried to recall something interesting the earl had said. "A ball. Perfect." A quick word in his father's ear to plant the idea of hosting a shoot in conjunction with the ball. Unfortunate accidents often happened when there were people with loaded guns wandering all over the place.

Confident his father would remain in the drawing room drowning his pathetic sorrows, he edged out of the concealed doorway that led onto the foyer. There was nothing he could do about the mucky footprints left behind as he made his way across the tiled floor and entered the library.

He went straight to his father's desk, but all three drawers were locked, convincing him the will likely resided in one of the compartments.

He was casting about for something to prize open the locks when the library door creaked open and in walked Springer. Arthur's hackles rose. He'd never trusted the oily fellow who'd shown only a passing interest in Anthea—until her brother was shipped off to Jamaica.

"Looking for something?" his brother-in-law asked.

"A book," he replied, cursing the hasty reply when Springer gestured to the shelves, eyebrows raised.

Aware Springer had every reason to betray him, Arthur sauntered out of the library. "Another person the world should be rid of," he muttered as he tackled the stairs leading to his chamber. A double shooting accident was beginning to look very appealing. He'd like to include Farnworth, but three bodies might raise suspicion. He'd seek the Watchman's advice on the matter, though the prospect of venturing into Ancoats again tied his gut in knots. However, the first priority was planning how to steal the horse.

SHARING THE NEWS

"Y OU LOOK TIRED," Rebecca remarked when Susan arrived in the morning room of the dower house.

"I didn't sleep well," she admitted.

"Oh?" her friend replied, eyes wide. "Why is that?"

Susan would never divulge anything of the intimacy she and Griff had shared. Emma and Gabriel should be the first to know of the engagement, but she itched to tell Rebecca who clearly suspected. "I was worried after our earls returned from Withins Hall last evening. Something's going on."

"*Our* earls?"

"Very well," Susan replied as heat rose in her face. "I suppose you've already guessed Griff asked me to marry him."

Rebecca nigh on shook with anticipation. "And you said?"

"I accepted."

Her grinning friend reached for her hand. "I'm so happy for you. It's plain to see you are both in love."

Susan couldn't rid herself of niggling doubts. "I have deep feelings for Griff, but I doubt he loves me. He simply sees the match as advantageous."

Rebecca gaped. "Did he say as much?"

"No, but logic says he's marrying me because it's his obligation to sire an heir, and he wants to gain control of Orion."

"I didn't get that impression when we were at Clifton Heights. He seemed to enjoy your company. However, I suppose the kind of thinking you describe is true of most aristocrats, but I'm surprised you would agree to marry under those circumstances."

Susan understood her friend's skepticism. "I know I'm not the kind of woman rakes are normally attracted to," she admitted with a smile.

Rebecca frowned. "If you hope to change his ways, you should reconsider. I naively thought I could persuade Waterman to give up the gin. It was the biggest mistake I ever made."

Susan shook her head, unable to think of a single thing she would change about Griff Halliwell. He was a skilled lover, a man who adored horses and who'd hidden his grief and loneliness behind the veneer of a roguish lifestyle. On top of that, he aroused her sexually and she couldn't imagine living without him now that long-denied side of her had been unleashed. He was as essential as the air she breathed.

But she could share none of these innermost thoughts with Rebecca. Emma, on the other hand, was the closest things she had to a sister. "I wanted Emma and Gabriel to be the first to know, although, last night, I got the feeling your son already knew of Griff's proposal."

"Perhaps he learned of it on the drive to Withins Hall?"

"If Gabriel knows, then Emma certainly does. Still, I'd like to go over to the main house shortly so we can tell everyone."

She didn't mention she could hardly wait to see Griff again, though she hoped he wasn't having regrets.

They'd barely finished breakfast when Jenkinson entered the morning room. "Pardon the interruption," he said. "Lord and Lady Farnworth, Lord Pendlebury and Miss Crompton have ridden over from the main house."

A wave of heat swept over Susan. Every nerve tingled. Perhaps Griff was also anxious to reunite. "Show them into the drawing room," she replied as she stood.

GRIFF FEARED SUSAN may have changed her mind now that she'd had a chance to reconsider her acceptance. He wouldn't blame her. He'd tried to convince himself his proposal was the act of a madman, but the joy on her face when she entered the drawing room of the dower house swept aside his doubts. He genuinely wanted her as his wife.

She greeted everyone, but it was to him she offered her hand. The love in her eyes was only for him.

"I'm afraid I've let the cat out of the bag," he confessed after brushing a kiss on her knuckles.

"We had to come," Emma exclaimed, kissing Susan on each cheek. "Gabriel and I are delighted by the news."

Griff put his arm around Susan's waist, glad her best friend's congratulations were genuine. He wasn't sure how it had come about that the members of this family accepted him, rakish reputation notwithstanding.

"Is it true?" Patsy asked as she trailed in after the others, Wellington squirming in her arms. "I had to go after this naughty dog. He was chasing squirrels again. What did I miss?"

"Your aunt and I are engaged to be married," Griff explained.

The next thing he knew, Patsy had thrust the poodle into her stepfather's arms and rushed to hug Susan. "I'm very, very happy."

Then it was his turn. Beaming a broad smile, the child bobbed a curtsey and asked, "Will that make you my uncle, Lord Pendlebury?"

"Yes, I suppose it will," he replied with a chuckle, liking the sound of Uncle Griffith.

"I'd suggest Jenkinson bring coffee," Rebecca declared, "but I think the occasion calls for something stronger."

The butler had withdrawn to await his instructions by the door "May I bring sherry for a toast?" he asked.

"Ugh, sherry," Patsy exclaimed, her sweet face contorted into a grimace of disgust.

Much laughter, hugging, handshaking and convivial conversation ensued. Tentative plans were made to formally announce the betrothal at the Farnworths' ball. Griff privately agreed with Patsy about the taste of sherry, but he dutifully drained his crystal glass of the stuff, all the while exchanging heated glances with Susan.

The realization he'd been welcomed into a loving family warmed him as much as the fortified Spanish wine.

SUSAN COULD HARDLY think when Princess and her yapping brood arrived in the drawing room, having apparently followed Wellington from the main house.

Gabriel came to the rescue. "Please get those infernal poodles out of here, Patsy," he pleaded.

She scooped up Wellington and called his family to follow her outside.

Everyone breathed an audible sigh of relief when silence reigned once more.

Rebecca spoke first, stunning everyone when she suggested, "Why don't you come to stay at the dower house, Lord Pendlebury. I believe I'm a suitable chaperone and I'm sure you and Susan would like to spend time together planning your nuptials."

Susan risked a glance at Emma. Though they never spoke of it, she had a strong suspicion Gabriel and Emma had been intimate before their marriage. That didn't mean they would agree to the improper suggestion.

Griff looked to her, a question in his eyes, but she wasn't sure how to respond any more than he was.

And what would Patsy think of such a situation?

"I'll probably be going back and forth to Clifton Heights,"

Griff eventually replied. "I want to make sure all is in readiness for when Susan and I take up residence."

"Still," Emma said, "when you are here, it would make sense to stay in the dower house. We'll be busy preparing all the guest chambers at Thicketford Manor for people coming from a goodly distance."

To Susan's amazement, Gabriel nodded his agreement.

ST. JOHN'S

"I FIND IT hard to believe Gabriel and Emma agreed to this," Griff told Susan as they stood in the foyer of the dower house and watched Frederick trundle his master's valise up the stairs to the guest chamber, Jenkinson leading the way. He squeezed her hand and wiggled his eyebrows. "Especially given my reputation."

"They know I trust you," she replied, leaning into him.

"Keep pressing those lovely globes against my arm and I might turn out not to be so trustworthy."

As they strolled to the drawing room, she avoided his teasing gaze but her blush aggravated the turmoil in his nether regions.

"I can't explain how it is I've lived so long with no interest in sexual matters," she said shyly, "and, now, I crave the sensations."

Griff cautioned himself not to express surprise at Susan's tendency to openly discuss matters ladies were supposed to know nothing about. He also resisted the urge to strut like a proud peacock. "Ah, but you'd yet to meet the roguish Earl of Pendlebury," he countered, kissing her forehead. "However, much as the aforesaid rake would love to whisk you upstairs and have his way with you, I think we should wait until no one else is about. This evening, shall we say?"

"Yes," she murmured, her blush deepening as she looked up at him. "Tonight."

"You know," he teased, "you really should see a physician

about whatever is in your eye."

She swatted his arm, but her smile assured him she enjoyed his teasing.

"This afternoon," she said, suddenly back to being the businesslike Susan, "we'll go to St. John's Parish church in Preston and make the arrangements."

"I suppose that's where Cromptons traditionally get wed, is it?"

"Yes, and try not to laugh at Canon Parr, he tends to be rather pompous. I wouldn't be surprised if he interviews us with the billycock still on his head."

"Billycock?" Griff asked.

"You Manchester people probably call it a bowler."

The image of a parson who sported a bowler hat sobered Griff. "I hope he doesn't ask about my church attendance. I've been somewhat derelict in that duty."

"He might, but don't worry. Gabriel is his largest benefactor."

He chuckled. "Knowing Lady Susan the Crusader as I do, I'm sure she'll rush to my defense if the parson decides to be stubborn."

"You know me well," she replied with a shrug.

AFTER THEY'D ENJOYED luncheon with Rebecca, Griff assisted Susan to climb aboard his carriage in order for Frederick to drive them to Preston. "Alone at last," he quipped, drawing her closer as they set off.

Susan was a lifelong believer in the natural order of things; the dictates of so-called proper behavior often went against nature. One had only to consider the requirement some ladies deemed *de rigueur*—corsets that made it difficult to breathe. Or the belief wealthy men had the right to own other men and treat them like animals. It therefore felt right to snuggle into Griff and put her hand on his chest. "You always give off such heat," she told him.

"That's your doing," he replied, tilting up her chin.

His kiss bombarded her senses—the warmth of his lips, the taste of the wine they'd sipped at luncheon, the subtle aroma of his cologne, the hunger of his growl as his tongue mated with hers.

"Emma always talks about the Six Mile Kiss," she said breathlessly when they finally broke apart. "I never understood what she meant."

"Let's see," Griff replied, tracing a fingertip along her lower lip. "Six miles to Preston, right?"

"Of course," she exclaimed. "We'll have to prolong the next kiss if we want it to last six miles."

Shaking his head, he brushed the backs of his fingers over her nipple. "You can't expect a man to kiss you for six miles and keep his hands to himself."

Susan's overactive brain immediately set about solving the looming problem of how Griff might get his clever mouth on her nether lips while seated in the confined space of a moving carriage.

In the event, it was his expert fingers that danced up her skirts and brought her to ecstasy while she suckled his tongue. The compulsion to cry out her euphoria was powerful but his tongue was insistent it be as far inside her mouth as possible.

Soaring on clouds of bliss, she gradually floated to earth in his arms. "That was indescribable," she whispered, laying her hand on his maleness. "But what about your pleasure?"

He covered her hand with his own. "We're just coming into Preston, but there's always tonight, remember?"

The unflappable Susan Crompton wondered what it was about the sound of his deep voice promising sexual delights that made her giddy with anticipation.

As she righted her clothing and prepared to alight outside St. John's she hoped the perceptive Canon Parr wouldn't guess what they'd been up to.

"At least now I understand the Six Mile Kiss," she told Griff as they walked through the well-tended graveyard to the main door of the church.

"It's six miles back too," he reminded her.

She inhaled deeply, trying desperately to get her mind off sexual congress before she faced the parson.

AS HE ENTERED the dark portico of the church with Susan on his arm, Griff was preoccupied. His own restraint amazed him. It wouldn't have been the first time he'd thrust inside a woman whilst in a moving carriage—an acrobatic and surprisingly erotic experience as he recalled. He'd simply derived more satisfaction from watching Susan respond to his touch. Who would have thought a passionate woman lurked beneath the bluestocking veneer? The anticipation of what they might do later rendered the waiting that much more—what was the word?

Difficult.

However, he was confident that claiming Susan would be worth the wait. Some things had to be lingered over, savored.

He chuckled, thinking how proud his parents would be that he seemed finally to be thinking like a mature adult.

"My mother would have loved you," he declared as they explored the dingy corridor of offices behind the main church, looking for the parson.

They eventually encountered a tall, gangly young man Susan introduced as Reverend Whitworth, the curate.

"Call me Stephen," he gushed, nigh on crushing Griff's hand when he learned the identity of Susan's companion.

"Is Canon Parr about?" she asked.

"Unfortunately, he's away giving the last rights to an elderly parishioner. May I be of help?"

"Lady Susan and I wish to marry in your church," Griff explained, acknowledging Susan's restraint in deferring to him.

"Splendid," Whitworth exclaimed half-heartedly after briefly frowning at Griff, clearly taken off guard by the notion any man would wish to wed a woman well-known locally for her views on the shortcomings of all men everywhere.

"We'd like the first reading of the banns to take place next week," Griff added, surprising himself and Susan if her wide-eyed response was an indication.

"I'm sure there'll be no problem," Whitworth replied, gesturing for them to sit on two wooden chairs in his cramped office. "Subject, of course, to Canon Parr's approval."

He removed a leather-bound ledger from a nearby shelf, dipped a quill in the ink well, fanned away the dust motes that flew into the air when he opened the ledger, and asked, "May I ask your full name, my lord?"

"Griffith Clifton Halliwell, third Earl of Pendlebury, son of the late William Clifton Halliwell and Alice Griffiths, born 24th of March, 1792 at Clifton Heights, Lancashire."

Pride and sorrow filled his heart as he recited his pedigree. The warmth of Susan's hand squeezing his and the admiration glowing in her eyes finally swept away all doubts like chaff on the wind.

With painstaking pen strokes, Whitworth scratched the information into the ledger, then read it back.

"I'm sure we have all your pertinent details here, Lady Susan," he said, patting the ledger. "There'll be no question as to your ancestry." He cleared his throat. "And spinster status."

Griff bristled, though he supposed the curate was correct. His name and rank would have to be verified, but the young man didn't have to blush so deeply when mentioning Susan's unwed status.

"The Earl of Farnworth can vouch that my fiancé is who he says he is," Susan declared, cutting to the heart of the matter.

"Good," the red-faced curate replied. "He can perhaps drop

by and meet with Canon Parr."

Susan was predictably having none of that. "I suggest, Stephen, that you make an appointment to see the earl at Thicketford Manor at the earliest opportunity."

"Of course," Whitworth agreed. "Thoughtless of me. So, we'll set a date for the ceremony, shall we?"

"The week after the third reading of the banns," Griff replied.

AFTERNOON DELIGHTS

FTER LEAVING ST. John's, Susan and Griff strolled arm in arm to Carr and Sons tailoring shop, sharing amused remarks about the curate. Susan noticed the wide-eyed stares of several passersby. "People are wondering who you are," she told him. "And how it is I'm on the arm of a gorgeous man like you."

"Let them gawk," he replied. "We make a handsome couple."

Unsure what to do with a compliment from a male, she stored it up in her heart.

Carr greeted them with his usual effusive politeness, assuring Griff the items he had ordered were almost ready.

"I'll also need a new outfit for a special occasion," Griff told him.

"Oh?" the tailor asked, eyebrows raised.

"A wedding," Griff explained, winking at Susan.

"He's prolonging the suspense, Mr. Carr," she said. "The earl and I are to be married."

The genuine delight that blossomed on Carr's face was heartwarming. He shook Griff's hand. "May I congratulate you both. Splendid news. Now, let's get you measured, my lord. If I may suggest…"

He paused, frowning when Susan followed the men through a green velvet curtain into the fitting room area behind the shop. "Er…you might be more comfortable on the chaise, my lady," he said, gesturing to the couch in the shop designed for ladies to wait for their gentlemen.

"I'm perfectly at ease with my fiancée observing the proceedings," Griff told him. "She'll no doubt have input into your suggestions."

Apparently realizing there was little to be gained in objecting, Carr indicated a plush sofa in the fitting room and slid his tape measure from around his neck.

Susan sat and arranged her gray silk skirts, looking forward immensely to her first experience of watching a man being measured for new clothing.

GRIFF HAD BEEN measured for new clothing time without number. It was usually a tedious experience, but then he'd never undergone the process with a woman watching.

Susan's avid perusal and endearing blushes—especially when the efficient tailor took measurements of his inside leg—turned the mundane into the erotic. If Mr. Carr noticed the swelling at Griff's groin—and how could he not—he carried on in his usual businesslike manner.

Watching Susan squirm in her seat, Griff was seized by a lunatic notion to unbutton the front flap of his breeches, take out his throbbing lance and let her look her fill. "This is for you," he'd whisper.

"I beg your pardon, my lord?" Carr asked, dragging Griff's errant thoughts back to earth.

He cleared his throat. "Just musing aloud."

The arousing notion of Susan finally setting eyes on the most intimate part of his body persisted as final arrangements were made with the tailor. Perhaps in the carriage on the way back to Thicketford Manor?

Upon leaving the shop, he was relieved to see Frederick had brought the carriage around to the door. Susan seemed as anxious to board as he was. They were locked in an embrace and kissing passionately before Frederick had climbed back into the driver's seat.

SUSAN HAD NEVER behaved so recklessly in her life, but then she'd never been in love before. A little voice in the back of her mind insisted she was behaving like an animal as she shoved Griff's frock coat off his shoulders, tore at his cravat and pawed his chest, all the while suckling his tongue as if her life depended on it.

His growl led her to believe he liked her aggression. He cupped her breast with one hand and hiked her skirts up to her hips with the other. When his talented fingers played with her needy nubbin, it seemed the next logical step to reach for the buttons at the front of his breeches.

With their lips still locked together, he helped her unfasten the flap and guided her hand inside his smalls. Curling her fingers around his silky hardness nigh on moved her to tears. She recognized her first touch of intimate male flesh as the most meaningful experience she'd ever had. "Griff," she murmured into his mouth.

"Susan," he rasped in reply.

Lost in a haze of one rapturous release after another, she vaguely worried his groans meant she was squeezing too hard. As the carriage entered Thicketford's gates then passed the main house, he leaned his forehead against hers. "Your touch inflames me," he panted. "We'll have to hurry if I'm to make it to the bedroom."

Her initial instinct was to suggest they remain in the carriage and continue to bring each other pleasure, but Jenkinson's face rose in her mind's eye. "I'll follow you to your chamber," she whispered, reordering her clothing as he refastened his breeches.

"I'm afraid your cravat is a lost cause," she said with a chuckle.

With a mock sigh, he removed it, exposing the tempting flesh of a strong neck she wanted to nibble. "I suggest you hold it to your breasts," he said with a naughty grin, "otherwise your butler might wonder about the damp circles around your nipples."

She looked down hastily, tempted to laugh, but Frederick had opened the door and was taking down the step.

She accepted the footman's hand to alight, very aware of Griff behind her. She flounced past Jenkinson in the doorway of the dower house as if she hadn't been engaged in scandalous behavior. Hopefully, Rebecca was nowhere about.

If her butler found it curious she clutched a cravat to her bosom, he showed no sign of it.

STRUGGLING FOR CONTROL

GRIFF NODDED POLITELY to Rebecca who emerged from the drawing room, hastening up the staircase to his chamber before she engaged him in conversation. The earl's widowed mother would immediately recognize a man's arousal when she saw it. He hoped she wouldn't detain Susan too long. He was ready to burst after the intimacy in the carriage. He dithered about removing his clothing while he waited for Susan to arrive. If the imminent tryst had been with a mistress, he'd have disrobed without hesitation. Susan was a lady, and his betrothed—a woman he respected. However, if he didn't soon remove his breeches…

Throwing caution to the winds, he tore off his outer clothing, deciding at the last moment to leave on his smalls. No use frightening the woman, although she must have some inkling of his size after…

He reached for the bedpost, leaning his forehead against the cool wood when the memory of her touch made him dizzy with need.

He swiveled his head to the door at the sound of a soft click. Susan stared for only a second or two before hurrying toward him, her gray eyes full of lust and longing. He'd been concerned she may have begun to regret the intimacy in the carriage. His fears melted away when she put both hands on his chest, stood on tiptoe and licked a nipple.

He no longer needed the bedpost as his anchor. Susan was his rock, the woman who would keep him afloat when life's challenges threatened to swamp him, the Lancashire lass who would defend her man against all comers. "Susan," he growled, taking her hands in his. "Let me undress you."

⇒⇒⟫⟨⟪⟨⟨

SUSAN TURNED HER back to Griff lest he detect her hesitation. "There are tapes and hooks," she explained, suddenly feeling silly. As if she were the first woman he'd undressed.

Apparently sensing her concerns, he put his hands on her shoulders and turned her to face him. "You and I are embarking on a long journey together, Susan," he said. "It's important we have trust. I admit I've bedded other women, but I've never felt for any of them what I feel for you."

"I'm just nervous," she admitted. "It's ironic I consider myself an expert in all things, but I don't know the first thing about pleasing a man."

He took her hand and curled it around his arousal. "Does it appear to you I am not pleased? Your touch sets me alight."

Fascinated by the dusting of dark hair on his chest, and the warm fullness in her hand, she found it difficult to be rational. "I agree we must be honest with each other. I confess my original intent was to make you think I was smitten with you."

She wished she could take back the words. Now, he would doubt her sincerity.

He gathered her into his embrace, threw back his head and laughed heartily, which wasn't the reaction she expected. "You're not angry?"

"Well, I'm curious as to your ultimate goal."

"To alarm you into rushing back to London and forgetting all about Orion."

"And my plan was to make you think I was enamored with

you in order to persuade you to part with Orion."

"My plan went awry," she murmured.

"As did mine," he echoed, easing her away and peeling her bodice down to her hips.

"You're an expert at this," she allowed. "I didn't even know you'd begun undoing the fastenings."

She held on to his shoulders, eyes closed while he efficiently completed the task of stripping her. Finally, standing naked under his perusal, she prayed he would like what he saw.

"You are incredibly beautiful," he rasped. "I can't wait to make you mine."

Drawn by insatiable curiosity she took hold of the waistband of his smalls. "I want to see all of you," she whispered, peeling down the undergarment when he nodded.

She gasped when his manhood sprang free, a thick lance jutting from his body. A whole host of theories about male and female relationships suddenly made sense. She and Griff were made to fit together. "I want you," she confessed.

Again, his chuckle wasn't the response she expected. "I was afraid you'd be intimidated. I'm not a small man."

"But, you're so…"

Intoxicated by the sight and scent of an aroused male, she had difficulty finding the right word, finally remembering Orion. "So magnificent," she exclaimed, falling to her knees. She licked the swollen tip, then took him into her mouth and suckled. It was an act of submission Susan the Bluestocking would never have agreed to.

Groaning, Griff gripped her shoulders.

The taste, the texture, the intimacy—all new, all heart-stoppingly wonderful. But it struck her with blinding clarity this joining wasn't an act of submission at all. It was one of trust.

GRIFF HARDLY RECOGNIZED the highly aroused man who stood naked, gripping the shoulders of an equally naked woman while she suckled.

The realization that Susan wouldn't deny him if he insisted on making love to her filled his heart to bursting.

He cupped his heavy sac, hoping the needy words would emerge. "Play with me," he rasped, his thighs trembling when she squeezed him gently.

The Griff who sought only to flee his responsibilities and indulge his own pleasure would already be thrusting his greedy shaft deep inside his bedmate.

The Griff who had stumbled upon a priceless jewel in Susan Crompton struggled for control. "I want desperately to join our bodies," he admitted. "However, like selfish male bastards everywhere, I've harbored the assumption I would deflower my bride on our wedding night."

She let out a long slow breath and rested her head against his rapidly beating heart. "If ever I allowed myself to fantasize of one day being married, I assumed I would come virgin to my bridal bower. That was before I met you and it doesn't lessen my craving for you to take me now."

She put her arms around his neck and nestled into him when he lifted her off her feet.

"We'll wait," he said. "But there are ways to bring each other pleasure that making the waiting bearable."

MAKING PLANS

SUSAN AND REBECCA had very quickly become firm friends. They'd never had any difficulty sharing and appreciating each other's ideas about the latest goings-on in the world. Mealtimes were always filled with lively conversation.

The evening she and Griff dined with Rebecca after their tryst in his chamber, Susan was afraid her friend would immediately sense what had transpired if she made any attempt to speak.

She might opine on the abysmal state of the post-war economy, but her voice and the longing in her eyes would betray a preoccupation with the exhilarating sensations wrought by Griff's talented mouth on her most intimate woman's place.

If Susan looked at her betrothed across the table, Rebecca would easily see her craving to rush back upstairs. She thirsted to relive the joy of Griff's shout of completion when he spilled his seed between her breasts before collapsing atop her. She wanted to bear that weight again and run her fingertips through the sheen on his broad back.

She risked a glance at him, shuddering inwardly when he licked his lips and smiled.

Wretch! He was teasing her, knowing full well she was in agony. The promise of a life with a playful man made her giddy.

"Tell me about your journey to Preston," Rebecca said after finishing her soup.

"Well," Griff replied, "it's only six miles, as you know. Barely enough time to get comfortable in the carriage."

Susan's nipples tingled at the memory of *getting comfortable*.

"Yes," Rebecca confirmed. "My son is forever reminding me of the distance, as if I'm too senile to remember."

Susan chuckled. It seemed Emma and her husband continued to indulge in a degree of intimacy during the ride to Preston. She wondered if they still referred to it as the Six Mile Kiss. Susan and Griff had gone beyond kissing. Perhaps they could call it the Six Mile F—

"And how was Canon Parr to deal with?" Rebecca asked, jolting Susan out of her reverie.

"Er…he wasn't there. We arranged the banns and the ceremony with the curate."

"Which reminds me," Griff said, "I must mention Stephen's impending visit to Gabriel before I leave on the morrow."

Susan's stomach turned over. "Leave?"

He reached for her hand and meshed his fingers with hers. "I have no wish to depart, but it will be necessary to go to Clifton Heights for a day or two. The house should be perfect if I'm to bring my bride there."

His smile and the touch of his hand calmed her racing heart.

"Also, I want to make sure arrangements are made for Orion's eventual arrival, and the stud farm we plan to set up. I'm hoping Tom Glazebrook is willing to come north to take over running that side of things."

Accustomed to making her own decisions, Susan's reaction was to balk at Griff's assumptions. However, she was elated he seemed to be saying he wanted to make his home at Clifton Heights, rather than in London. She'd have willingly moved to the big city with him, but Lancashire was where they both belonged. She deemed it better not to object to his making all the decisions. A wife was expected to defer to her husband. Squeezing his fingers, she resolved to learn how to make him think she was deferring to him.

THE FOLLOWING MORNING, after another stolen night of partially satisfying intimacy with Susan, Griff bade farewell to Thicketford Manor.

She was close to tears as they kissed each other goodbye outside the dower house. He too felt strangely bereft at leaving her, though he'd only be gone a few days. "I'll miss you," he whispered, nibbling her earlobe.

"It's just for a little while," she replied, forcing a brave smile. "I'll be kept busy with the seamstresses Emma insists must begin the dressmaking process immediately."

"You speak of something most women love as if it's torture."

"For me it is," she confessed. "You must know by now I'm not very feminine."

"I beg to differ," he countered. "I find your womanly attributes intoxicating."

"Be gone, before I drag you upstairs."

Chuckling, he bowed to Rebecca before boarding his carriage.

He returned Susan's wave until Frederick had driven them out of sight. Settling back to enjoy the journey, he cupped the pleasant arousal Susan's threat had given rise to. "Three weeks of waiting and I might go mad."

As the miles sped by, he reminisced about his disdain of Edwina Waxenby when she'd waved goodbye outside Tattersalls. Life had changed dramatically in the short time since then. He had changed. Susan had resurrected the Griff who'd buried himself in dissolute pursuits for too long. "You're a lovesick fool," he chided, though he had no regrets about his besottedness. So, why hadn't he confessed his love? In the throes of sexual madness with women whose names he couldn't even recall, he'd cooed insincere words of *amour éternel*.

He was in love with Susan, but hadn't summoned the backbone to tell her. He supposed he was a typical male in that regard and resolved to remedy the situation as soon as they reunited.

AFTER LUNCHEON ON the day of Griff's departure, Susan embarked on a trip to Byrom's, Manchester's premier mercers. Emma and Rebecca accompanied her. Purchasing fabric for a wedding dress was a bridal rite of passage, one Susan had never thought to experience, and she was excited, as were her friends.

Lively conversation about recent royal weddings seemed to shorten the journey. Emma was particularly enamored of the gown worn by Princess Charlotte when she married Leopold of Belgium the previous year. However, Rebecca reminded them only royal brides were allowed to wear silver.

Susan's preference was for a simple gown of muslin, or perhaps cotton, fancied up with embroidery. As for color, she'd thought a lighter shade of gray than what she normally wore.

Emma and Rebecca wouldn't hear of it, especially after the shop assistant at Byrom's showed them a print in the latest edition of *Ackermann's Repository*. The petite woman insisted a white satin dress with an overdress of striped gauze was *de rigueur* for any aristocratic bride.

They spent a pleasant afternoon drinking copious cups of tea and sampling delicious petits fours while perusing several books of fashion plates. It was eventually agreed *Ackermann's* white satin and gauze overdress trimmed with Brussels lace would be the perfect thing.

Susan had never worn such a beautiful creation. She'd normally have been the first to criticize extravagance, but her perceptions had changed. She wanted to look beautiful for the man she loved. The occasion warranted frivolity. She chuckled inwardly, marveling at the frivolous side of her character Griff had resurrected. Life had been too serious for too long.

"Pearls, I think," Emma suggested.

"My mother left me hers," Susan replied.

"White satin slippers and white kid gloves," the sales clerk said. "I recommend Archer's for those. They're not far from here."

"What about a veil?" Rebecca asked.

"Old fashioned," was the terse reply, accompanied by a sour look from the shop assistant.

Emma charged the purchases to the Farnworth account. Byrom's man of work loaded the packages wrapped in brown paper into their carriage.

Susan instructed Conrad to head for home instead of following the directions to Archer's. "I'm sure Timpson's in Preston can procure the satin slippers," she told her friends as she boarded. "And I have Mama's white gloves."

"It's good luck to have something of your mother's," Rebecca said with a yawn.

Given the loveless marriage her mother had endured, Susan doubted the veracity of that thought. She leaned her head back and closed her eyes, soon lulled to sleep by the movement of the carriage. She dreamed of Griff's wide-eyed delight when he saw her walking down the aisle.

Jolted awake when a wheel lurched into a pothole, she realized things had gone strangely quiet. Opening one eye, she discovered Emma and Rebecca had also dozed off.

Their spending spree had worn everybody out!

AFTER AN UNEVENTFUL journey that seemed all the longer as the distance between him and Susan increased, Griff was delighted by Potts' announcement that Tom Glazebrook had already taken up residence in the servants' wing of Clifton Heights.

He hurried to the stables where he found the man he was confident could help him establish a successful stud farm. "You're a sight for sore eyes," he exclaimed, pumping Tom's hand. "Thank you for coming."

"Right enough, my lord," Glazebrook replied with his usual dour expression. "To be honest, I'm a Lancashire lad at heart. This is where I belong."

Griff regretted it had taken him so long to realize the man had never really been happy in the big city. "Well, let me tell you about Orion while we walk and you can share your thoughts on how we should proceed."

Rogerson soon joined them. Tom explained his recommendations regarding rearranging the stables to accommodate the thoroughbred away from the mares. "Like at Pendlebury Stables," he said.

They agreed on the need for a separate stable to eventually be built for Orion. The current stable would have to be expanded. Rogerson took charge of both projects.

Lengthy discussions ensued about how to convert Clifton's paddocks into something resembling the set up at Pendlebury. Griff wasn't surprised when Tom asked, "And what do ye intend to do with the operation down south, my lord?"

"It's a good question," he replied. "I can either sell the farm and the horses, or we can figure out a way to bring some of the best mares here."

"So, ye intend to move north for good?"

Griff might have expected his northern stable master to ask forthright questions—ones he should really have been asking himself. "I mean to hold on to the London townhouse for when I attend sessions in the House of Lords, but I see no reason to keep the farm. I've discovered I'm a Lancashire lad at heart too."

"Always knew it were so," Tom replied with a rare grin. "This Lady Susan must be a rare prize."

Satisfied with his productive afternoon, Griff spent the hour before dinner luxuriating in a hot bath. Fantasizing about sharing the big tub with his *rare prize* resulted in the inevitable arousal which a few firm strokes quickly assuaged. "You need to be more patient," he rasped to his flaccid cock as he stepped out of the tub. "Less than three weeks and you'll be home."

After the accident, he'd loathed dining alone in the enormous dining room. This evening, the delicious meal of Cornish hen, roasted potatoes and carrots assured him Potts had staffing of the kitchens firmly in hand. Content and replete, he leaned back in his new Sheraton chair and envisioned Susan seated beside him at the satinwood table, and, God willing, a bevy of intelligent, healthy and curious children.

After thanking Potts for replenishing the bar with an excellent brandy, he retired for the night, the resourceful Frederick serving as his valet. It wasn't the first time he'd had erotic dreams but, tonight, the woman in his fantasies had a face and a name.

"Susan," he rasped upon awakening with a rock-hard morning erection.

WHAT'S GOING ON HERE?

NXIOUSLY EXPECTING TO see Arthur, Tillie's heart sank when she exited the almshouse. One of the Watchman's thugs lounged against the brick wall.

Terror-stricken, she tried to fathom how they'd found her. Arthur was the only person who knew she was in Preston and he would never betray her.

She tried to hurry past him but he grabbed her arm. "Come with me," he growled.

Her only hope was to create a fuss. Surely some Good Samaritan would come to her aid, although it was a drizzly afternoon and there weren't many about. She yanked her arm as hard as she could. "I'm not going back to Manchester," she screeched.

"Arthur's waiting for ye at Withins Hall, stupid cow," he hissed, tightening his grip.

Confused, she let him drag her along, not truly believing Arthur had sent him. "You're 'urting me," she whined as they crossed the footbridge over the Ribble.

"Stop complaining and I'll be gentle," he said, his voice laden with sarcasm. "We've a long walk ahead of us."

He let go of her arm when she nodded. She'd thought Arthur might come for her in a carriage. Instead, he'd sent a hoodlum whose presence would make the long trek seem even longer. And what was her beloved's connection with the Watchman's lackey? "I'm beginning to wonder about you, Arthur Coleman," she muttered under her breath.

She almost had to run to keep up with the lumbering lout. The rain had held off but it was muggy. She was panting hard when he led the way through a gap in the thick hawthorn hedge bordering the Whiteside estate. It seemed Arthur still hadn't smoothed things over with his father. She'd have to make it clear she was running out of patience.

Emerging from the thorny hedge scratched and bleeding, she espied Arthur, waiting outside the folly in the distance. Overcome with relief, she waved, disappointed when he didn't wave back.

"What took so long?" he growled when she finally reached him. "I've been waiting an hour."

She tried to organize her thoughts. There was something she'd meant to tell him, but was too exhausted to think. Close to tears, she tried to nestle against him. If he would just put his arms around her and…

"Get off me," he exclaimed, backing away. "You'll bloody my shirt.

⇛⇚

"WE'VE GONE OVER this ten times," Arthur said. "What is it you don't understand?"

He was just about at his wits' end with Tillie. She'd done nothing but pout and complain of being thirsty since she'd arrived at the folly an hour ago. Truth be told, he'd be glad when the Red Bandanas took her off his hands.

"I don't know 'ow to ride," she whimpered for the umpteenth time.

The thugs snickered.

Arthur prayed for patience. "You have to ride the horse. We're too heavy. It's only a short distance over the fields from Thicketford Manor to our stables, and Wiggo here will have hold of the halter."

He cringed when she sniffled, then wiped her sleeve across her runny nose. He'd thought the folly would be a good place for a bit of slap and tickle while they waited for twilight, but she looked decidedly unappealing.

Plus, his father stood in the way of setting up Orion as a stud at Withins Hall and the details of the shooting accident hadn't been finalized with the Manchester men, so he needed at least one of them to stay.

It probably wouldn't be the first time they'd watched people *in flagrante delicto*, but he didn't fancy the Red Bandanas gossiping about the lamentable state of his bed partner. They'd deem him weak and weak men never prospered.

All in all, the escapade was taking its toll on his nerves. Inhaling deeply, he gathered Tillie into his arms, reining in his temper when she slobbered all over him. "Just remember. Wiggo will lead the horse out of the stable. Then, he'll help you to mount and lead the nag across the fields to Withins Hall. Simple as that."

"But why can't 'e lead the beast 'ere without a rider?"

Arthur couldn't let on the only reason for her presence was so the thugs could take her back to Manchester with them. "He's a racehorse," he improvised. "He won't go anywhere without a rider on his back."

"Oh," she replied. "I see. I didn't know."

Breathing a sigh of relief that she was as dimwitted as he'd always thought, he eased her down to the floor. "Why don't you get some sleep?"

"All right," she replied. "I am tired, but I worry I'll be too late getting back to the poorhouse if I don't go soon."

"You'll be safe here at Withins," he lied.

A FOOT PRODDING her backside jolted Tillie from a dream of sleeping in Arthur's soft feather bed. For a moment, she couldn't grasp why she was lying on the cold stone floor of the torchlit folly.

"Get up," Arthur growled. "It's time."

The knot in her belly tightened. The horse.

"I'll wait in the stables," he hissed, shoving her toward Wiggo.

The lout took her arm and dragged her into the darkness of the meadow. A terrible memory of the last time she'd traversed this same field came flooding back. When the attempt to kidnap Patsy Crompton had gone terribly wrong through no fault of hers, she'd fled back to Arthur, trusting him to protect her. Instead, he'd sold her to the Watchman in order to clear his gambling debt.

Foreboding twisted her innards. She'd been such a fool. Sexual delights and empty promises had blinded her to reality. This escapade wouldn't end well. Once he had the horse, Arthur intended to send her back to the Watchman. There was no other reason for her to be involved. All that nonsense about needing a rider...

However, there was no point whining to Wiggo. She could expect no help from him. "Just watch for an opportunity to escape," she told herself, gulping air in an effort to calm her racing heart.

A groom raised his lantern and challenged them as they crept into the Farnworth stables. Wiggo sent the lad flying with a ferocious backhander, retrieved the lantern and thrust it into her trembling hands. Paralyzed by fear, Tillie glanced over her shoulder at the lights of nearby Thicketford Manor. Even if she had the breath left in her lungs to run, Wiggo would quickly overtake her. And he'd be angry. The stricken groom slumped against the stall might be dead for all she knew. The thug wouldn't dare kill her but he could inflict some serious damage.

She knew all was lost when Wiggo emerged from a stall, pulling the biggest horse she'd ever seen. Tossing his head, the snorting beast stamped the ground with his hoof. She couldn't run, but neither could she mount the angry dragon.

Overwhelmed, she fell to the ground in a dead faint.

PACING THE STABLES at Withins Hall under the irritatingly watchful eye of Wiggo's fellow gang member, Arthur threw up his arms in exasperation when he heard Wiggo's gruff voice not far away. Judging by the colorful language and the snorts and whinnies of an unhappy horse, he'd say the thug was having a difficult time with the beast. His hackles rose when Tripp lumbered out to aid his comrade. Arthur had run off the stable boys, but it was important to get Orion into the stables without creating a disturbance. His father had to be kept in the dark a little while longer. It wasn't a big concern. Baron Whiteside rarely ventured into the stables.

It was tempting to laugh when Wiggo finally appeared, the angry stallion balking at every step and Tillie slung over his shoulder.

His amusement was short-lived when the mares in the stable became agitated. He almost wished he'd let the grooms stay. They would have known how to calm the mares' panicked cries. Wiggo hefted Tillie into a pile of hay and set both hands to the rope pulling Orion. Nostrils flared, the stallion reared, hooves flailing.

"Get him in the stall," Arthur hissed.

Dodging the deadly hooves, Wiggo swore a blue streak.

The more Wiggo heaved on the rope, the more frenzied the horse became. Arthur's temper was close to snapping when a voice he recognized only too well demanded, "What the devil's going on here?"

"Father," he replied, forcing a smile. "We're having a spot of bother. Farnworth has loaned us this horse, but..."

To his surprise his father calmly approached the stallion, all the while cooing silly noises. Astonishingly, the horse soon quieted, even allowing his nose to be stroked.

His sire then took hold of the rope, led the now docile horse into a stall and tied him to a post.

Suddenly, the way ahead became clear to Arthur. His father now knew of Orion, and likely didn't believe the tale of Farnworth making a loan of the horse. As his sire turned to confront him, Arthur nodded to Tripp. It took only one mighty blow of the thug's cosh across the back of his head to fell Bertrand Coleman. With his father dead, Arthur could now claim the title. No will would deprive him of the right of inheritance.

Murderous Intent

AFTER BREAKFAST, SUSAN spent a tedious hour with the seamstresses hired by Emma. The two local women were skilled and the wedding gown was taking shape. It was bad luck for a groom to see his bride in her gown before the ceremony, but Susan wished Griff had returned so she could at least show him the material.

She decided to don her riding habit instead of the gray muslin she'd worn earlier to the morning room, though she didn't plan to go for a ride until after luncheon. It wasn't her favorite pastime, but a good canter would fill a lonely afternoon and take her mind off Griff.

She and Rebecca were waiting for luncheon to be served when a red-faced Jenkinson ushered in the earl's valet.

Susan's throat tightened as she rose. Bradley's deep frown and his unexpected arrival were sure signs something was amiss.

"Orion," he declared without preamble. "He's been taken."

"Taken?" she parroted, gripping the back of her chair, overwhelmed by the possibility she had lost her beloved horse.

"The earl and Lady Farnworth intended to take a leisurely ride to Preston today to arrange for musicians for the ball. Upon arrival at the stables, they discovered Orion's stall was empty, save for a stable lad who'd been knocked out cold. My lord thought you should know."

"Could he have struck the boy and bolted?" Rebecca asked.

Bradley shook his head. "The door to the stall had been unlatched, but wasn't damaged."

"Jenkinson," Susan said. "Get my horse saddled and brought round. I'll accompany Bradley back to the manor house. And send a message post haste to Lord Pendlebury at Clifton Heights."

Ten minutes later, she rushed into Thicketford Manor, almost bumping into Gabriel on his way out.

"Any news?" she asked, though Emma's stricken face and the rifle suddenly in the valet's hands indicated there wasn't.

"Bradley and I followed Orion's tracks," Gabriel explained. "I hate to say it but they seem to lead across the fields to the Whiteside estate."

"Since Griffith was so rudely turned away from Withins Hall, we've been worried Arthur Coleman may be back," Emma added.

Susan seethed. This was all too reminiscent of Patsy's kidnapping. "You think that twerp is responsible for stealing my horse? I'm coming with you."

"No," Gabriel said firmly. "This could be dangerous. You and Emma stay here and don't let anyone enter the house. We'll ride over to Withins Hall to investigate."

"Come into the drawing room, Susan," Emma coaxed. "I've rung for tea."

"I need something stronger than tea," she replied, wondering how on earth she was going to explain to Griff the loss of the thoroughbred on which he'd placed all his hopes for the future of Clifton Heights.

⤐⤐⤐⫷⫷⫷

SATISFIED POTTS AND Glazebrook would tend to the remaining tasks necessary to bring Clifton Heights up to snuff for Susan, and feeling somewhat superfluous, Griff had decided to leave early and surprise his fiancée by arriving a day earlier than planned.

Leaning back on the padded wall of the carriage, he closed his eyes, anticipating the smile that would blossom on her face.

He opened them again, puzzled when the carriage rolled to a halt on the outskirts of Chorley. He assumed the new driver hired by Potts had lost his bearings.

He hurriedly stepped out of the vehicle when a rider wearing the Farnworth livery came alongside the window. "My lord," he panted. "I was on my way to Clifton Heights with a message when I recognized the carriage."

His belly suddenly in knots, Griff feared something dire had happened to Susan. "What is so urgent?"

"Lady Susan wanted you to be aware Orion has been stolen."

Relief washed over him. He'd been on edge ever since his rude reception at the baron's home. He'd a sneaking suspicion Gabriel's hunch Arthur Coleman had returned was correct. There was no love lost between him and Susan, but she was apparently safe. "Right, Lever," he told the new driver. "On to Thicketford Manor with all possible haste."

Halfway into the carriage, he decided to trust a little voice that whispered Arthur might possibly be involved in Orion's disappearance. It would be reassuring to hear from Bertrand that such wasn't the case. "On second thought," he said. "We'll go by way of Withins Hall first."

Fifteen minutes later, he had the brass knocker in hand, his jaw clenched in case the same rude young man appeared. He relaxed when Whiteside's butler opened the door and ushered him into the foyer.

"I'm afraid the baron has gone out to the stables, my lord," Judson explained. "It's a place he rarely visits, so I expect him back momentarily if you'd like to wait."

Gooseflesh crept over Griff's nape. Could it be the baron was involved in the theft? "If it's all the same to you, I'll make my way there."

Judson hesitated.

"It's a matter of some urgency and I'm sure your master won't mind," Griff insisted, already halfway out the door.

"To your left, my lord," the butler shouted. "All the way to the rear of the house."

Griff glanced up at Lever still seated on the driver's bench of his carriage. Frederick would have been a handy person to have at his side, but the young footman was still at Clifton Heights. Lever was too elderly and frail to be of much use if an altercation arose.

Cursing the inevitable crunch of his boots on the gravel pathway, he cautiously entered the torchlit stable, furious when he saw the same young man who'd turned him away threatening a frenzied Orion with a horsewhip. Striding to confront the wretch and wrest the whip from his hand, he stopped dead when he saw a young woman kneeling by Bertrand Coleman's body.

Preoccupied with trying to recall where he'd seen her before, he failed to pay attention to the glint of warning in the woman's eyes. He fell to his knees and surrendered to a sickening darkness when something struck him hard from behind.

⇒⇒⇒✦⇐⇐⇐

VAGUELY AWARE WIGGO had coshed an intruder, Arthur hurried out of Orion's stall. He was disappointed it wasn't Stringer lying in a heap in the straw. However, getting rid of Susan Crompton's fancy man would be immensely gratifying.

"Ye've killed two men," Tillie wailed, still on her knees beside his father. "I want no part of killing."

She cowered away, sobbing when Wiggo threatened to smack her.

"Wot we gonna do wiv the bodies?" Tripp asked.

Arthur had to think quickly. Everything was happening too fast. "The earl must have arrived in a carriage. Go get it from the front of the house."

"Wot about the driver?"

Arthur gritted his teeth. Was he expected to solve every problem? "Deal with him."

Left alone with Tillie, he bristled when the earl moaned.

"'e's not dead," she said.

"Well, he soon will be," he replied, retrieving a length of baling twine from a hook. "Bind his hands and feet."

She shook her head, until he raised his hand. "No good will come of whatever you're planning, Arthur," she said as she reluctantly did his bidding.

"That's Baron Whiteside to you, my girl. And nobody will find the bodies when Wiggo and Tripp send the carriage over the edge of Woltham Quarry."

"But it flooded years ago."

"Precisely."

ORION'S REVENGE

T HE EARL CAME to a moment or two before Wiggo and Tripp arrived with the carriage. Clearly infuriated to find himself bound hand and foot, he began to berate Arthur, all the while struggling against his bonds. Tillie could have told him it was a waste of time. Arthur tore a strip off her petticoat, gagged his captive and checked the bindings. She'd tried not to tie the rough twine too tightly so it wouldn't hurt as much, but Arthur pulled the knots tighter.

She retreated to a dark corner of the stables as the protesting nobleman was carried to the carriage by the thugs and dumped inside. The baron's body was hefted in next. She prayed Arthur wouldn't decide to consign her to the deep lake at the bottom of the quarry. If she was dragged off to Manchester, another opportunity for escape might eventually arise.

She breathed again when Arthur slammed the door and sent his henchmen on their way with directions to the quarry.

She cringed when he swaggered over and brandished a dagger under her nose. "Come on, Lady Matilda," he mocked. "One last tup, for old time's sake."

If she tried to deny him, he would punish her, but her own gullibility had brought her to this coil. Loathing for him and for herself boiled over. "You're a disgusting murderer."

His smile turned to a scowl. "You'll pay for your insolence," he spat, raising his blade.

Tillie held her breath, convinced the last sound she would ever hear would be the restless cries of the Whiteside mares, clearly upset by Orion's presence. The racehorse hadn't stopped pacing, snorting and whinnying. He'd kicked the boards of his stall more than once. Splintering wood suddenly drew Arthur's attention.

She screamed, paralyzed by fear when the horse flew out of his damaged stall like an enraged Pegasus come to life. Transfixed by the beast's awesome power, she stopped breathing when he reared. Risking a glance at the flailing hooves, she stared in disbelief when a deadly hoof crashed down on Arthur's head.

He crumpled to the straw like a broken doll with its head split open.

Trembling with the certainty she was about to be stomped to death, she whimpered like a child when Orion tossed his head, turned and galloped out of the stable.

She scrambled to her feet, wrenched the dagger from Arthur's grip and fled, just in time to see the horse disappear into the darkness, heading toward the Farnworth estate.

Anxious voices alerted her to the arrival of others. At all costs, she mustn't be found with Arthur's body. She'd be blamed—and how to explain the baron's disappearance? And the earl's?

As she fled into the night, following the path Orion had forged through the long grass, reality suddenly became clear. The only way to save herself from a charge of murder was to do everything she could to prevent the despicable crime Arthur had set in motion.

"PACING WON'T HELP matters," Emma said. "Come and sit down."

Susan only vaguely heard her friend's advice and kept on wearing a path in the expensive drawing room carpet at Thicketford Manor. "I have to keep moving," she replied, frantically worried for her horse. "I'm trying desperately to come up with a way to explain all this to Griff."

"He's perhaps received your message by now and set out. He'll probably be here later today."

The adder coiled in Susan's heart hissed that Griff might leave her if the horse wasn't recovered. "Orion means so much to him," she murmured.

"He cares more about you," Emma assured her. "He'll be angry that you are overwrought."

Peering into the glowing coals of the dying fire in the hearth, Susan looked in vain for some sign that Emma's words were true. She swiveled her head when Frame burst into the room without the customary polite cough. Indeed, she barely recognized the red-faced, disheveled man who seemed unable to choke out the message he'd come to deliver. A dreadful premonition wrapped its tentacles around Susan's stomach.

"What is it?" Emma asked as she rose from the sofa, thankfully more in control of her voice than Susan.

"The horse, my lady," Frame panted, gesticulating wildly. "Outside."

Susan later had no memory of how she arrived at the front of the house. It was tempting to fall to her knees and give thanks when she espied her beloved Orion stomping one hoof on the gravel driveway, but the greater need was to reassure the snorting horse he was safe. She tried to think what Griff would do.

"Careful," Emma warned as Susan stretched out her hand and slowly reached for the halter, all the while uttering soothing words. Wherever Orion had been taken, he'd escaped and somehow instinctively known Thicketford Manor was where he belonged—with her and Griff.

The animal calmed when she took hold of the halter and stroked his nose. "He hasn't come far," she told Emma, reinforcing her belief their wretch of a neighbor had stolen him. "He's barely winded."

Orion tossed his head, baring his teeth when a wild-haired apparition emerged from the darkness and collapsed on the driveway.

Intent on keeping her horse calm, Susan was grateful when Emma gingerly approached the sobbing intruder, but she wasn't prepared when her friend exclaimed, "It's Tillie."

Emma tried to help the girl to her feet, but Tillie gulped air, seemingly unable to rise from all fours.

"The…earl," their former maid stammered.

"Lord Farnworth?" Emma asked, alarm evident in her voice. "What of him?"

"The other one," Tillie croaked, shaking her head.

An icy hand gripped Susan's innards. "The Earl of Pendlebury?" she shouted.

"Woltham," Tillie gasped, nodding like a marionette.

"The quarry?" Emma asked. "Why would Lord Pendlebury go to Woltham Quarry?"

Susan already knew the answer. "Has Arthur taken him there?"

"Arthur's dead," Tillie wailed mournfully. "The beast killed 'im. 'is 'enchmen took the earl."

Not for the first time in her life, Susan gave thanks for her ability to immediately see to the heart of a problem. She'd be damned if she was going to allow Griff Halliwell to end up broken at the bottom of an abandoned quarry, which had clearly been Arthur's intent. Acting on instinct and pure adrenalin, she stood on tiptoe. "Will you trust me?" she whispered close to Orion's ear.

"Give me a leg up," she commanded Emma when the horse nodded.

"Surely you're not…"

"Help me, please," Susan begged, swamped with relief when her friend acquiesced and helped her scramble to sit astride the dancing thoroughbred.

It wasn't elegant, but she didn't care.

"Wait," Tillie exclaimed, holding out a dagger to Emma. "She must take this."

Susan steeled herself to be courageous as she took the weapon Emma handed to her without hesitation. This was no carefully crafted romance novel. She was about to ride into danger to save the man she loved. She'd never used a blade before, but would if necessary.

"Be careful," Emma rasped. "I'll send riders to Withins Hall to alert Gabe and Bradley."

Fisting one hand in the thick mane, Susan urged Orion forward. "I know you have bad feet, but Griff's life is depending on your speed."

She held on for dear life as the horse surged forward into the night.

BRAVE AND BEAUTIFUL

FLICKERING TORCHES AND raised voices indicated a commotion was going on behind Withins Hall. It prompted Gabriel to remain mounted when he arrived. "We'll carry on to the stables," he advised Bradley.

There, they found the source of the racket. Gaping servants clustered together watching a tableau that might have been a scene from an opera. Wailing loudly, Lady Anthea knelt beside a body.

Her husband stood over her. "He's not worthy of your tears," Springer growled.

"But he's my brother," she sobbed.

"What's going on here?" Gabe demanded as he dismounted.

"It's Arthur," Springer replied, striding over to him. "Judging by the hoof-print, his head's been caved in by a horse," he added, pointing to the shattered walls of a stall. "However, all our mounts are accounted for."

"Is he dead, my lord?" Bradley shouted from the edge of the meadow.

Still sobbing, Anthea nodded woodenly.

Gabe found the situation mildly amusing. Arthur had stolen Orion and the stallion had killed him. It was as if…

He shook the ludicrous notion from his head. "So, where's the horse now?"

Bradley pointed toward the Farnworth estate. "Looks like he

escaped this way."

Anthea suddenly struggled to rise as Gabe headed for the meadow. "Wait! More importantly, where are my father and the earl?"

"The earl?" Gabe queried, thinking grief had muddled the woman's thoughts. She tended to be addlebrained at the best of times.

Judson stepped forward. "The Earl of Pendlebury called earlier, but we found his driver unconscious in the driveway. His carriage has disappeared, along with two unsavory characters Arthur kept hidden away in the folly. He thought I didn't know, but..."

Dread crept into Gabe's heart as the butler carried on his explanation. "We didn't pass the earl's carriage on the road."

Approaching hoofbeats heralded James Footman. "My lord, Lady Susan has gone in pursuit," he yelled as he reined to a halt amid a collective gasp from the scattering servants. "No time to lose."

"In pursuit of what?" Gabe asked.

"Lord Pendlebury's carriage, headed for Woltham Quarry."

As Gabe and his valet raced for their horses, he cursed under his breath. He'd lived in Lancashire a relatively short time and had no idea of the quarry's location. However, he didn't doubt the intentions of Arthur's henchmen. "Do you know the way, James?"

"Aye, milord."

"Lead on," he commanded, praying he and Bradley got to the quarry in time to save Halliwell and Lady Susan.

LYING ON THE floor of the racing carriage alongside the baron's body, Griff had no opportunity to brace himself against being jostled against the seat. He had to be grateful the boards no longer reeked of chicken shit. It seemed to take an eternity, but he eventually managed to contort himself into a sitting position.

"Thorry," he spluttered through the wet gag.

Clearly, panic had stolen his wits. He was apologizing to a dead man because his long legs were sprawled across his body.

It came as a short-lived relief when Bertrand moaned. Now, he had to think of a way to save the old man's life as well as his own. He'd overheard mention of a flooded quarry, which didn't bode well.

If he could untie the rope around his ankles, an opportunity to flee the carriage might present itself. However, with his hands bound behind his back and the breakneck speed at which they were traveling, there wasn't much chance of that.

The length of his legs made it difficult to finally brace his feet on the floor, from where, with considerable effort, he levered himself up onto the seat.

Sweating from the exertion and fearing his arms had been wrenched from their sockets, he swiveled to lie across the bench with his feet against the wall. If the fall didn't kill him and the vehicle ended up in water, perhaps he could kick open the door and swim out. That would still leave the baron to drown, and swimming with his hands bound…

Anger at his helplessness threatened to choke him. He didn't want to die at the very moment he'd found happiness. As the carriage slowed, he closed his eyes and conjured an image of Susan's smile. "I should have told you I love you," he rasped.

SUSAN FELT NO fear for herself as she clung to Orion's mane. If the horse's feet pained him, he gave so sign of it as he chewed up the miles at lightning speed. It was as though he too understood the urgency.

Jaw clenched, she imagined she was Boadicea riding to rid

Britain of the Romans, except she meant to survive and do whatever it took to save Griff. She'd never told him she loved him and it was of the utmost importance she remedy that oversight.

Undaunted, she urged Orion on when a full moon cast its light on the dire scene at the top of the quarry. A man was leading a horse away from the carriage. At least they'd thought to spare the animal, probably to use for their getaway. The wheels were still on terra firma but the rear end of the vehicle teetered over the edge of the abyss. Another man leaned his back against the front, legs braced to push.

Righteous anger transformed Susan from the mortal Iceni queen into the immortal Tisiphone, most vengeful of the Furies. Howling like a she-wolf bent on protecting her pups, she kept her gaze fixed on the carriage, willing it to remain where it was as she thrust the point of the dagger into the air.

The moon illuminated the pale, astonished faces of the two thugs moments before they fled into the darkness. It seemed the sight of a demon horse ridden by an avenging fury was more than they were willing to confront.

Two shots echoed nearby, followed by screams of pain; Gabriel must be close, but Susan's concern was to get Griff out of the carriage. Praying he was alive, she slid off Orion when he snorted to a halt, and ran to yank open the carriage door.

A maelstrom of emotions swirled in her heart when she looked into Griff's eyes—relief he lived, anger he'd been trussed up like a chicken for the spit, surprise to see the baron on the floor, gut-wrenching fear when the groaning carriage shifted, and, yes, a modicum of amusement at the shock in Griff's beloved gaze.

He shook his head as she clambered aboard. "Get out, Susan," he panted when she pulled down the gag. "We'll go over any second."

"No," she replied, sawing at the rope binding his ankles. "We'll get you both out. Gabriel is on his way."

"You're an incredibly stubborn woman," he rasped. "I regret I've never told you how much I love you."

"I was bothered by a similar regret," she replied hoarsely. "I love you, infuriating man."

As soon as his legs were free, they jumped from the doomed carriage, landing inelegantly in the grass. Susan had never felt more alive. She'd saved the life of the man she loved.

"Free my hands," he growled, getting to his knees.

She hurriedly carried out the task, choked by renewed terror when he climbed back into the teetering conveyance as soon as she'd cut through the rope. "No," she mouthed.

Shouts heralded the arrival of Gabriel and Bradley. The valet tossed aside his rifle and both men reached up to heave on the traces, leaning all their weight to prevent the fall into the quarry.

Susan recovered her wits and ran to help Griff drag the baron the rest of the way out of the carriage.

As they collapsed in a heap, Gabriel and Bradley let go of the traces. The creaking carriage hovered for only a breathless moment before plunging into the dark waters below.

Heavy breathing was the only sound until a faint splash echoed.

Bradley and Gabriel hefted the baron and carried him away from the edge.

Griff gathered Susan into his embrace. "You saved my life," he whispered close to her ear. "You are brave as well as beautiful."

Clinging to him, she breathed in his familiar scent, shaken by the realization of how close he'd come to death.

The woman who disdained men had come to rely on this man's strength. Life without him would have been unthinkable.

A snort from Orion drew Griff's attention. "What are you doing here, Boy?" he asked, holding out a hand.

Susan dithered when the horse nuzzled Griff's palm. The two had clearly bonded and her fiancé might be upset if she'd injured the stallion in any way. "I rode him," she murmured. "When

Tillie alerted us, it seemed the fastest way to get to you."

Orion bared his teeth and shook his noble head as if to confirm how difficult a ride it had been.

Griff put his hands on her shoulders and eased her away, a frown marring his handsome features. "Well, that explains how you knew what was afoot here, but I take back what I said. You're not just brave. You're bloody incredible."

THE BALL

TWO WEEKS AFTER the near catastrophic events at Woltham Quarry, Lady Emma Crompton-Smith stood beside her handsome husband at the entrance to the ballroom of Thicketford Manor. Nervously scanning the spacious, glittering room one last time, she was reassured the string quartet was playing at a suitable volume, the refreshment table was piled high with sweets and savories, the bewigged footmen looked immaculate in their new livery. "All is in readiness," she told Frame.

The butler descended the staircase in his usual regal manner. Emma wasn't sure how he managed to get the attention of the guests assembled for cocktails in the foyer without even a slight cough, but a hush gradually fell.

"Lord and Lady Farnworth welcome you to Thicketford Manor and invite you to ascend," he intoned.

It had been years since Emma had taken part in a receiving line. Her first husband's funeral was likely the last occasion. She barely remembered anything about that stressful day, except for her outrage at Arthur Coleman's shockingly suggestive behavior.

This grand event was the first ball she and Gabe had hosted as earl and countess. They knew some of the guests, but many were strangers. They'd invited local gentry as well as powerful industrialists who were reshaping Lancashire's economy. Some had come from as far away as Bolton and Liverpool. The guest chambers here and at Withins Hall were full. Rooms were booked at all the inns in Preston. It was a relief her sister had sent regrets. She didn't need Priscilla's judgmental eyes on everything she did, nor her husband's disparaging remarks about the idle rich.

Emma was glad Gabe was by her side. Neither of them had been born into the nobility, but her handsome husband—resplendent in his officer's uniform—had an easy way with people that would make up for any gauche missteps she might make.

It was a relief when Susan appeared on Griffith's arm. Her former sister-in-law looked stunning in pale green satin. Emma noticed she'd taken to showing off more cleavage since the Earl of Pendlebury had come into her life.

Emma's husband had turned out to be a more than satisfying sexual partner. She suspected Susan had found a mate who would carry her to rapturous heights. The perpetual frown had all but disappeared and been replaced with a hungry craving every time she set eyes on Halliwell.

"Thank you," Emma whispered to her friend. "I can practice on you."

"You'll be fine," Susan replied pecking a kiss on her cheek. "You're a natural at this."

Emma bobbed the required curtsey to greet Griffith. "My lord, welcome." It was tempting to tell him how handsome he looked. His forest green frock coat and full-length form-fitted trousers complemented Susan's gown. Cut a little short to reveal the plum-colored waistcoat subtly embroidered with a delicate yellow motif, it clung to his broad shoulders. A perfectly tied white cravat and snowy white shirt completed the impression of a wealthy young man comfortable in his own skin. Emma recognized Mr. Carr's handiwork in every stitch.

Griffith bowed, bestowing a polite kiss on Emma's gloved hand. "I hope to gain some pointers this evening, my lady, so Susan and I may one day host an event as grand at Clifton Heights."

"I'm so pleased we can announce your engagement this evening here at Thicketford Manor," she said sincerely.

"As am I," he replied, his eyes locked with Susan's adoring gaze.

As they moved on into the ballroom, Emma exchanged a smile with her husband, pleased to see the same happiness for Susan in his expression that she felt.

Emma's mother-in-law came next, but she was clearly in a dither about something. "What's wrong, Rebecca?" she whispered close to her ear.

"I'm concerned for Bertrand. He's having a devil of a time with the stairs. Anthea's fussing over the dilemma, but you know how inept the girl can be."

Everybody had been mightily relieved to learn Baron Whiteside was recovering from his injuries, though he was still obliged to rely heavily on the aid of a cane. Delighted he'd agreed to attend, Emma fretted. She hadn't given a thought to the stairs.

"I believe the problem has been solved," Gabe said with a chuckle when John Springer and Dr. Adrian Henry appeared carrying a wicker chair on which sat Bertrand Coleman.

"You brought your own bearers," Gabe jested, shaking the baron's hand.

"Yes," their guest replied without smiling.

Emma's heart went out to him. He seemed a shadow of his jovial self. She supposed knowing your own son had tried to murder you would be a source of sorrow for any man. She wondered how he felt about the manner of Arthur's death, but would never mention it. Was he as relieved as everyone else that Arthur was gone for good? The baroness hadn't fared so well. She'd collapsed in a dead faint when told the news, and never regained consciousness. She and Arthur were quietly interred together in the family cemetery behind the folly.

"How well you look, Bertrand," Rebecca gushed, offering her hand as she approached.

Smiling for the first time, the baron extricated himself quickly from the chair and kissed Rebecca's hand. "Kind of you to say so, m'dear."

Gabe raised his eyebrows as they watched the two toddle off toward an alcove near the refreshment table. "Interesting!" was all he said.

Next, they greeted Springer and his wife. Emma struggled to keep a straight face when Anthea asked, "Will there be an opportunity to perform this evening?"

Springer rolled his eyes.

"Unfortunately, no," Emma replied, tempted to address her guest as *Silly Goose*. "We'll be showcasing Susan and Griff's announcement during the intermission, and we wouldn't want to detract from that, would we?"

Anthea pouted. "I suppose not."

Thankfully, Springer pulled his wife into the ballroom.

Gabe was already shaking Dr. Henry's hand when Emma turned her attention back to the queue of guests. "Thank you again for coming so quickly that terrible night, my friend," he said. "It was a miracle Bertrand didn't succumb at the quarry while we waited for the carriage from Thicketford Manor."

"And another miracle you were here to treat him as soon as he arrived," Emma added.

Adrian nodded in his usual modest way. "I did what I could and it's mainly thanks to Lady Susan and her fiancé he's alive at all. I fear the limp and the impaired eyesight might be permanent. And, of course, he'll never recover from Arthur's treachery."

"I believe my mother is doing her best to help him cope," Gabe said with a chuckle. "Enjoy yourself tonight."

"I will."

Feeling more confident the evening was going to be a success, Emma prepared to greet the next guests in line.

CUDDLING WITH GRIFF in a loveseat in between dance sets, Susan surveyed the happy faces of the guests. "I must congratulate Emma," she told him. "The musicians have played a wonderful selection, numerous guests have commented on the quality of the refreshments, and this ballroom looks magnificent. It all brings back happy memories."

He meshed his fingers with hers. "Tell me."

She was worried he wouldn't be interested in her childhood reminiscences. "It was so long ago."

"But I want to know everything about you."

"My mother loved entertaining. Looking back, I think she was determined to counteract my father's stern nature. He hated frivolity. I was just a child, but my mother insisted I be allowed to attend the balls for a short time before I was whisked off to bed."

"Patsy told me she's only permitted to be present for the grand announcement later," he said.

"Yes, she's disgusted about missing the rest of the ball. I expect she's whining to Miss Ince. That woman has the patience of a saint."

They shared the humor, then Susan continued. "I'll always remember the swirl of colors as the ladies danced by gracefully. Mind you, in those days, it was mostly minuets and quadrilles, although there was apparently some gossip about scandalous waltzes at the Farnworth balls."

She lifted his hand to her cheek. "I never imagined I'd one day find my own perfect dance partner."

"I'm not much of a dancer," he protested modestly.

"Nonsense," she retorted. "All I've done this evening is follow your lead. I don't have a clue about the steps."

She didn't mention the exhilaration of waltzing in his strong arms, her breasts pressed against his hard body, the tantalizing aroma of his cologne in her nostrils. It was as if they were the only two people on the dance floor.

A few other gentlemen had asked her to dance, but she sensed their discomfort under Griff's scowling scrutiny. She loved that he was clearly jealous.

He took a sip of his punch. "Be sure to get the recipe for this delicious concoction. We'll serve it at Clifton Heights when we host our first ball."

Daughter of an earl, Susan had grown up among the aristocracy. Nevertheless, the imminent prospect of becoming Griff's countess filled her with immense joy and a degree of trepidation. Clifton Heights was enormous, and there was much to be done to repair both the house and relationships with the local people. However, she'd never been one to back away from a challenge.

Griff took her glass and put it aside with his own when the musicians struck up another waltz. "You know," he told her as he led her by the hand on to the dance floor, "Thomas Raikes, the well-known diarist, once wrote that no event ever produced so great a sensation in English society as the introduction of the waltz in 1813."

She had known of Raikes' comments but preferred not to appear a know-it-all, which struck her as hysterically funny. "Really?"

"Now, they play a waltz almost every second set," he added, taking her into his arms. "Gentlemen everywhere can't help but applaud."

"And we ladies can blame those naughty Germans," she replied as she melted into his warm embrace.

GRIFF MADE FLIPPANT comments about men loving the intimacy of the waltz but, the more he danced with Susan, the more difficult it became to keep his hands to himself and his cock from splitting his new trousers. He should perhaps have instructed Mr. Carr to make them a mite less snug. That's what came of listening to the tailor's advice that a well-endowed man shouldn't be shy about showing off God's generous gifts.

The fit had certainly had the desired effect on Susan who rarely took her eyes off his crotch when they weren't dancing.

All in all, it was torture and he couldn't wait for the wedding to be over and for Susan to finally be completely his.

Tonight's guests were generally aware an important announcement was to be made. They'd likely already read the news in *The Times*. A portly man Griff recognized as one of the judges from the trial took him aside and expressed relief Clifton Heights would once again be occupied by the earl and his family. He quietly hinted he was *pulling strings* to get the tenants' sentences reduced.

When Gabriel asked everyone to gather around the dais temporarily vacated by the musicians, people hurried to comply and a hush fell quickly.

Dressed in a full length white gown, her black hair bound up in a very sophisticated style, Patsy appeared at her stepfather's side and gazed up at him with adoration.

"That's our cue," Griff said, leading Susan by the hand as the smiling crowd parted like the Red Sea.

They stood arm in arm. Patsy grinned at them knowingly as if she alone were privy to a great secret, and Gabriel began his speech.

"Firstly, I want to thank my wife for her tireless efforts to make this evening a success."

Standing beside her husband, Emma blushed deeply as shouts of *hear, hear* resounded.

"Secondly, it's my distinct pleasure to make an announcement concerning a member of my family."

Susan tightened her grip on Griff's arm.

"Lady Susan Crompton and I may not be related by blood," Gabriel continued, "but she's my wife's dearest friend, and the closest thing to a sister I've ever known."

Griff patted Susan's hand, sensing she was close to tears. "He holds you in great esteem."

She nodded, struggling to maintain her composure. "I will not cry," she murmured.

"Susan is a rare gem, a woman of compassion and conviction who has never stood idly by when confronted by injustice.

"Some men—myself included when I first met her—might be intimidated by such a strong woman."

A hint of polite laughter rippled through the assembly.

Gabriel narrowed his eyes at Griff. "A strong woman needs a partner who recognizes that her strength will make him stronger."

Pride swelled in Griff's heart as he nodded. Gabriel had said it perfectly. Susan had strengthened him.

"And so, I am delighted to announce that Lady Susan Crompton and Lord Griffith Halliwell, Earl of Pendlebury, are to be married Wednesday next at St. John's Parish church in Preston."

Loud applause resounded as Griff assisted Susan to mount the dais. Gabriel shook Griff's hand. Emma hugged Susan. Patsy jumped up and down with glee, to the detriment of the complicated hair-do.

The applause ebbed when Griff held up a hand. "I'm grateful to Lord and Lady Farnworth and to Patsy for welcoming me so warmly into their family."

More applause.

"However, my greatest thanks goes to Lady Susan Crompton. Most of you probably already know of her heroic actions that saved my life a fortnight since."

"Mine too," Baron Whiteside shouted.

Louder applause.

"What you don't know," Griff continued, "is that Susan has saved my life in more ways than one. She has made me a better man, and I am honored she has agreed to be my wife."

He reached into the pocket of his waistcoat for the surprise he had concealed there, took hold of Susan's hand and slipped the ring on her finger. He hoped the simple circle of pearls with a diamond at their heart would please her. "This belonged to my mother, Susan. I ask you to accept it as a token of my love and esteem."

Tears slid down her cheeks as she stared at the ring. "I love it," she declared, standing on tiptoe to kiss his lips. He drew her into his embrace and deepened the kiss. It probably wasn't appropriate behavior but the whistling and cheering seemed to indicate no one was offended. They were among down-to-earth northern folks, after all.

A WEDDING

A WEEK LATER, Griff stood before a stern-faced Canon Parr, awaiting his bride. He hadn't set foot in the church since meeting the curate, and the parson chastised him for his absence as soon as they met for the first time fifteen minutes before.

Swallowing his annoyance, Griff apologized, mumbling an excuse about responsibilities at Clifton Heights.

Turning to scan the crowded pews, he easily picked out the old maids with the Book of Common Prayer clutched to their copious bosoms.

Elderly bachelors sat separately. He recognized the tailor and Gabe's friend, the doctor who'd tended Bertrand and seen to Griff's own rope burns and sprained shoulder muscles.

Many of Thicketford Manor's servants were in attendance, including James Footman who'd willingly walked Orion home from the quarry.

He suspected the men with plump wives and rosy-cheeked daughters carried on trade of some sort. Lawyers and other professional men were easily identified by the manner in which they looked down their noses at the millworkers who completed the throng. Susan had explained the cotton workers attended church only on special occasions.

As Griff waited in the crowded church, he was chuffed—a delightful Lancashire word his father was fond of—that his marriage had clearly been deemed a special occasion.

Griff wondered what the attendees thought of his decision to ask a servant to be his best man. He couldn't think of anyone he'd rather have at his side on this momentous day than his faithful butler. He might have known Potts would consider his black frock coat with tails, black waistcoat, knife-edged black trousers and starched white shirtfront as the most appropriate garb for the day. The only concession to the joyful nature of the occasion was the white bowtie that had replaced the usual black. Griff stopped fretting when Mr. Carr nodded his approval upon their arrival at the church.

A murmur of excitement rippled through the congregation. The carriage bearing the bride had arrived. Griff straightened his shoulders, gasping when he beheld Susan standing beside the font, a shimmering beacon in the shadowed porch.

SUSAN APPRECIATED THE reassurance of Gabriel's gloved hand on her arm as she prepared to walk down the aisle with him. "It doesn't seem all that long ago since you and Emma were married in this same place," she said.

"You're right," he replied. "We were fortunate to find each other. Sometimes, life has a way of bringing people together in unlikely circumstances. Just like you and Griffith."

Susan recognized the truth of her good fortune. "Emma told me then that I would find the right man one day."

Gabriel arched a brow. "She did?"

"I snarled at her," Susan admitted.

"You look beautiful, Aunty Susan," Patsy said.

"Thank you for being my bridesmaid, darling. One day, you'll walk down the aisle to wed the man of your dreams."

"Ugh," Patsy replied, scrunching up her nose.

"Sorry. What did I miss?" Emma asked as she joined them, adjusting her gown after feeding Rafe in the vestry. "Sometimes babies choose the most inopportune times."

"Ready?" Gabriel asked.

"More than ready," Susan replied.

She and Gabriel began the measured walk down the aisle, followed by Emma hand in hand with Patsy. Susan kept her gaze fixed on the handsome man standing with his butler. She couldn't say Griff was the man of her dreams since she'd never dreamed of becoming a married woman. But they loved each other and that was all that mattered.

❈

GRIFF TOOK SUSAN's hand when Gabriel gave her over into his safekeeping. He couldn't fail to miss the stern warning in his fellow earl's eyes but, when her warmth penetrated his skin, he knew he'd made the right choice. He would be a good and faithful husband.

"Dearly beloved," Parr intoned, obliging Griff to drag his gaze away from Susan's gray eyes, "we are gathered here together in the sight of God…"

Most of the preamble washed over him, only the words *ordained for the procreation of children* snagging his attention and making Susan blush.

To avoid fornication gave him pause for only a moment; it was true he and Susan had shared intimacies but he didn't consider that a sin, just practice for when their bodies finally joined.

A cough from Potts jolted him to his senses. Parr was addressing him. "Griffith Clifton Halliwell, wilt thou have this woman to thy wedded wife, to live together after God's ordinance in the holy estate of Matrimony? Wilt thou love her, comfort her, honor, and keep her, in sickness and in health; and, forsaking all others, keep thee only unto her, so long as ye both shall live?"

"I will," he replied, never more sure of anything in his life.

"Susan Crompton, wilt thou have this man to thy wedded

husband, to live together after God's ordinance in the holy estate of Matrimony? Wilt thou obey him, and serve him, love, honor, and keep him, in sickness and in health; and, forsaking all others, keep thee only unto him, so long as ye both shall live?"

Susan turned to look at him. "I will," she replied.

He knew he ought to fall to his knees in humble thanksgiving for the love this woman bore him but, next thing he knew, her warm right hand was in his and he was repeating his pledge to her. "I, Griffith Clifton Halliwell, take thee, Susan Crompton, to my wedded wife, to have and to hold from this day forward, for better for worse, for richer for poorer, in sickness and in health, to love and to cherish, till death us do part, according to God's holy ordinance; and thereto I plight thee my troth."

Susan took his hand in hers and pledged herself to him. "I, Susan Crompton, take thee, Griffith Clifton Halliwell, to my wedded husband, to have and to hold from this day forward, for better for worse, for richer for poorer, in sickness and in health, to love, cherish, and to obey, till death us do part, according to God's holy ordinance; and thereto I give thee my troth."

Clearing his throat again, Potts placed the wedding band on Parr's book. Griff took the golden circle and slid it onto the fourth finger of Susan's left hand.

Looking into her loving eyes, he followed the parson's lead, though he had no need. He had practiced the words over and over in preparation. "With this ring I thee wed, with my body I thee worship, and with all my worldly goods I thee endow."

Drowning in Susan's gray eyes, Griff absorbed little else, except Parr's pronouncement that he and Susan were now man and wife.

❧❧❧

ON TO CLIFTON HEIGHTS

USAN AND HER late father had never tolerated each other, yet she found herself wishing he were present at the wedding breakfast in Thicketford's dining room, a place where he'd often loudly admonished her interest in learning and social justice. "See, Papa," she'd whisper. "Some men appreciate a bluestocking."

"What are you smiling at?" Griff asked, squeezing her hand under the table.

"Just a memory," she replied, heat sweeping over her when he placed her hand on his arousal. "Griff," she breathed, trying to remove her hand. "People might see."

"Don't go all prudish on me now," he chuckled. "We're among family and they understand we want each other."

It was true they were celebrating with a small group...

"But Potts..."

Griff chuckled. "His look of censure is permanent. It wouldn't matter what we were doing. You'll notice he's directed it at every one of the footmen who've waited on us."

"Baron Whiteside," she tried.

"He's too busy flirting with Rebecca," Griff replied wiggling his eyebrows. "He wishes he had the courage to do what I'm doing."

Susan had to smile. Gabriel's mother and their widowed neighbor did seem immersed in each other's company. Judging by Anthea's pout, she'd also noticed. Springer, on the other hand, looked wryly amused.

"Patsy's too busy chasing those infernal poodles," Griff added.

"And playing big sister to Anthea's little girl," she agreed.

"I think we should slip away," he murmured, nibbling her ear.

"But Emma has gone to so much trouble," she began, not sure why she was being so coy. Every intimate part of her body was urging her to remove her clothes, then Griff's. And Clifton Heights was two hours away. Part of her wished they'd accepted Gabriel's invitation to spend their wedding night at Thicketford Manor, but Griff had politely and understandably insisted on Clifton Heights. "I intend to deflower my wife in my own bed in my own home," he'd told her privately, igniting the increasingly wanton cravings in unmentionable places.

Griff's arousal swelled when he curled his hand over hers. "You know very well Emma would be the first person to encourage our departure," he retorted. "In fact, the hunger in Gabriel's eyes when he looks at his wife leads me to believe Lord and Lady Farnworth might also spend the afternoon in bed."

"I suppose I'm simply playing the part of the shy virgin bride," she said, fluttering her eyelashes while moving her fingers on him.

He sucked in a breath. "That was the wrong thing to say to a man who's thirsting to do away with said maidenhead."

Her heart raced when he stood and bowed to the guests. "Pardon the interruption," he announced, taking her hand. "Lady Pendlebury and I have a long journey ahead of us."

Susan, who prided herself on never blushing, felt the heat rise in her face when everyone cheered and clapped as they hurried out of the dining room.

Fifteen minutes later, their luggage had been loaded and they were boarding the Farnworth carriage Gabriel had generously loaned. Potts was none too pleased when her new husband told him to ride up top with Conrad, although, as Griff had pointed out, it was difficult to discern the butler's true feelings on any matter.

Griff kept her mouth busy during the two-hour journey, so it was unlikely the prudish butler heard any of her muffled euphoric screams.

She tried in vain to give her husband pleasure in return, but he insisted gruffly on waiting until Clifton Heights.

GRIFF REGRETTED REBUFFING Susan's attempts to relieve the pressure building in his loins during the carriage ride but, if she'd so much as touched a fingertip to his cock, he'd have gone up in flames.

He'd always had a healthy, some might say prodigious, sexual appetite, but the raw hunger to claim Susan was eating him alive.

In the past few weeks, they'd eased some of the tension of waiting by bringing each other pleasure in very intimate ways. In those stolen moments, he'd learned how little suckling it took to start her moaning. She exploded when he applied just the right amount of pressure to the little nubbin that tasted sweeter every time he feasted on her juices.

To his delight, he'd discovered a passionate woman beneath the prickly armor. He could scarcely wait to enrich their love life with some of the more erotic positions he'd read of. After all, Susan loved learning new things.

He shook his head as the carriage rolled to a halt outside Clifton Heights. He was getting ahead of himself. The first order of business was to bring her to the edge of rapture, then plunge his already hard cock into the warm sheath he knew awaited. The excruciating wait was almost over.

SUSAN EXPECTED POTTS to be out of sorts, but the butler scooted down from the driver's bench with amazing agility and proceeded to organize the staff. Servants poured out of the house and Potts soon had them lined up for inspection.

Susan was pleased to note the Fazakerlys were still among them, but wished she didn't look quite so disheveled for her first meeting as the new countess.

Potts gestured to a young maid who curtseyed to Susan. "Olivia here is assigned as your personal maid, my lady."

"Ma'am," Olivia murmured, her eyes studying the steps.

The butler clearly intended to move on, but Susan wanted to speak to the shy girl who'd done an adequate job of lady's maid to Susan and Rebecca during their visit. "I'm sure we'll get along fine," she said with a smile.

Olivia curtseyed again. "I hope so, Ma'am."

"Your ladyship," Potts corrected.

"*My lady* will do, Olivia," Susan said, hoping to remove the nervousness from the girl's eyes.

"As ye wish, my lady."

Frederick stepped forward.

"I've taken the liberty of appointing Frederick to the position of valet, my lord," Potts told Griff.

Her husband nodded his approval, but Susan knew he didn't want to linger on the front steps inspecting the troops, which was what Potts seemed to have in mind.

Surprisingly, it was Mrs. Fazakerly who came to the rescue, obviously having taken note of Griff's untied cravat and overall rumpled appearance. "I expect Lord and Lady Pendlebury are anxious to freshen up in their chambers. Everything's ready, my lady," she assured Susan with a wink.

INDESCRIBABLE

"INDEED, MRS. FAZAKERLY," Griff replied, breathing a sigh of relief at the woman's good sense. "We'll perhaps meet with the staff in the morning, when we're not so fatigued."

The housekeeper's knowing grin proved she wasn't fooled.

He had a hard time keeping his face composed as he scooped up his bride and carried her over Clifton Height's threshold. "The wise woman knows I'll be far too fatigued in the morning to even get out of bed," he whispered.

Susan clung to his neck as he carried her upstairs. It was tempting to simply carry her into his own chamber, shut the door and get on with it. However, Olivia and Frederick were hurrying up the stairs right behind them, so he supposed the proprieties had to be observed.

Susan gazed around when he deposited her on her feet in the chamber adjoining his. "I've only been in this room once before," she said. "When Rebecca and I were planning redecorating, we decided it was charming enough to leave as it is."

Her words pleased him. "As you've guessed, this is the chamber of the mistress of the house. My mother chose the pale yellow decor, so I am pleased you like it. However, I don't intend for you to use this room much."

"I thought earls and their countesses slept in separate bedrooms," she teased with a glint in her eyes.

"Not this earl and not this countess," he retorted, tearing off the cravat that had come undone during the journey.

He longed to strip her of the wedding gown, but suspected it might be more challenging than it looked—and the ensemble looked daunting enough. Besides which, Olivia hovered just inside the door, her adolescent face as red as a winter beetroot.

"I expect Frederick awaits in my chamber, so I'll leave you in Olivia's capable hands, my love. Don't be too long."

He kissed her hand and left through the adjoining door, almost laughing out loud when he beheld Frederick standing to attention, holding up an ankle-length linen nightshirt. "I assure you I won't be needing that," he declared.

His valet's shoulders relaxed as he rolled up the garment. "Potts insisted, my lord," he explained with a trace of a smile.

"My butler never married," he replied, sitting on the edge of the bed so Frederick could remove his boots. "I won't need it. I usually sleep in the buff anyway, but especially today."

Within minutes, he was naked. Rubbing his hands together, he dismissed his valet and stared at the door, willing Susan to appear soon before his need exploded.

Frederick paused with his hand on the doorknob. "If I may suggest, my lord," he said. "Even the most eager bride might tend to be overwhelmed by the sight of an unclothed, aroused man ready to pounce."

Griff was tempted to laugh, but the sound of Susan's voice thanking her maid banished Frederick from the chamber. Taking the advice to heart, Griff dove under the bedcovers seconds before his bride entered.

"Olivia had laid out this nightgown," she explained, peeling the flimsy negligée off over her head. "I didn't have the heart to say no."

Griff had seen Susan naked before. It wasn't the first time he'd reveled in the sight of her thick, dark locks draped around her shoulders. The hungry look in her eyes as she stared at his chest wasn't new. None of those previous delights mattered to his overjoyed cock. The Griff who'd preferred fair-skinned blondes must have been out of his mind. His alluring gypsy bride was the only woman for him.

He threw aside the linens to welcome her into bed.

Greedy eyes fixed on his manhood, she climbed into the enormous four-poster, startling when he came to his knees.

"Don't be alarmed," he said, reaching to close the heavy curtains. "I want to shut out the world so there's just you and me in our cozy nest."

Nodding, she stood to pull the opposite curtain closed, teetering on the soft mattress.

The sight of thrusting breasts, a delectable bottom, firm thighs and the prize he sought so near was all too much. Growling, he clamped his arms around her hips to steady her and nuzzled his nose into the dark curls. She put her hands on his shoulders, thrust back her head and cried his name. It was an easy matter to lay her down and let his tongue follow where his nose had led.

He lapped her honeyed juices like a man who's crossed a barren desert, savoring her arousal. She fisted her hands in the sheets when he reached to roll rigid nipples twixt finger and thumb. Wanting her pleasure to last, but fearing he might soon spill, he flicked his tongue in and out of her sweet folds.

She arched her back and babbled his name as rapture took her. Needing no further encouragement, he knelt between her legs, dipped the swollen tip of his cock in her juices and thrust.

He expected her to cry out in pain when her hymen surrendered to his assault, but she clamped her legs around his hips and rose to meet him stroke for incredible stroke.

"I've tried to imagine what you would feel like inside me," she said seductively, looking into his eyes. "It's indescribable."

Was it his imagination, or had her voice deepened? Held in the thrall of the most incredible sex of his life, he decided not to worry about it.

Striving for a release he knew instinctively would be the best he'd ever had, he lost control, plowing into her like an animal.

His skin heated. His biceps quivered with the effort of preventing his body from collapsing on top of her. The contented smile never left her face, until he reached between them and pressed his thumb to her jewel.

When her eyes rolled back in her head and she stopped breathing, his cock recognized its moment of glory had arrived. He shuddered as his balls drew up and catapulted his seed to its destination. His semen erupted inside her warm sheath. "Susan," he shouted, shaken to his core by the sheer beauty of their joining.

"Griff," she sighed a while later when his breathing had steadied.

He ought not to have collapsed on top of her after his climax, but the delicate touch of her fingertips tracing patterns on his back had him hypnotized. "What?"

"You're mine at last."

"Forever," he replied, not caring that he was drooling into the pillow.

EPILOGUE

Ten months later

"I'M EXCITED," SUSAN admitted as Thicketford Manor came into view at the end of the avenue.

"Not nearly as excited as Patsy, I'll warrant," Griff replied. "Gabriel told me she was driving her mother mad with questions before our son was even born."

Susan gazed down at the babe asleep in her arms. "Let's hope he wakes soon, or she'll be disappointed."

"The poodles will probably make sure he does," Griff remarked.

As they expected, a large welcoming committee awaited. Servants applauded as Emma took Bryn from Susan's arms and nestled him atop her baby bump. Even Frame cracked a smile. Gabriel grinned, shaking Griff's hand. "Well done. I know the wondrous feeling of becoming a father for the first time."

"And you've another on the way," Griff replied.

"I want to hold Bryn," Patsy whined, trailing after her mother as everyone trooped into the house.

"We talked about this, young lady," Emma replied, rolling her eyes. "He's only a week old. When we get settled in the drawing room, you can hold him on your lap. Remember how careful we had to be with Rafe?"

The toddler in question tugged at his mother's skirts. "I hold him too?"

"Me first," Patsy insisted, making a beeline to sit next to her mother when they reached the drawing room. "Why did you call him Bryn?"

"It was my Welsh grandfather's name," Griff replied.

Susan wedged herself into a loveseat next to Griff. Her family had gathered to meet her son for the first time. She was safe among people who loved her, but Griff and Bryn were her family now. She could never be far away from her loving husband. Just looking at him kindled reminders of the erotic delights they shared.

The pleasant afternoon unfolded predictably. Patsy was eventually allowed to hold the still sleeping Bryn on her lap for a few minutes. Rafe touched a careful finger to the babe's forehead then lost interest and hurried off to chase one of the poodles. Wellington and Princess wandered about aimlessly, more docile than Susan remembered.

Gabriel asked about Orion and the new Pendlebury Stables which was the only cue Griff needed to talk at length about the phenomenal success of the enterprise he'd worked so diligently to get off the ground. Orion's heroic role in Griff's rescue had also enhanced the reputation of Pendlebury Stables. The horse was a legend in his own right.

Susan inquired after Emma's health now that she was expecting again.

Rebecca asked about the progress of renovations at Clifton Heights, expressing her understanding when Susan admitted she hadn't done much while she was pregnant.

Susan was curious and saw nothing amiss with asking about Baron Whiteside. Emma's correspondence had hinted at a continuing friendship. Susan was glad of it since Rebecca now lived alone at the dower house. She wished the question unasked when the color drained from Rebecca's face and she glanced nervously at Emma.

"We weren't sure whether to tell you or not," Gabriel said

after clearing his throat. "But you'll probably hear of it soon enough."

Susan was confused. Surely she would have heard if the baron had died?

"A short while ago," Rebecca said softly, "my son's friend, Dr. Henry, attended a woman in labor."

Susan glanced at Griff, who looked as confused as she felt.

"The woman gave birth to a son," Rebecca continued. "But she died soon after."

Susan shivered. She'd been lucky to breeze through the birthing process with almost indecent ease. "I still don't understand…"

"This all took place at the poorhouse."

Susan was losing patience. It was regrettable that an unfortunate pauper had died in childbirth, and heaven knew she and Griff had campaigned for…

Gooseflesh suddenly crept across her nape. "What was her name?" she asked, though she already knew the answer.

"Tillie."

She leaned into her husband when he put his arm around her shaking shoulders. "A motherless child born into poverty will have no chance in the world," she whispered close to his ear. "Tillie caused a lot of grief, but I believe Arthur manipulated her."

The sudden silence was bothersome. There was something else they weren't telling her. "I assume the child was Arthur's. Does the baron know?" she asked.

"Yes," Rebecca replied, her chin quivering. "He's petitioning the Poor Law commissioners, determined to extricate the lad from the orphanage. He wants to adopt the baby and bring him up at Withins Hall."

Susan's feelings were mixed. The child was Bertrand's grandson, so it was understandable he felt some responsibility. Tillie had eventually recognized the error of her ways and Griff's life had been spared as a result. Still, the thought of Arthur's spawn growing up so close to Thicketford Manor made her skin crawl. John Springer probably wasn't happy about the idea either.

"There's no guarantee he'll grow up to be like his father," Rebecca noted optimistically.

"Only time will tell," Gabriel replied stoically.

Bryn chose the moment to open his eyes, scrunch up his darling little face and wail loudly.

Griff hurried to take the squirming babe from Emma, holding him close and cooing daddy words in an unsuccessful attempt to stop the ear-splitting wailing. After a few moments, he held his child out at arm's length, his nose wrinkled. "I believe the problem lies with my son's bottom."

Susan thought he was probably right, but she wondered again how long men would survive without women to deal with life's unpleasant moments.

If you missed Gabriel and Emma's love story, *EVERY EARL HAS A SILVER LINING*, it is also available.

Book 3 of the series, *SLOW AND STEADY WINS THE EARL* will feature Lady Patsy Crompton, all grown up and ready to take the London scene by storm.

About the Author

Thank you for reading *Wild Earl Chase*. If you'd like to leave a review where you purchased the book, and/or on Goodreads and BookBub, I would appreciate it. Reviews contribute greatly to an author's success.

I'd love you to visit my website and my Facebook page, Anna Markland Novels.

Tweet me @annamarkland, join me on Pinterest, or sign up for my newsletter.

Follow me on BookBub and be the first to know when my next book is released. I'm also on Instagram. @annamarkland

As an amateur genealogist (aka an addict of family tree research) I became obsessed with tracing my English roots back to the Norman Conquest in the 11th century.

This turned out to be a pipe dream since I am not descended from the nobility and records were not kept for "common folks" until much later. Even then, early parish records are often indecipherable.

As a result, I began to write stories about a medieval family I conjured from my imagination. The Montbryces were born.

Like many people, I had an inner craving to write one good book. What was originally intended as that one book about my fictional family eventually became the 12-book series, The Montbryce Legacy.

In other words, writing superseded genealogy as my principal addiction, and I have since published more than 60 novels and novellas. Almost all are historical romances that feature Vikings, Highlanders, medieval knights or Regency earls. You can find more details on my website annamarkland.com.

I've lived most of my life in Canada, but I was born in the UK. The years spent in English schools instilled in me a love of European history which continues to this day. While I may boast of being a proud Canadian, I'm still a Lancashire lass at heart.

Before becoming a full-time writer, I was an elementary school teacher, a job I loved. I then worked as administrator for a worldwide disaster relief organization.

I love cats, although I haven't been able to bring myself to adopt another one since unexpectedly losing Topaz a few years ago.

I have few domestic skills. You'll notice most of my heroines hate sewing!

I try to follow a few simple guiding principles in my writing. I give my characters free rein to tell their story which often turns out to be different from my original version! I'm a firm believer in love at first sight. My protagonists may initially deny the attraction but, eventually, my heroes and heroines find their soul mates. It seems only natural then to include scenes of intimacy enjoyed by people who love each other deeply. I believe such intimacy is wholesome. Historical accuracy is important to me, although I have been known to tweak history when necessary. I write romance because I find a happy ending very satisfying.

Many thanks to the members of my critique group, Sylvie Grayson, Reggi Allder, Jacquie Biggar and Liz Ann Carson, and to my editor, Scott Moreland. A special thank you to my beta reader extraordinaire, Maria McIntyre. The value you all add to my work is much appreciated.

www.ingramcontent.com/pod-product-compliance
Lightning Source LLC
Chambersburg PA
CBHW071753190726
48292CB00003B/967